MORE, PLEASE

KATE ASTER

Cover design: The Killion Group, Inc.

DEDICATION

To every reader who wrote me asking for
"More, please!"
My heartfelt thanks for your enthusiasm and support.

PROLOGUE

SEVEN MONTHS AGO

- LOGAN -

Maeve traces her manicured hand up the length of my tandem kayak and the movement is enough to make any man drool.

She turns sharply toward me, her face incredulous. "*Ohio*? What the hell are you moving to Ohio for?"

I crack a smile, her harsh tone pulling my gaze away from her French-tipped fingernails and over to her eyes—the eyes of a very happily married woman and a good friend these past months. And even though I might have easily fallen in love with her had I been given the chance, I'm not unlike any other man who has met her. She's just one of those women who would be easy to love.

Her husband is one lucky Lieutenant.

"That's where I'm from, Maeve." I'm not surprised I never told her, and doubt she or Jack ever asked. In the Navy, the question is usually *Where have you been stationed?* rather than *Where are you from?*

I'm guessing people look at a Navy uniform and assume the guy in it must have been raised someplace near the water to appreciate this way of life. But my childhood memories center around farmhouses and grassland, not ocean waves and sailboats.

She tsk-tsks quietly. "Is that why you're parting with this? There's no water where you're headed?"

Her eyes drift back to the kayak I've got leaning against a stately oak on the northeast side of the campus of the U.S. Naval Academy. The tree's leaves are golden yellow now, as bright as a dandelion, and it pains me to think I won't be here to see them fall to the ground.

I knew this would be my last tour. I was supposed to have left this summer, but separating from the Navy comes with a mountain of paperwork and bureaucratic red tape, and I haven't fought it because Annapolis is a great place to be stuck for a while.

I shrug, moving the kayak to lay flat on the ground as an autumn wind threatens to topple it. "Not where I'll be, anyway. There's a creek, but not deep enough to kayak in for more than a quarter mile without crashing into rocks." I frown at the sight of the kayak, unmarred and unused. "Besides, it's a tandem kayak."

"So your girlfriend isn't following you." She says it like a statement rather than a question, and I suddenly can imagine her snuggled up in bed with Jack as they shake their heads, lamenting what poor taste I have in girlfriends.

And I'd be the first to agree with them.

"No," I answer, making sure to keep my tone level and unemotional.

She shakes her head, as I predicted she would. "Jack and I didn't like her anyway."

They'd like her even less if they knew why she left me.

Her back straightens and lightly tanned arms fold across her chest, looking again at the kayak. "You sure you want to part with her? She's a beauty."

I'm assuming she's talking about the kayak. Not my ex-girlfriend.

"Yep. You'll be doing me a favor, taking it off my hands. And I figured with the way Jack likes to kayak, maybe a tandem would be in your future sometime soon."

Jack doesn't wear the SEAL Trident on his uniform like I do. But he's stationed right now as an augmentee for one of the Teams down in Little Creek, Virginia, even though he and Maeve spend any moment they can up here in Annapolis.

Her brow furrows in thought. "How much are you asking for it?"

"For you? Nothing."

Cocking her head, her knuckles move to rest on her trim waistline, a classic Maeve pose. "No way. This is practically new, Logan."

Brand new, I want to say, but I won't. "Seriously, just take it. I owe you big time for the decorating you did on my house when I got here."

Her eyes roll lavishly. "Oh, please. You would have been happy to live in a bachelor pad with a picture of dogs playing poker on the wall. You only let me decorate as a favor to Jack and me."

She's actually right. She was starting her own interior design company and needed to build up her portfolio. And how could any man say no to a woman like Maeve? "Maybe. Just take the kayak, Maeve. Consider it a wedding gift."

"You already gave us a wedding gift."

"A second wedding gift then. You can send me photos of all the places you go in it and make me cry while I'm land-locked in the Midwest."

Wincing from the image she likely had of me in the middle of a cornfield, she touches my arm sympathetically—a friendly gesture that would have stirred me up a while back. But now I only see her as the big sister I always wished I had.

"You're sure you belong in Ohio? I thought you'd head back to San Diego when you were done here."

Uncomfortable suddenly, I stoop to lay the paddle on the inside of the vessel as my heart rate climbs. "My family needs me now. You know the deal."

It has nothing to do with the way my hands are suddenly clammy, and I feel like I'm suffocating.

"Well, don't dig those roots too deep, okay? We're still hoping you'll come back to us," she says, her innocent words unintentionally having a double meaning because I really do feel far away sometimes, 7,000 miles from everyone else.

My eyes drift to the water as she climbs into the kayak to get a feel for it. The brackish water here flows into the Chesapeake Bay and then intermingles with the waters from every ocean on the planet.

And the thought calms me. This time, just like always.

CHAPTER 1

TODAY

~ ALLIE ~

"So... what do the rooms look like here?" I'm actually stunned that the words slipped from my mouth. They're so unlike me that I nearly glance over my shoulder to see who said them.

My mother would be ashamed, but my friends would probably rise to their feet applauding. It had been that long.

It's not that I'm a prude when it comes to sex. I can tell a room full of half-sloshed women how to effectively play with a guy's balls while they give a blowjob. Or, without even blushing, I'm able to stoically discuss the best angle to find your G spot.

After all, that's what helps pay the bills.

But I am all talk, no action. I mean, *no* action. Not for over a year, closing in quickly on two. And after what the last guy did to me, it's no wonder. Especially now that my world has been expanded by sex toys and I've discovered that I can give myself a much better orgasm than my last boyfriend ever did.

The man sitting across the table from me is different, though.

I'm okay-looking and on a good day I'm a solid 7. But I'm not really the social butterfly type. If I try something like the hair-flip-while-giggling move that I see executed by other women at this bar, it usually looks like I have an acute neck spasm.

So the guys I attract seem to fall into the average range—not the "drop your panties" kind of men like the guy I am sitting across from right now. He has Hollywood A-lister looks. Chiseled features, piercing eyes, and a wide jaw that makes him look a bit like a football star. I'm not sure why he's even sitting here with me, and certainly clueless as to why he bought me dinner after sharing a drink at the bar. Yep, actually *bought* me dinner, picking up the bill without the slightest hesitation the way men do in those old movies I watch on cable at 2 a.m.

And when he told me he was a SEAL—*a freakin' Navy SEAL?*—my mouth went dry and my heart did its own version of *Riverdance*.

"Nothing too special," he answers me. "But I hear the room service is good. Maybe we could order dessert in the room?"

The timbre of his voice is like liquid gold, warm and smooth. The kind of voice that flows through the air casting a warm sensation across my breasts.

Dessert? The only dessert my starved libido wants to devour is him.

"Sounds perfect." I try to sound like the confident woman I'm not. I have never picked up a man in a bar, and certainly hadn't intended to tonight. I'm here only because I was supposed to meet one of my sales reps, who stood me up via a text message forty minutes after we were supposed to meet.

Logan—yes, a guy who looks like this could never have an ordinary name like Mark or John—bought me a drink while I waited. A drink that led to dinner, that led to a tantalizing conversation that made me want to lick his entire body like a lollipop.

As I stand, he pulls my chair out for me, a gesture I'm not even sure what to do with. The last time a guy pulled a chair out for me, I was trying to sit down, which resulted in me crashing to the ground with the cackles of my third grade classmates in the background.

This time is different. Instead of feeling like a humiliated eight-year-old, I'm feeling like the horny, sex-deprived 24-year-old I am. This man has all the moves, the moves that are making my knees give way and my lips want to meld themselves to his.

His hand touches the small of my back as he guides me toward the mirrored elevator doors in the hotel's lobby, sending tiny shivers down my spine. I've had drinks here a few times before, but I've never actually seen one of the hotel rooms. Here in the far, far-reaching suburbs of Dayton, Ohio, this hotel and conference center is the only option for happy hour drinks outside of meeting at Applebee's.

He reaches for the "up" button and I can't help noticing his hands. I've always had a thing for guys' hands. Logan's are rough and imperfect, the way I like them, with long, sensual fingers. I imagine they are calloused in all the right places.

So as one of those long, rough fingers presses the button, it is then that hesitation grips me. No, not quite hesitation exactly. More like sheer terror. I see my reflection standing next to an impossibly hot man. Me, in my sensible skirt and lightweight blouse, teetering on heels that I only wear under duress.

This is not something I do. This guy is just passing through town. He said his home is in San Diego. He's probably leaving tomorrow or the next day.

This is destined to be a one-night-stand.

My *first* one-night-stand... which anyone would figure out if they learned I'd had one solitary sex partner in my entire life, my college boyfriend who dumped me for being "no fun anymore" after my dad died unexpectedly.

A one-night-stand is not in my playbook.

But I need this. I need to feel this man's hands on me, to remind me that sex is not intended to be a solo sport.

We step into the elevator and I immediately wish for another drink. I am sober as a judge, so tomorrow morning when I slink out of his room to do my walk of shame, I won't even be able to blame alcohol.

I am ready to bolt, till he stands next to me in the otherwise empty elevator and the doors shut. His arm gently wraps around my waist, and his warmth seeps through the clinging fabric of my skirt. Lightly, his finger traces the tiny cleft in my chin as he says, "You're sure you wouldn't rather have dessert in the restaurant?"

Arrgh. I curse my own transparency. *Don't you dare pull a "nice guy" routine on me,* I think. *I need a Bad Boy tonight. Not a nice guy.*

I know this for a fact because I hear plenty of sordid tales of nights with Bad Boys while I'm peddling my sex toys for the multi-level marketing company I work for. You have no idea how women talk at these parties as they are drinking their Chardonnays and filling out sales forms for overpriced vibrators and candy-scented lubricants. I listen to more post-coital confessions than a psychiatrist specializing in sex addicts.

I hear these stories of hot, creative men, and wonder what the hell my selfish-in-bed last boyfriend was thinking with his usual missionary-style sex that lasted just long enough for him to get off, while I usually had to finish myself off after he dozed next to me.

I've been missing out. Big time. And while I might be able to talk a good game when it comes to sex, I'm pretty much sticking to the script that the company gives me. And yes, they really do provide a script.

So I do what any hot-blooded female other than me would do at that moment: I push him against the mirrored wall and say, "They're not serving what I want for dessert in that restaurant."

Then, just as a smile touches his lips, I press my mouth against his and taste him for the first time, swirling my tongue across his teeth and entwining it with his. My hands are pressed against the mirrored wall on both sides of his head and his fingers channel into my hair. He consumes me, kissing me in a way that makes my pelvis arch against him unconsciously.

My, my. He is a big boy, isn't he? I can feel his erection pressing against me and it sends my entire mind into a whirlwind like one of those carnival rides that whip you around in circles upon circles until you can't even remember your own name. He is bigger than the new UltraMag vibrator model that just came in last week complete with a clitoral stimulator, retailing at $199.95 (but $100 off if you host a party for me in the month of June).

Spinning me 180 degrees so that my back is now against the wall, his rock-hard chest is pressed against mine, entrapping me. I feel his hands grip mine, lifting them above my head as he plunges his tongue into my mouth in a needy, suggestive rhythm. His kiss is addictive, and had he broken it off right then, I would have grabbed his face and demanded, "More, please."

The heat between us is searing. I can feel the steam rising from my skin. His body is hard and big and broad and makes me feel tiny.

I like this feeling. I like it a lot.

Releasing me from his possessive grip, his hands travel along my body, down my sides, the pads of his thumbs lightly brushing against the curves of my breasts. I ache to strip this silk blouse off me and feel him against me with nothing in between us.

As the elevator gives a final ding, and the doors open to an empty hallway, my knees nearly buckle. He must have felt me start to go limp because, giving a quick glance over his shoulder, he lifts me off my feet and carries me out of the elevator. The last time I was lifted by a man, I was nine years old and had twisted my ankle during gymnastics class, and the guy was my dad.

My dad, who would be shaking his head at me right now.

Guilt threatens to extinguish the glorious feelings that are shooting off like fireworks throughout my torso. I fight my good-girl conscience, my hands moving to the sides of his face as I kiss him while he walks down the hall with me in his arms.

He's surprisingly adept at being able to walk down this hall, somewhat blindly with his face firmly attached to mine. It makes me wonder how many women he has carried down this hall.

Maybe this is his shtick—picking up women in the bar downstairs and taking them to his room. Maybe I am one of a long string of women during his visit to Ohio.

No, no, no. I'm battling my sensible, paranoid mind as it lectures me with every step he takes down the hall. I focus on the taste of him, a mix of the beer and steak that he had for dinner, as I dip my tongue further into his warm, inviting mouth. And the smell of him. I inhale it deeply—a simple, soapy scent that intoxicates me. He sets me down gently to fumble for a key card in his pocket and I glance at his door. *His* door. That leads to *his* room. That has *his* bed. That I am going to have crazy, mindless, hot monkey sex in.

Holy shit.

Trying to banish the hesitation that is building in my conscience, I nudge him against his door before he is even able to slip the card into its slot. I splay my hands against his chest, the thin fabric of his shirt warm to my touch.

And I feel them.

Oh, yowza, I feel them: real, honest-to-God six-pack abs that are so firm I could bounce a penny off them.

Right there in the vacant hallway, I can't resist pulling his shirt out just a little so I can slip my fingers underneath the bottom and touch them.

I purr in response. I've never touched anything so fine in my life, except maybe that time my college roommate wore a mink coat (even though morally I find fur coats reprehensible, I'll admit it was soft as sin).

My hands seem to sizzle against his skin, sending a shimmering sensation from my fingertips all the way to my core.

I touch my mouth to his and tentatively trace his perfectly formed lips with my tongue. I feel him moan, low and mildly menacing, and he drops the key card to the floor, digging his fingers into my hair again. His hands then move to my back, pulling me closer so that I can feel just how much he wants me right now. And I can't help but wonder if he's visually impaired because I'm not nearly as smokin' hot as he is.

But who cares? I'm not caring *what* he sees in me as he does something completely incredible with his tongue, titillating me in a way that simply cannot be replicated by any of the toys in our most expensive line.

My body is thrumming in a rhythm that seems almost primal in reaction, and I'm wondering what other parts of me he could spark to life with that gifted tongue.

He pulls his mouth from mine and bends over to retrieve the key, just long enough for me to check out a truly remarkable ass. From behind him, I wrap my arms around to his front to feel those abs again. I wonder if he has any tattoos on that shredded bod of his. Or maybe a bad-ass body piercing, though he doesn't quite seem the type. I wonder if he'll let me trace my tongue along the hills and valleys of those sculpted muscles.

I wonder… if I can do that without having to take off my own clothes in the process.

Oh, no, I suddenly think as he slips in the key and the tiny green light on the door lights up. I am going to have to get naked with this man.

Me, in my sensible undies and legs that I skipped shaving this morning.

Do I have any stubble in my armpits? That would really suck.

Maybe he's the type that likes it with the lights off?

Truth is, I don't know. I don't know anything about him. And I sure don't know how men like to fuck women they pick up in bars. Because technically, this will be just a fuck.

I've never had just-a-fuck in my life.

Just as he starts to nudge the door open, I panic. I panic like any God-fearing cafeteria-Catholic would panic in this situation. This is out of my realm. Beyond my comfort zone. This is a huge mistake.

"Oh, God." I say it out loud, though I hadn't meant to.

He turns to look at me. "What's wrong?"

"I—"

I've had one sex partner in my life. The only sex I've had in a hotel room was at a sex toy conference and I was very much alone at the time.

And I'm a spineless scaredy-cat.

But rather than saying any of these truths I do what any spineless scaredy-cat like me would do. I lie. "I left my phone downstairs."

"Want me to go get it? You can make yourself at home in the room."

"No. It'll just take a minute. I'll be right back."

"Okay," he says, a smile in his eyes. "While I wait, I'll order dessert." He presses his lips to mine again and I almost have to swallow the cry that is singeing my throat. I memorize the feel of his brief kiss, the way his hard body melds so nicely with mine, the feel of his muscles as they bunch when he moves his hand to my face in a light caress.

I memorize it, because I know I'll never have it again. Guys that look like this only come along once in a lifetime.

And here I am, too chicken-shit to take advantage.

As I step into the elevator, I lean my head against the mirrored wall, noticing the smudge marks from when I had plastered my hands at either side of his head, kissing him.

On a whim, I snap a picture of the smudge with my phone. I know it's weird. But it's the only proof I'll have that for five precious minutes out of my life, I had thrown caution to the wind.

CHAPTER 2

~ ALLIE ~

If a stray cat walks by, I'll be dragged into the street.

I have three dogs attached to me, one in each hand, and a third whose leash has somehow wrapped itself around my ankle. It is the best I can do under the circumstances. Two of my volunteers have yet to show up, and two more texted me saying they're sick.

Sick. Yeah, right. The sky is the color of the blue topaz pendants that sparkle in the window of the jewelry store just five doors down from where I sit, and a warm breeze is blowing in from the South. It is a perfect day in May in America's heartland, and I swear I can smell the moist soil being tilled on Len Kroger's farm a mile south of town.

My deadbeat volunteers are probably lounging on their hammocks, sipping a Starbucks right now, or writing up a grocery list for a spontaneous neighborhood barbeque because it's just that kind of day in Newton's Creek. That's what I'd be doing if I didn't feel the weight of adorable furry lives bearing down on me every day.

Sinking my back into the uncomfortable folding chair outside Sally Sweet's Pet Boutique, I watch the slow but steady trickle of traffic on Anders Road, which is pretty much our town's Main Street.

I like this street because it seems frozen in time. My dad used to tell me that half the stores he had shopped at as a kid were still open here, even if they are struggling now in today's economy. There's a five-and-dime across from me where Dad used to buy me balls of cherry blast gum or a pretzel rod for a nickel anytime we visited. It is the kind of street where people always greet me as I sit with my rescued dogs trying to find them homes.

Even after spending half my night wallowing in my humiliation after bailing on the hottest man alive, I'm feeling pretty content sitting out here just like I do every Saturday morning for two hours with my canine friends.

Life is like that. You fall in a pile of mud. You get up. You move on.

I spot Cass hauling ass across the street toward me, dragged by a 75-pound husky mix on a leash. I sigh with relief and longing when I see the cardboard tray she holds sporting three large coffees, mine heavily spiked with cream and sugar if she got my text fifteen minutes ago.

Slow down, Snowball. Don't make her spill my coffee.

"Sorry I'm late," she says as she sets the coffee down on the concrete beside me and takes one of the leashes from my hands.

"Don't worry about it," I respond, greedily taking the cup and sucking in a hot mouthful of caffeinated decadence. "Thanks."

"Am I the only one here so far?"

"No. Maddie and Lila are inside with the little ones," I say as I give a toss of my head in the direction of the pet store entrance. The little ones are a Chihuahua and a Maltese, both likely to have homes by the end of the week from the number of applications I have in hand for each of them. It is so much easier to rehome the little guys.

I unwind Crocco's leash from my leg and put it in my hand, getting licked by Snowball in the process.

Cass's eyes meet mine briefly as she gives Crocco a pat in greeting. "You look tired."

I know she's talking to me, not Crocco, despite his permanently weary bloodhound eyes. He is a mutt in the extreme, and I struggled to choose a breed in his listing on our website. Even my dad, who was a vet for twenty-five years, would have had a hard time nailing it down. But Crocco's eyes are all bloodhound.

I grunt my reply, not exactly ready to explore my indiscretions of last night. Or my lack of indiscretions, as the case may be. Cass is my friend, and a pretty good one, even though I've only known her a matter of weeks. But really, as the founder of this shoestring rescue organization I need to keep some measure of dignity.

"You sick or something?" Her big, blue eyes—the exact shade of the sky this May day—are prying open my bounty of secrets from last night. But I clamp my mouth shut.

Cass is gorgeous. Freaking gorgeous. She moved here from New York City for a summer job at an amusement park called Buckeye Land, Ohio's second rate Disneyworld knock-off. I've never been there since it opened up after I had outgrown the I-wanna-be-a-fairy-princess stage of my life.

Cass doesn't even need a costume to look like the princess she was hired to portray. She has platinum blonde hair and a pearly white smile that could make a man's head do a 180 as he plows his Lexus into a telephone pole. If I had her looks there would be no way I'd hang out in front of a pet store with a bunch of dogs when I could be sitting in front of a mirror somewhere just admiring myself.

But that's just me. And I guess the thrill of being gorgeous would wear thin after a while.

"Not sick. Just was out late last night," I finally confess.

"Oh, that's unusual for you, isn't it?"

I raise an eyebrow. I know she didn't mean it in an insulting way. I work two jobs and foster dogs in my little one-bedroom condo. My free time is usually spent walking down Anders Street with three dogs and a fistful of poop bags. So unless it's for business, I tend to go out about once or twice a Presidential administration.

"What'd you do?" she asks.

"I was supposed to meet Mary. She said she had a great idea for booking more parties this summer. You know how things slow down. But she never showed."

"Didn't she cancel on you last week?" She shakes her head. "I don't know why you put up with her."

I shrug. Mary books about twelve sex toy parties a year, and since I was the one who signed her up as a rep, I get a piece of the pie every time she makes a sale. So I'll put up with her.

Granted, selling sex toys wasn't what I wanted to do when I was growing up. And it sure wasn't why I slogged through college.

But my *real* job working as an executive assistant for a nonprofit based in Cincinnati barely pays enough to cover my mortgage, let alone dog food for three and vet bills.

I moved to Newton's Creek just two days after I graduated from college, not the best place for new grads to go looking for a job unless you majored in agricultural sciences. My mom had gotten remarried—too quickly after my dad's death, in my humble opinion—and something inside me wanted to move to my dad's hometown.

I don't know why. I was probably chasing ghosts. Or just wanting to keep him with me in any way I could.

When I was a junior in college my dad died of an aneurism. He had seemed healthy as a horse only two months prior when I kissed him on the cheek and promised I'd come home to Cleveland for Thanksgiving.

Sometimes, like right now when I'm thinking of him, I can still feel the warmth of his cheek against my lips and see the sheen of tears in his eyes as he said good-bye to me. I was Daddy's little girl—Daddy's only child, actually—and he had hated to see me go. He spoiled me every day of my life. Not with things, because we didn't have the money for that. But with love.

And with pets. Dad was a vet with a very special place in his heart for abandoned and neglected animals, so much so that people started dumping their unwanted pets at our house rather than at the local pound.

So when I settled here in his hometown, the first stop I made was the county shelter. I had thought I'd adopt a dog, but instead of just walking out with one dog for myself, I walked out with three… and a mission.

My "day job" boss, Nancy, who started a nonprofit of her own about ten years ago, helped me establish my fledgling rescue organization as a 501(c)(3) charity. Then I put a sign in Sally Sweet's Pet Boutique asking for volunteer foster homes. It was really a lot simpler than I had dreamed it would be.

I smile now at the memory of when I placed my first rescue dog in his new home. That was 53 dogs ago. Yet still not enough.

"Where'd you go?"

"Hmm?" Cass's voice snaps me back to the present. "Bergin's. The hotel bar."

Barely registering as a blip on the GPS, the town of Newton's Creek doesn't have many places to meet up for happy hour. So if you're over 21 and single in Newton's Creek (I think there are about twelve of us), you are definitely familiar with Bergin's.

"Hmm." She stretches her lavishly long legs in front of her. Cass actually modeled in New York, and I think it's really odd that she seems content for the moment in Newton's Creek. "So what was his name?" she asks me.

"Who?"

"The guy you don't want to talk about."

I slump in my chair, signaling my spaniel mix up onto my lap, while Crocco tugs mercilessly on his leash, attracted to the smell of the donut shop two doors down.

"Logan," I mumble. To hell with keeping my dignity. I have three layers of dog spit on my shirt. Who am I kidding?

"Logan," she repeats, glancing over at another one of my volunteers walking toward us on Anders Street. "Sounds like a made-up name."

"Well, whoever he was, he bought me a nice dinner when Mary didn't show up."

Cass's eyes widened. "Wow. A man who actually buys dinner. Last time I got invited to dinner here in town, we went for fast food, and he still asked me to split the bill."

This is hard to believe coming from Cass. With her looks, she could seduce a prince or a sheik or a billionaire oil mogul. Or any combination of the above. But I guess there aren't many of those in Newton's Creek.

"What's he do?" she asks.

"What do you mean?"

"I mean, what is he? Pilot? Lawyer? Doctor? Sports agent?

They're never just carpet salesmen or accountants at a hotel bar. They always come up with something good."

I hate that she is right. "SEAL," I mumble, giving a wave to my friend Kim about a hundred feet away as our eyes meet.

"A seal?" Cass's face is scrunched up.

I can tell by her expression she's picturing a marine mammal at the Cincinnati Zoo, balancing a ball on its nose and going, "Ar! Ar!"

"SEAL. Like, as in Navy SEAL," I clarify.

She bursts out laughing just as Kim approaches, reaching out for Crocco's leash.

"What's so funny?" Kim asks.

"Allie met a guy at Bergin's last night who told her he was a Navy SEAL."

Shaking her head, Kim's eyes narrow into tiny slits. "That bastard. I've heard about guys like that. They lie and pretend they're heroes to get free drinks and stuff."

"Or to get laid," Cass adds with enough authority that I suspect she's met a fake SEAL or something similar in her past.

My face droops, Basset-hound-style. I hadn't considered that. "Well, he actually might be one. He told me a lot of stuff about their training and the places he's lived."

"Probably read some stuff in a book or something." Kim shakes her head. "Haven't you seen all those stories recently? Total losers pretending to be in the military? It's all over the news these days. It *so* pisses me off."

I actually have seen those stories. I surf the web as much as the next girl. But I hadn't suspected he was a fake last night. Nothing seemed fake about that guy, especially not those magnificent pecs that I had ogled while we ate. Even now, remembering the way the smooth fabric on his shirt seemed to showcase his sculpted torso makes my body hum.

"I don't know. He was pretty convincing. I mean, you guys didn't see him. The guy had six-pack abs."

Cass raises a single eyebrow at me. "Allie, we're in Ohio. The only Navy SEALs you'll find around here are the ones in my fantasies. The guy was a fake."

Kim reaches down and lets Crocco slather wet kisses on her arm. I've known Kim since I started this organization. She's never been able to foster a dog because she lives with her parents right now. But I can't remember a single Saturday when I couldn't rely on her to help handle the dogs. "Wait a minute. How would you know he had a six-pack?" she ponders. "What'd he do? Strip down in the bar?"

My gut tightens. I'm caught. I hadn't intended to tell anyone how I had followed him up to his hotel room, only to race back to the elevator in a fit of blind terror. "I could just tell. His arms were ripped. You know." *Arms, yeah. Focus on those arms and don't get tempted into telling your friends that you had dared to touch a set of abs so fine they should be cast in bronze.*

"Oh. My. God. You slept with him, didn't you?"

"No," I deny. I didn't sleep with him. If I had, I might be sporting a wide Cheshire cat grin right now, and have a brain filled with dirty memories to last a lifetime.

Kim's eyes widen. "You did. That's totally out of character for you. He didn't slip something in your drink, did he?"

"No, no," I say. *Not unless it was a pint of estrogen.* "And I didn't sleep with him. I swear it. We had dinner and that was it."

"And you know about his abs, *how* exactly? Did he Vulcan mind-meld you?" Kim is a bit of a sci-fi geek and not afraid to show it.

"I might have felt one or two of them when we kissed." Or three or four. Not that I was counting.

Unconvinced, Cass bites her bottom lip thoughtfully. "Is he a good kisser, anyway?"

I blush from the memory of his lips on mine. "Damn good."

Kim tightens up the leash on Crocco. "Well, thank God you didn't sleep with him. Navy SEAL, my ass. Can't believe you nearly fell for that. Probably uses that line all the time. He could have been an axe murderer, or a carrier of every STD around."

I should have expected this reaction from Kim. She is a single mom of a four-year-old who swears anxiety is as much a part of motherhood as stretch marks.

"Shut up, killjoy. Besides, she would have used a condom. Right?" Cass glances at me for confirmation.

"Of course I would have." I nod vehemently.

Kim raises her eyebrows. "Yeah, and if condoms were foolproof, I wouldn't be a mom right now."

I shoot her a silencing look as an older man approaches, about my dad's age if he were still alive. He pets our dogs for a while and talks about one of the dogs he had seen online. My heart does a happy dance when he tells me he already filled out an application—a sign that he's serious about adopting. I pull a small stack of applications I printed out this morning from my backpack and find his close to the top.

Giving him an encouraging grin, I point him in the direction of the pet store's door where Lila has the Chihuahua. Hope wraps itself around my heart. The man seems perfect for Dollie. No kids. An apartment that allows dogs. All I'll have to do is swing by for a house check and call a few references, and I'll have one more open slot in a foster home.

And one more dog I can save from the county shelter. That is enough to make me take a sip of my latte, imagining it is celebratory champagne.

"He's perfect for Dollie," Kim comments, and I'm happy that we've moved on to a different topic. "Seems very calm.

That dog is so hyper. I'm surprised you even had Lila bring her today."

I toss my shoulders upward. "She's okay if we keep her indoors. And she's easier to manage than Streamer." Streamer is Lila's other foster, a MinPin that pees every time he meets someone new. I don't have enough volunteers to bring all of our dogs to these Saturday events, and have to pick the ones who make the best impression. Streamer is definitely not the cream of the crop among our rescues.

The second hour of our event approaches, and we're starting to see more traffic.

As another couple hands me their application and gives Crocco a final pat on the head, I feel a strange prickling up my spine, as though someone's hand is touching the nape of my neck.

And I see him approach, feeling the air rush out of my lungs.

Logan?

What the hell?

For a split second, I'm thinking the guy is stalking me. I know. Laughable, considering he has this spectacular Greek god bod, and I'm just... me. But when I see the complete shock in his eyes, I know he isn't exactly expecting to run into me either.

Then the humiliation settles over me like a wet blanket, remembering how I ditched him last night. As he walks toward us, I just stare at him, dumbfounded, suddenly oblivious to what Kim is saying to me as I nod in response, completely on auto-pilot.

I hear Cass give a low whistle as Logan nears and I know she must have spotted him. You can't *not* see a guy like Logan approaching. At least, not if you're a heterosexual female under the age of 80.

Logan stands above me, towering over my speechless

form as I melt into my folding chair from his mere presence. Even in the daylight, the guy is hot. No, he is hotter. No wonder I nearly got naked with him.

"Alexandra," he says, and I hear Cass whimper at the sound of his voice uttering my name. The guy could be a phone sex operator with a voice like that. Come to think of it, if I signed him on as a sex toy rep, sales would quadruple and I could retire ten years earlier than planned. "What are you doing here?" he asks.

"I—uh—" I stammer. What *am* I doing here? Oh, yeah. "I run a dog rescue. We're here every Saturday morning so that people can meet and uh, maybe adopt a dog." The words are stumbling from my mouth, but I'm not even sure what I am saying. Being close to this much testosterone in the morning is inebriating. Two more minutes in his presence and I'll turn into a blithering idiot.

"I know," he replies. "I'm here to see Kosmo."

Kosmo. Seriously? This guy wants to see the chocolate Lab mix I've been fostering for the past six months? No one wants to see Kosmo. They all ask how he's doing, but no one wants to actually *adopt* him. I had taken Kosmo home from the shelter, not knowing that he'd end up being our most costly foster ever. Not that that would have stopped me. There was something about his soulful eyes that had drawn me to him, and once I took his face in my hands and stroked his furry cheeks, I was a goner.

But Kosmo turned out to be a special needs dog. He has a valve in his heart that won't close all the way, requiring expensive medication and a surgery as soon as I can afford it. Donations for the heart procedure are trickling in. But as of now, the medicine is paid for straight out of my sex toys sales, like so many of the other expenses that come with my fosters. Who would have thought I'd be selling dildos for dogs?

"I filled out an application online last week," he adds.

"Oh," I murmur, still shell-shocked.

Cass sends me an inquisitive look, obviously trying to figure out how I know this guy. "And your name is?" she asks him in her breathiest tone. Is she flirting with him? And can I blame her if she is?

Logan's dazzlingly blue eyes shoot over to Cass. "Jake Sheridan."

My gut seizes up. The lying piece of shit. "*Jake*?" I ask. "I thought you said your name was Logan."

Coughing, Cass spits out a mouthful of coffee. Obviously, she is putting two and two together.

"Are you okay?" Logan—I mean, Jake—asks her.

Her cheeks are flushed. "Yeah. Sorry. Went down the wrong hatch."

My eyes are still locked on his as I await his answer.

"Logan's my middle name."

I glance sideways at Cass who is giving a slight eye roll. Don't say it, Cass. Don't say it. But I'll think it: *Lying SOB*.

"I'm Jacob Junior, so I've always gone by Logan, my middle name. But I probably put Jacob on the form."

Yeah, right. Jake, Jacob, Logan. If I talk to him for ten more minutes, I'm betting he'll toss a few more names my way.

Cass spots his application and hands it to me. I can see her pointer finger placed appropriately at the line where he listed his occupation. And my stomach roils at the words "Construction Manager." Prick.

Navy SEAL, my ass. I can hear Kim's words echoing in my brain. She was right, and I hate that. The guy is slicker than the best lube I sell.

How could I have been so stupid?

"Well, Jake—" I begin.

"Logan," he interrupts.

Whatever. "—Kosmo isn't here today. I only had enough volunteers to handle six dogs."

"Okay. So how can I meet him?"

Insistent guy. He'll do well in... construction management.

"Well, normally one of us will take the dog to meet you at your home. We always do house checks, anyway, before we adopt out a dog. You know, to make sure someone's not living in a place that's unsuitable for a dog. Like, say... a hotel." I frown at him.

A half-grin sidles up his cheeks, and my heart rate picks up in pace by 10% despite the fact that this guy is a compulsive liar.

"I was just staying there a couple nights. I'm renovating my townhouse and had no plumbing."

"Really." Unconsciously, I draw the word out three or four syllables. "I thought you said you live in San Diego."

"No, I lived in San Diego. A while back. I still consider it home, though."

Sure thing, Slick. "Mmm, okay. Well, I'm not sure it sounds like you're ready for a dog then." I set his application back down on the pile.

"Of course I am."

"Well, you said your townhouse is undergoing construction. With workers coming and going, I don't think it would be the best place for a dog. He might slip out an open door. And I'm sure you must have seen on our website that Kosmo is a special needs dog. He needs a calm, stable home. Not a construction zone." I know I sound patronizing, but I hardly care.

What an idiot I was. Sitting there last night, listening to him talk about life in the SEALs, which he no doubt learned about by picking up a few bestsellers. How many other women did he use that line on?

"My plumbing's fine now. The townhouse is nearly complete. I have a fenced-in backyard. There's nothing dangerous there for a dog." His gaze on me is heavy.

"Okay. I'll call you if he's still available. There's been a lot of interest in him lately."

Kim shoots me a look and I silence her with a stifling glare. There has been no interest in Kosmo. Few people want to adopt a dog that comes with such a hefty price tag.

Logan—or Jake, Jacob, or whatever the hell his name is—inhales deeply, broadening his chest in a way that is, frankly, scary as hell. "I think we should talk," he says. Then, glancing sideways at my two friends, he adds, "Alone. Maybe we could take one of the dogs for a short walk?"

If I wasn't in a public place, I would be paralyzed in fear right now, especially with Kim's suggestion that he might be an axe murderer still floating around in my brain.

"Sure." I toss my shoulders carelessly to make it seem like my heart isn't palpitating behind my ribcage. I stand up, suddenly feeling like a munchkin next to his 6-foot-plus frame. I am a Maltese to his purebred German shepherd.

Feeling Kim's and Cass's eyes watching me, I give my dog's leash a little tug and walk down the brick-lined side-walk toward the smell of coffee pouring out of Pop's donut shop. It is busy every Saturday morning. Plenty of witnesses in case this guy turns Jekyll-and-Hyde on me.

When we are out of earshot from my friends, I turn to him. "So?"

"So. Small world, huh?"

I nod. "Small town."

"You disappeared on me last night. I was worried about you when you didn't come back. I even checked the restau-rant and the front desk downstairs. But no one remembered you leaving."

That is the one good thing about being average-looking

like me. No one really notices me coming and going. I kind of fade into the woodwork.

"Well, I had second thoughts," I tell him.

"I figured that must be it." He stares at me for a beat. "You could have just told me that."

He seems so damned sincere. I have to remind myself that, in the span of a few hours last night, this guy lied to me about his name, his job, and where he lives. He probably has a wife and kids waiting at home for him.

"You didn't mention last night that you were looking for a dog," I say.

He laughs. "And you didn't mention you rescue dogs. I thought you said you work in some kind of sales."

I glance at him, nearly sucked into the vortex of his baby blue eyes. *Noooo,* a silent scream wails inside my hormone-laden brain. "We're an all-volunteer organization. I have two other jobs to pay my bills." My voice is clipped. "The dog rescue is just something I do on the side."

"Good for you. I wish we had talked about it last night. I love dogs. I've wanted one for years," he says, sounding so sweet I can feel cavities forming in my teeth. He touches my arm lightly and I hate the way my body reacts, blood surging south, warmth pooling just below my naval.

I square my shoulders toward him, and give him my deadliest glare. I don't have time for this. I have more respect for myself than to give another minute to a guy who lies to me within minutes of meeting me. And pretending to be a SEAL? Hell, that's just unpatriotic.

"Listen, as nice as it is to talk about old times, I really do have to get back to my volunteers."

He takes a step backward, looking confused. "And Kosmo?"

"What about him?"

"I'd still really like to meet him. I think I could give him a good home."

I nod curtly. "I'll be in touch." I turn on my heel and walk away. Yet pulling my eyes from him is almost painful. Such a waste of good looks on a complete liar.

And my thoughts seem to echo those of my friends. Thank God I hadn't slept with him.

CHAPTER 3

- LOGAN -

My niece is tearing a path across my parents' front lawn toward my truck and, just like that, my world lights up.

Hannah is beyond adorable in her two tight braids with her glasses that are just a little too big for her face. Despite the sour attitude of her mother, my niece seems to have retained that special joy that comes from being seven.

She's at that age when she doesn't mind me calling her names like Peanut, Sugar Puff, and Pumpkin. Which is good, because I think I'll always think of her as Pumpkin. She still takes me on fairy hunts in the woods that line the banks of the creek beyond my parents' house. And she closes every day saying it's X number of days till Santa comes.

I think we're about at day 230 now.

"Did you get the doggie? Did you get the doggie?" Hannah chants as soon as I open my door.

The smile that had just been on my face threatens to

disappear. I've tried to forget about Kosmo and the bat-shit crazy girl who seems to like playing God with the animal. It's been a week since I saw her in front of the pet store, and I still haven't heard a word about my application.

I've rewound the 24 hours I had known her a few times in my head, and for the life of me, I can't figure out why she turned into a cold-hearted ice queen overnight.

Thank God I hadn't slept with her.

Seriously… I bought her dinner. She pretty much invited herself to my room, plastered me against the elevator in a kiss that was off-the-charts, then disappeared on me as I sat waiting in my room with two orders of lava cake (which I managed to eat later by myself). Then she treats me like I committed a crime the next day.

But my niece, in all her wide-eyed innocence, has reminded me why I'm really pissed off.

That woman has blocked me from getting the dog I want.

"No, Pumpkin," I answer. "Not yet, anyway. But hopefully soon."

Her hazel eyes are sad, ripping the heart out of my chest, until she brightens only three seconds later. "Want to hunt for fairies?"

"You bet." I love the way her mind works—changing direction as quickly as the wind. My niece has ADHD, and I always joke that between her ADHD and my PTSD and my brother's OCD (though he'll never admit to it), we've got enough acronyms in our family to sound like a branch of the federal government.

She is a whirlwind of energy, a whirlwind that her teachers complain about relentlessly, according to her mother.

"Just let me drop these groceries in to your grandma." I take her hand and walk up the paved driveway to my parents' house.

I can never seem to call this place my home, even though I have many memories here. This house is luxurious, and I don't feel like I fit in. Especially not after five deployments and countless missions that showed me how most of the people of the world live. This is the kind of opulence that almost makes me feel a sense of shame.

Don't get me wrong. Even though it was my grandfather who started JLS Heartland, my dad worked his ass off to get the company to where it is today, and I give him a lot of credit for that. He never even went to college, and started working for JLS the Monday after he got his high school diploma. With Dad at the helm, JLS grew from a solid construction company to a housing development empire. JLS Heartland has developments in 32 states now.

Even since his diagnosis, Dad still manages to work eight-hour days, doing most of his work from home. "Eight hours is a short day for me," he is always quick to remind my mother when she nags him to rest. And he's right. Fourteen-hour days were always the norm for him. I barely have any memories of my father because of it.

My mom smiles at me as I walk into the kitchen.

"I still don't get tired of seeing you walk through my door, Logan," she says. I know she's referring to the years I was away. They were hard for her, and I still feel a pang of guilt for putting her through that. But she understands why I felt the need to serve.

Which is more than I can say for my dad.

I smile in reply. "I picked up the stuff you asked for," I tell her as I set a bag of groceries on the counter. My mom is chopping some vegetables for tonight's Sunday dinner. She could easily hire someone to do the cooking for her, but she politely refuses. She won't hire a driver to take Dad to his doctor appointments and, until last year, wouldn't even hire someone to clean her house.

She is a proud woman who thinks she can do everything herself. Which is one of the reasons I came back to Ohio. She needs help with Dad. And even though I have brothers, I know that as Dad's dementia progresses, she'll need all her sons here.

I share a conspiratorial look with Hannah as I witness her snatching a cookie from the plate Mom has reserved for dessert.

Over her shoulder, my mom asks, "So, I don't see that dog with you today. Did you not get him yet?"

Again, with the dog. Obviously, sharing the idea with my family was not the thing to do. "No. I put in an application, but haven't heard from the woman who runs the rescue organization yet."

"Maybe she didn't get your application. I never trust all those online forms they have these days. I always think it's better to hand things to someone in person."

Sure, I think, *unless the lady apparently hates you with a vengeance.* "She got the application. I saw her in person last week. I just think she doesn't want me to have the dog."

"Why on earth not?"

I sigh. I'm not about to tell my mom that I had nearly slept with the woman. "For some reason she doesn't like me."

My mom drops her knife and eyeballs me. "Why on earth would she dislike you?"

I crack a smile. My mom is always saying *why on earth* this and *why on earth* that.

"Maybe she has something against military guys." There actually are women that do. I've known a couple kids of service members who had some resentment toward a line of work that took away one of their parents for most of their lives. I can't blame them in the least. I even dated a girl briefly who was terrified she'd fall too hard for me, and then just be waiting around all the time like her mother did for her Navy dad. Waiting for me to come home. Waiting to get orders that would send me away again. Waiting for that dreaded day when a Casualty Assistance Calls Officer might show up at her door and tell her that I wasn't coming home again.

There is a lot of waiting in the military.

But Alexandra didn't seem to mind that I had a military background when we talked over dinner that night. I can't remember all that I told her, but she definitely got that predictably dazzled look in her eyes when I told her about my life as a SEAL a while back. Damn, she had been cute with those dark eyes and gentle curves, and a wholesome façade hiding the inner witch that I got to see the morning after.

"Are you just giving up, then?" my mom asks.

I glance over at Hannah before I answer. I never want that little girl to think that her uncle gave up on anything. "Just trying to figure out what my next move is."

"You could just go to the county shelter and adopt a dog there."

"Yeah, but this one really needs some medical help."

My mom glances my way. "Taking on another hard luck case, are you?" She smiles, probably remembering all the injured animals I used to bring home as a kid. "Well, then just do what you always did when you were a SEAL." My mother perks up a smile as she reaches for the refrigerator door.

"What's that, Mom?"

"Command. Take the lead. Tell that woman what you want and 'don't give up the ship.'" She ends her statement with a famous Captain James Lawrence quote. I have to love the way Mom is always weaving some Navy heritage into the conversation. You'd think she had been married to an Admiral all these years.

She is right, I realize hours later as Hannah and I are deep in the woods looking for fairies, armed with flashlights and magnifying glasses, and covered in some kind of apple-berry scent that she said would attract them. And yeah, I realize that my brothers in the SEALs would never let me live it down if they knew I let my niece douse me in perfume.

My mom is right. I don't need to retreat. Time to march forward.

I slip away to the front porch just after dessert with my phone and start typing out a message to the contact email address I found online, when one of my brothers steps out on the porch.

"It was nice of you to come," he says.

Ryan is my younger brother by ten months, which classifies him as my Irish twin, I guess. "I always do," I tell him.

"Yeah. Keep it up, okay?"

"I will."

"I know Dad appreciates it."

I nod slowly, knowing immediately where this conversation is headed. I'm the eldest son—the one Dad always imagined handing over his business to one day. Even though I enjoy construction, I love actually building something with my own two hands. Dad's business has gotten so huge that the only place for me in his company is something behind a desk, wearing a suit, and having godforsaken business lunches with people I don't give a shit about.

I know; I interned there in high school before I got accepted to the U.S. Naval Academy, breaking my father's heart.

"He's glad you're home. We all are. Especially now."

I sigh deeply, wanting to ask him something, but not really ready to hear an honest answer. "How's he been, anyway? He always seems fine at dinner." About a year ago, when I was stationed in Annapolis, I got a call from Dylan, my youngest brother. He had received a phone call from Dad asking when Dylan's plane was going to land and where he needed to be picked up.

Trouble was, Dylan wasn't flying on any planes that day.

My dad is pretty stubborn, and he insisted that Dylan had told him that he was flying into Ohio that day. We all shrugged it off. Dylan does travel a lot, and Dad was under a lot of stress at work.

But then about a month later, he called me from his car. He didn't know where he was. Not just like his car had made the wrong turn and he was in an unfamiliar part of town. He didn't even know what state he was in.

I'm not sure why he called me, actually, but I'm glad he did. Because if I hadn't heard it for myself, I never would have believed it.

He hung up the phone with me against my pleas, and I called the police to try to get some help finding him. They found him in Pennsylvania two hours later.

The diagnosis was vascular dementia.

That day when I had flown to Ohio to meet my family in the hospital, I learned that the man I knew as strong and determined and successful would slowly wither away into someone who didn't even recognize me. It would take a while—maybe five or so years depending on how quickly it was advancing, the doctor said. But it was inevitable.

"He's doing well," Ryan tells me, and I fight back the hope that always churns up inside of me when I hear things like this. I can't help thinking sometimes that the doctors have made a mistake. But then another episode happens, and reality stabs me in the gut.

"He'd really love it if you came to work for the company, Logan."

I roll my eyes childishly at the statement.

"It wouldn't have to be running the show. But right now,

while he still knows what's going on around him, don't you think it would be a good thing?"

I know what he's insinuating and I hate it. I could work for him for a while, until Dad reaches the point when he doesn't know who I am anyway. I don't like thinking about that. "Ask Dylan."

Ryan cocks his head. "You know he has no place at JLS Heartland. Never had any interest. Even Dad knows that."

My youngest brother Dylan had been blessed with enough talent to eclipse any plans my dad had for him at the company. He went to college on a full wrestling scholarship, spent every free moment training, and ended up with a medal at the Olympics. So while I was deployed to third world countries armed with an HK416 and wondering if I'd come home in a body bag, Dylan was raking in millions from cereal and shaving endorsements.

I'm happy with my choices in life, don't get me wrong. But Dylan's a pretty hard guy to relate to.

"Besides," Ryan adds, "he's busy now. Got another gym opening up in LA."

And I'm *not* busy is what he's really saying, just renovating a handful of little townhomes. In this family, that classifies more as a hobby than a job.

"I'd go crazy locked in an office all day, Ryan. Besides, I've only started renovating my townhomes. You'd know that if you ever stopped by," I add. Hey, if he's going to toss a little guilt my way, I can throw it right back at him.

I bought a strip of townhomes that were in foreclosure when I moved here, and am fixing them up one by one. I love the work. I love taking something that has been neglected and turning it into something that shines. If I stick around after I sell these ones, I might do it again. Sadly, there are plenty of foreclosures in our area these days.

"Sorry. Been meaning to, but I've been a bit chained to my desk now that Dad's unable to take the lead on projects."

My point exactly, I want to say. But I don't. I know Ryan enjoys his work to some degree, but I also know there is a trace of resentment toward me for not stepping up to bat when Dad wanted me in his company years ago.

"Just think about it," he finishes, rising from the wicker chair and stretching his back as he gazes at the sunset.

I see the way he looks at the stand of trees leading up to the creek as he stretches, and it saddens me. I never pictured Ryan taking over for Dad. Not Ryan, who liked backpacking and hiking and rock climbing. Looking back at the two of us as we were growing up, I'm a little surprised that he wasn't the one who ended up a Navy SEAL rather than me.

But he has a responsible streak in him a mile long. And I'm damn grateful our family has him. "I will think about it. Promise." And I will. After the townhomes are renovated and sold, I might be looking for another challenge to fill my time.

I'm clueless, though, how a mission-driven guy like me would thrive at JLS Heartland.

Nodding and giving my shoulder a pat, he walks back into the house. The silence of the night somehow bothers me —it always has since my last year in the SEALs—as though I'm waiting for a firefight to erupt or an IED to explode beneath me. My heart picks up its pace, and my throat feels like it's closing.

I know it isn't. This, I can control now.

I suck in a deep breath, reminding myself that oxygen is not scarce and look back down at my phone to distract myself. I start tapping out a message:

"Alexandra, I'm writing to follow up about Kosmo since I haven't heard from you. I'm still interested in him and know that I could provide a good home for him. I would appreciate it if you

would contact me ASAP to conduct the house check you mentioned."

I gaze out at the final rays of sun as they disappear behind the trees in the distance, remembering the image of the refreshing woman that I shared dinner with. She had that kind of sweetness that guys like me eat up. Such a stark contrast to how she was the next morning.

Coming from a band of three brothers, the intricacies of the female mind continue to evade me.

"I'm not sure what happened between the time you departed that Friday evening and the following Saturday morning that caused you to detest me..."

I pause, and delete the word "detest."

"...dislike me. However, it is imperative that Kosmo receives the medical care he needs and I can provide this without further delay."

That's right. Guilt her.

Through the open windows, I hear the laughter of my niece inside as she plays *Go Fish* with my brothers. My heart feels its usual tug.

"Regardless, I would like to offer to pay for any medical expenses Kosmo has, and would like to discuss with you and his vet scheduling the surgery he needs."

I close with my contact information, and hold myself back from adding my advice that she seek psychiatric help for her obvious multiple personality issues. After all, now is the time to focus on Kosmo.

CHAPTER 4

- LOGAN -

I had expected a reply. I hadn't expected it so quickly.

Within an hour of sending my email, she asked if she could do the house check tomorrow during the day sometime. She was surprisingly polite, and apologetic for not being able to do it after normal work hours, but she works most nights.

So now it's closing in on 10 a.m. and I'm rushing to finish painting this wall in the townhome that adjoins to mine before she arrives. I hate leaving a wall half-painted. My team is in the third townhome over, knocking down the wall between the kitchen and the living room, just as they had in this one last week. The noise is overwhelming, and I'm really worried she'll tell me that my house is too chaotic for a dog like Kosmo to recover from surgery. I plan on putting the heavy work on pause during that time anyway, but I just don't want anything to trigger this woman into going Ice Queen on me again.

The windows are open, and I'm surprised to hear a car pull up in front of my home ten minutes early. Leaning over to peek out the window, my hand slips and I end up with a thick, giant streak of beige paint on my blue shirt.

Dammit. *Way to make an impression.*

I open the door before she even is able to ring the bell next door. "Hi."

Glancing at the number on the door, she looks confused. "Oh. I thought you had written that you were in #1."

"I am." I step outside and move to my own door, swinging it open. "I'm just working on #2 and 3 now. I bought this row of townhomes and am renovating them."

"Oh," she says noncommittally and adds, "Wow," when she steps into my living room.

I have to admit, my house looks great. I bought most of the furniture and art pieces at Maeve's direction when I moved to Annapolis for my last tour with the Navy. There's nothing that looks "bachelor pad" here and that suits me fine.

"This is really beautiful," she says, her eyes darting around the room.

"Well, don't be too impressed. My friend Maeve is an interior designer."

"She's talented. Does she live in Newton's Creek?"

I suppress a laugh, trying to imagine Maeve in a small Midwestern town like this one. "No, she's in Annapolis, Maryland."

Her hand strokes the supple leather of the couch and I notice she seems to be appreciating the woodwork I installed. There's dentil molding along the ceiling and built-in bookshelves around the fireplace. I love books and I like to show them off.

She walks toward them. "You must read a lot."

"I try. I've only read half of these though."

"You could get an e-reader and not have to store all these," she says, making me grimace. I like e-readers—don't get me wrong. When I was deployed, it was the only way I could read as much as I liked since I couldn't fill my rucksack with books. But given the choice, I just prefer the weight of a good, heavy book in my hands.

"I guess," I reply. "But then what would I put on my bookshelves?"

She nods, her eyes wandering to the huge smear of paint on my chest.

I glance down apologetically. "Sorry. I was painting next door," I say.

Her eyes are still on my chest, but she seems to be staring at my pecs more than the paint. She bites her bottom lip awkwardly. "So, Kosmo is in the car. Shall I bring him in?" she asks, fluttering her lashes nervously as her eyes meet mine.

"Of course. I was expecting you to."

"Yeah. I just have learned to always take a quick peek at a house first. Sometimes applicants don't tell me about other dogs that might not get along with ours. Or once a house I visited had a definite hoarder situation going on. And another time there was a guy who greeted me at the door wearing nothing but a thong. I mean, who wants to expose a nice dog to that?" she finishes, stifling a laugh, and I swear her eyes glance down at my groin momentarily.

This woman completely baffles me. I'm getting the same vibe I did from her that night at dinner, the one that tells me she's attracted to me. But I'm still waiting for her head to start spinning as she mutates into the woman who stared daggers at me the morning after.

She heads toward the door, but stops abruptly at a framed

photograph of my team and me before my final mission with the SEALs. It's signed by all my SEAL brothers.

"What's this?" Her voice is faint and I can barely hear it over the circular saw two doors down.

"Just a photo of my team."

Taking two steps closer to it, she almost looks pale suddenly, and I'm clueless why. I'm a little freaked out by the expression on her face right now. She's eyeing my picture in a way I can't even define.

That photo means a lot to me and if she does something weird like sending it crashing to the floor, I'll be pretty pissed off.

"And that's you. Second from the right," she notices.

"Yeah."

She touches her fingers to her lips. "You were a SEAL."

My eyebrows arch. I'm positive that I told her that when we had dinner. "Yeah. We talked about that. Remember?"

"But your application said you're a construction manager."

"Um, yeah. I separated from the military last year. Got a little too banged up for it." I'm vague like I always am. If pressed for details, I tell people about my shoulder injury because it usually shuts them up. It's really no one's business that I came back from my last couple missions with moderate PTSD, as defined by the docs. I'm doing much better. And somehow talking about having it now just doesn't seem right to me since most the guys I know who have it are a lot worse off than me.

"Oh, no," she says quietly, her lower lip inexplicably quivering. "I really owe you an apology."

"Why?"

"I assumed that you had been lying about being a SEAL just to—um..."

"Get laid," I finish for her. I toss my head back and laugh. "So is that why you suddenly disappeared that night?"

"No. I didn't think that till the morning after when I saw your application and some other job listed as your occupation. And then when you said your name wasn't really Logan…"

"It is," I interrupt, trying hard to hold back a smile. "I only fill out forms with my legal name though. A habit from ten years in the military."

"Yeah, I get that now." She sighs, looking humiliated. "But you did tell me you were from San Diego."

"If I recall correctly, you asked me where home was. I only moved back here temporarily for some family reasons. If you had asked me where I lived, I would have said right here." I shake my head. "Look, I'm sorry if I wasn't specific enough for you. Maybe I should have made things clearer. But I don't lie to women."

That is the God's truth. Lies are like unexploded ordnance. You don't know when they'll blow up in your face, but they will.

"I'm really sorry," she says.

I touch her shoulder impulsively. I can't resist because she really looks defeated and I hate it when people look that way. "Not a problem."

"I'll get Kosmo." She walks out my door without even looking me in the eyes.

It's really not the big deal she thinks it is. It's not like she poured gasoline on my truck and lit a match. She just acted a little bitchy one morning.

Hell, my last girlfriend treated me like that once a month when she'd get PMS, and I wasn't mad at her about it.

I step to the open doorway and see Kosmo bound out of the car. He's big and burly and full of personality, I can tell already. I love how dogs just barrel through life. I've seen it before. They don't let things get to them much.

Got a heart valve problem? Oh well. Where's my toy?

Missing leg? No prob! Let's play anyway.

Blind in both eyes? So what. Got a bone for me?

I try to keep that attitude. It was hard when I was told that my time with the SEALs had come to an end. No one wants to hear that. But I just try to barrel through, same as Kosmo.

When they step in the house, I sit on the ground as Alexandra unhooks his leash, and let him sniff and lick me anywhere he wants. He immediately shows interest in the thick streak of wet paint on my shirt. Instinctively, I strip my shirt off quickly. "Hey, no, buddy. I don't need you licking paint off me the first time we meet." I ball up my shirt and toss it to the side. His fur is thicker than most Labs and I wonder if there's some husky or collie in him.

"Want to see your house?" I ask him. I know it's presumptuous to assume she'll let me have him. But at this point, I'll do anything for this mutt.

CHAPTER 5

~ ALLIE ~

Please put your shirt back on. The sight of your body will ruin other men for me.

I want to say it. I want to beg it. But I also want to just give one poke to that tantalizing V at the edge of his abs just to see what it feels like. His jeans are low on his hips, just low enough that I can see every precious ripple of muscle on his torso. What does a guy have to do to get a body like that?

"Be right back," he says and he bounds up the stairs, presumably to his bedroom to get a new shirt. Kosmo follows him.

I want to follow him, too.

Not a minute passes and he's in front of me again, covered up in a t-shirt that only turns my temperature down a degree or two. Truth is, he looks almost as sexy in that shirt as he did half-naked. Almost.

I follow him through the house as he gives me a tour. He

opens the fridge when we're in the kitchen and asks me if I want a soda. I nod, wishing I could pour the cold liquid over my body right now.

There's a box of dog treats on the counter that he says he picked up this morning, and he asks if it's all right for Kosmo to have one. I tell him yes, feeling a warmth settle into me as he sits on the ground and hands Kosmo the treat. Kosmo nuzzles him, looking for another and Logan wraps his thick arms around him in a hug.

I could cry right now. I could honest-to-God cry as I see these two together. It's like they were meant for each other, and I had nearly stood in their way.

Of course, I had intended to do a house check on him all along. I just let his application fall to the bottom of the bunch. After all, just because I thought he was a lying prick didn't mean he might not be a good pet owner. And like Cass was quick to point out, just about everyone lies when they are hanging out in hotel bars. Even *I* had dipped my toe in the water of deceit when I told him my name was Alexandra. It just sounds sexier than Allie, though no one uses my full name except for telemarketers.

But he hadn't been lying. He is a SEAL. Or was, specifically. And trying to remember what exactly he had told me that night, I'm willing to bet he never said he *currently* is a SEAL. Honestly, looking at him during dinner I was so damn focused on how gorgeous he was, the conversation had gone pretty much like this:

"Blah, blah, blah, Logan, blah, blah, blah, Navy SEAL, blah, blah, blah, blah, San Diego, blah, blah, blah, blah, Check, please!"

He shows us the upstairs next and my heart skips two or three beats as we step into the master bedroom.

He smacks the top of his king size mattress to urge Kosmo up onto it. Is it wrong to envy a dog? If he'd make the same gesture for me, I'd probably launch myself onto the mattress, too.

"So, is this where he'll sleep?" I ask.

"Yep, unless you think someplace else is better."

"It's perfect." Some dogs do better in crates at night, but definitely not this one. And I have to admit, I'm partial to letting a dog sleep with me at night. After all, it's the only company I get in the sack these days.

I doubt Logan can say the same.

"And I'm thinking I'll keep a water bowl upstairs in the bathroom here, and one downstairs. Your website said he gets a little more tired than other dogs right now, right?"

"Mmhm. But if the surgery is successful, that should change." I step into the master bath in the direction he's pointing, and my jaw drops. It's as big as my bedroom, and the tile work makes me feel like I'm in some boutique hotel in New York City. There are double sinks, a stand up shower, and a huge soaking tub. With the image of him shirtless still etched in my brain, I can't resist imagining him in that tub. And since it's big enough for two, my own likeness creeps into the fantasy. Of course, in my imagination, the ten extra pounds on my thighs and butt have miraculously relocated to my breasts.

I clear my throat. "Was this part of the renovation you were talking about?"

"Yes. I had to strip this place pretty much down to the studs. And I stole some of the space from the bedroom on the other side of this wall to make the bathroom bigger. Like it?"

"Love it," I reply without hesitation. I've never met anyone who's done a big project like this.

I step back into his bedroom where Kosmo is making himself at home on the four-poster bed. The room is definitively masculine with its dark wood and a leather recliner facing a television along the back wall. Another two bookcases stand on either side of a picture window. Glancing outside, I notice a fence around his yard—perfect for a dog like Kosmo. Just outside the fence, I see a rocky portion of Newton's Creek, the picturesque stream that gave its name to our town. The view is lovely, and I can picture Logan dropping a fishing rod into the water there with Kosmo at his side.

"You have a big yard for a townhome," I tell him.

"Let me show you it," he says, backing out of the room. "Since it's an end unit, I decided I'd fence off the side yard, too."

We walk down to the kitchen and he swings open the back door. Kosmo darts into the green space, sniffing and exploring. He's in heaven right now.

"He seems pretty happy here," Logan notices.

"He does," I agree.

He turns to me, suddenly looking serious. "Listen, I need to ask you something important."

I immediately brace myself. I knew this was too good to be true.

"How is he with kids?" he asks.

I expel the breath I was holding. I'm not sure what I was expecting, but when a man you barely know offers to cover a dog's $4,000 surgery, it's natural to think there might be some strings attached.

"You have kids?"

"No. But I have a seven-year-old niece who I spend a lot of time with when she's staying with her dad. I'd need a dog to get along with her." He pauses. "I'll pay his medical bills regardless, though. I just don't want her getting attached to a dog that might not get along with her. Life doles out enough rejection as it is."

I'm impressed that he even thinks on that level. So many

people don't see the big picture when it comes to adopting a dog. It's not all cuddles and long walks and games of fetch. "He plays all the time with my friend's four-year-old," I say, remembering how patient Kosmo was when Kim's son yanked his tail. "I mean, you really need to be cautious with any dog, and especially when he's recovering from surgery he might be crabby. But I haven't seen anything that would make me hesitate in letting you adopt him."

"So you'll let me?" He looks hopeful.

"Yes." I feel a little lump in my throat at the thought of handing Kosmo over to someone else. I always feel this way, though. "And it's written in the contract that you'll sign that if for any reason you can't provide a home for him, you have to give him back to us."

"Absolutely. So what happens now? Do you just leave him here?"

I almost agree to. I feel that certain Kosmo is exactly where he belongs. "Um, no. I actually have to check your references first. I usually do those after house checks because it sometimes takes a while to track people down, and half the time I get stood up for house checks, anyway."

"Really?"

"Yep. But anyway, that will give you time to buy the things you'll need. I'll give you a list and the brand of foods and treats he's been eating. I'd stick to what he's used to, at least for a while. And his medicine—" I begin, hesitating only briefly. "You'll need to stock up on his heart meds because he can't go a day without them. I have about a week's worth that I can give you. They're, um, pretty expensive," I warn him, ready to watch him bail.

"It's not a problem." He says it without hesitation, and I can't help but wonder how much this guy's banking as a construction manager. After buying a row of townhomes and putting all this work into them, I can't imagine he's got a lot of other projects right now. But I won't look a gift horse in the mouth.

"I can drop him off later this week, if that's okay. I'd really like to do it before Friday evening, if possible." I wouldn't ordinarily tell him why, but for some reason I'm compelled to. "The shelter euthanizes dogs then and since I'll have an extra space available in my home, I'd really like to pick up another dog who has run out of time."

His eyes are still fixed on Kosmo as he plays in the yard, but his expression changes. "Jesus," he says quietly. "Yeah, I'll buy everything I need tonight and be ready for him as soon as you want to bring him over."

"Great, thanks." I slap my hand to my thigh, and Kosmo charges to my side. "Well, I don't want to take up any more of your time today. I should probably get going."

He nods, heading back into the house, and I fight disappointment because I really don't want to go.

"Thanks for coming by, Alexandra."

"Allie," I say, hooking Kosmo back up to his leash. "Most people really just call me Allie."

"Really? You look more like an Alexandra to me."

I stare at him silently a moment. He probably doesn't know I am taking that as a compliment, but I am. When I look in the mirror, I don't see anyone as exotic or dramatic as an Alexandra staring back at me. I like the idea that he might see something different.

He walks me out the front door and up to the side of my car.

Bending over, he gives Kosmo a final pet and kisses him on the top of his head. That's one lucky dog, I'm thinking.

"See you soon, boy," he says, opening up the car door. I hope he doesn't notice that my car smells like a kennel.

Walking over to my side of the car, he asks, "So why did you leave?"

I'm caught off guard. Maybe it's the proximity to him that's causing it, but my brain seems to be short-circuiting as he gallantly opens my door for me. "Hmm?"

"That night at the hotel. If it wasn't because you thought I was lying about being a SEAL, then why did you disappear on me?"

Sighing, I sit in my car wishing I could come up with a good way of spinning the truth. "I just chickened out. That's… not like me. You know, following a guy up to his hotel room. I've never done that before."

He smiles. "Technically, you still haven't. You didn't make it over the threshold."

"I'm sorry about that."

"No need to be sorry. I just wish you had told me. I'd never push a woman into something she's not comfortable with."

This guy is too good to be true. I'm tempted to throw myself at him again like I did in that elevator, but I'm sure that train has left the station. After all, I haven't really made the best impression on him.

No need to humiliate myself further with this man.

"Well, I'm sorry, just the same." He'll never know how sorry. The mere sight of Logan does more for my sex drive than the best vibrator I sell.

As he shuts my car door for me, Kosmo sticks his head over the seat and licks my ear. Wish Logan would do that, but I can't be too sad about it.

After all, Kosmo's getting a home and the surgery he needs, and I'll be saving another dog this week.

Life is lonely. But life is good.

CHAPTER 6

~ ALLIE ~

"Seriously? He's really a SEAL?"

It's barely nine in the morning and I haven't had my coffee yet. I'm not ready for questions like this. But it's my boss, Nancy, talking to me, so I slap on a smile and respond.

"Was a SEAL," I clarify, talking into the little camera on my phone. Nancy likes to Skype our meetings, and I don't mind because I can do it in my pajama pants. I manage to put on a bra and a decent shirt just to make me look a little professional. But I've worked for her for over a year now, and I'm pretty sure she can guess I'm in slippers right now. "And he really does go by Logan. When I called his references, that's the only name they used for him."

"Holy crap. And you told me you were such a bitch to him that Saturday morning," Nancy reminds me.

It might seem odd that I even share details like that with my boss, but at this point she's really more like a friend who passes me a meager paycheck every two weeks. She runs her nonprofit out of her home in Cincinnati, but is on the road two-thirds of the time giving speeches and having meetings pumping up the health benefits of being vegan.

It's a hard sell in the heartland of America.

I take a sip of my coffee, laden with non-vegan creamer, and am glad she can't smell the bacon and cheese omelet I cooked up this morning. Nancy knows I'm not a vegan, but there's no need to rub her nose in it.

"Yeah," I answer her, pausing to swallow my coffee. "But he's still interested in Kosmo. And Crocco and Bullet look like they'll have homes by the end of the week, too."

"So you'll have no dogs?" she asks.

I nod. "I'll stop by the pound this week and pick up a few more," I say, even though I know that's not what she's insinuating.

Tilting her head to the side, she raises her eyebrows. "Or you could sell your place."

I sigh, trying to press the image of my real dream to the back of my brain. "I'm not ready to take that on." My voice stammers, not sounding very convincing.

Nancy is the dictionary definition of a Type A. There's nothing she won't take on if it means getting closer to her goal. If she gets an idea in her head, she'll pursue it to the ends of the earth. Which is why she has the balls right now to be calling from a hotel in Chicago—home to some of the best steakhouses on the planet, in my opinion—where she's been trying to convince schools to embrace the vegan lifestyle.

Good luck with that, Nancy.

We talk more about her schedule of meetings and I jot down notes about some calls I need to make for her.

Even though the pay is the pits and I make twice as much selling sex toys in the evenings, I love my day job working for Nancy because she lets me telecommute. So while the rest of the world is stuck in rush hour traffic, I can be at home with my dogs, half of whom need a refresher course in housetraining when I get them from the pound.

I finish getting dressed so I can grab another coffee at Pop's on Anders. It's only a short walk from my condo, and I love that I live in small town America but can actually do things without needing to get in my car.

Granted, there aren't many things to do in downtown Newton's Creek, unless I want to buy gourmet pet food at Sally Sweet's (which I certainly can't afford), or get a malted milkshake at the five-and-dime (which I do far too regularly), or drool over the diamonds in the local jewelry store (which, sadly, has been having its going out of business sale for the last two months).

There's a nouveau chic restaurant here, too, though I've never had enough in the bank to try it. It's got a five-star rating online and people drive all the way here from Dayton and Cincinnati to check it out when they spend a day in the country.

I pick up one of the free papers on the corner before I turn onto Anders. It's a warm late spring day and the humidity has kicked in just enough to make my hair frizz at the ends.

When I'm at the counter ordering, I put down my paper to pull my hair back in a ponytail.

"Hi, Pops," I say, my eyes meeting the older man behind the counter.

"Happy Tuesday, Allie," he greets me. Every morning, it's the same greeting. Happy Monday, Happy Tuesday, Happy Wednesday. And Pops has been plenty happy lately ever since the commuter bus started picking up here on Anders Street, doubling his business on weekdays.

I can't complain about it either since my condo's value

has spiked with more people wanting to live in the serenity of Newton's Creek and commute to the city.

"The usual?" he asks.

"Yes, thanks."

"Can I tempt you with a donut today?"

"No. Please don't," I beg him. I could easily be tempted, but something about meeting Logan has made my donut ritual seem a little less tasty. I know I blew my chance with the guy, but it reminded me that one day, maybe, just maybe, I'll want to get naked with a man again.

Glancing at my watch, I pick up my pace toward home. I'm meeting Cass at the pound today to photograph the dogs. Cass is really good with a camera. I guess she picked it up modeling in New York. So every Monday we meet at the pound to take pictures of the new intakes so that they can be put online. Before we started doing this, they didn't even have photos up of the dogs, and the only names they had listed were things like "HC128-SpanielX" and the like. There aren't many creative types who work at our local pound.

By the time I arrive, Cass is already trying to put a pink bow on a Westie. The dog's all brushed and I'm feeling guilty. "Am I late?"

"No. I got here early. Half of them are done already."

"Thanks."

"Figured I owed you after talking trash about your SEAL."

I scoff. "He's not my SEAL. And don't worry about it. I would have done the same thing if the tables were turned." I move to the Westie. "What's your name, pretty girl?"

"Boy. It's a boy."

"Then why the pink bow?"

"I didn't have a blue one. And it looks so cute. Don't you think?"

I shrug. It does look cute. This one won't even need my

rescuing, I'm betting as Cass snaps a picture. Someone will probably snatch him right up direct from the pound.

But there are so many others.

We walk Ice Cream (Cass apparently named him) back to his cage, and I frown at all the new faces around me. They all aren't as cute as Ice Cream. And worse, I see the familiar dogs, the ones I saw last week and the week before, who are likely running out of time. They might not be here when I come back later this week. I always let the County know when I've got space coming up, and they do their best to hold off on euthanizing them. But there's only so much room here, and I need both my fingers and toes to count how many times I've come for a specific dog only to discover they'd just been euthanized.

Death is a bitch. There's no "undo" button for it.

I feel my face droop. "Does this ever seem futile?"

Shocked, Cass turns to me. "What?"

"There are just so many we can't save. And they keep coming. I wish I could get more foster homes."

Cass frowns at my discouragement. "With the commuter bus now coming to town, more people are going to move here, Allie. Happens all the time. More people mean more fosters. And more people willing to adopt, too."

"I know..." My voice trails as my eyes fall to a German shepherd. His face seems wise and I wonder what he's seen in his life. Why would anyone give up such a beautiful dog? Will he still be here later this week when I have space? I make a mental note to ask before I leave today.

I turn to Cass. "Remember that property I was telling you about?"

"The foreclosure? Sure."

Pausing before I say anything else, I mull whether to even voice my thoughts. There's an old boarding kennel that went out of business before I even moved here, after a newer, fancier kennel opened up closer to the highway—one of those luxury pet resorts that offers tuck-in service, quilted bedding and dog massages. The older place just couldn't compete, so the property is in foreclosure—two secluded acres about fifteen minutes from town sandwiched between two farms. I snooped around it once and guess it could fit at least thirty dogs in there.

It's my dream.

Nancy told me about a nonprofit loan I could get, but I'd still need to come up with a good percentage of the money myself. Even though we get some donations, it's not nearly enough to secure the kind of loan I'd need to buy that place and fix it up.

"Do you have a couch?" The words slip from my mouth too easily.

"Umm, yeah. Why?"

I sigh as I retrieve a dog from his cage and hook him up to a leash. "I've been thinking more about that boarding kennel. And if these three adoptions go through this week, it will be the first time I've been dog-free in ages, right?"

"Right. But what has that got to do with the boarding kennel?"

"What if I sold my condo, and used the money to secure that nonprofit loan Nancy told me about. I could make a bid on the foreclosure."

"Where would you live?"

"Your couch." I send her a feeble grin.

"Oh, Allie. You'd hate where I live. The people in my building are freaks. Even I can't stand them, and I have a really high tolerance for freaks."

Frowning, I lead the dog down the long hallway toward the room where we've set up our makeshift photo studio. Cass's apartment is right outside of Buckeye Land, where most of the seasonal workers like her live. She's right. It sounds like hell to me. But it can't be worse than the hell I face walking in here every week and seeing all the dogs I can't save. "It would only be for a short while, till I hear back from the bank."

She picks up a dog brush. "You're welcome to stay as long as you need. My roommate is drunk half the time she's home anyway and probably won't even notice. I don't even think she's noticed I started fostering dogs. But I think it's a crazy idea. What if you go through all that and don't even get the place? I've heard foreclosures are weird like that. You put an offer on one and wait for months, and the damn thing ends up going to someone else anyway."

My shoulders slump. "But who'd want an old kennel? No one around here. It's been sitting vacant for so long, I can't imagine it's in good shape."

"All the more reason not to buy it, hon."

I sweep up a pile of fur that has collected on the ground. "I just can't get it out of my mind, Cass. I mean, it might be run-down, but it's a boarding kennel, already equipped for animals. How many times is an opportunity like this going to come up?" I take the brush from Cass and start on the matted fur on the dog's front legs, giving him a pet with my free hand. "When you decided to move to New York City to model, weren't you following your dream?"

"Yeah, and look how that turned out for me, genius. I'm playing fairy princess in the middle of freaking Ohio for the summer because that's the only thing my agent could get me."

"But you went for it. You went for your dream. You don't regret it, do you?"

"Every day of my life."

Okay, not the answer I was expecting. "But you'd regret it more if you hadn't tried. You'd be working somewhere wondering 'what if?'"

“Maybe. But at least I wouldn’t have to slap on a smile for another slobbery, germ-ridden kid who’s been in line an hour in the heat to get a photo op with me.” She pauses. “Oh, speaking of, they changed my schedule on me again, and I won’t be able to bring Moppet to the adoption event on Saturday.”

I nod, expecting this. Now that Buckeye Land is starting their summer schedule, I doubt I’ll be getting much help from Cass. “No problem. I can pick her up in the morning and bring her back if you give me your key. Or I’ll ask Kim. She’s running a party for me tonight, anyway.”

Kim only does a couple parties a year for me. Her parents frown at the notion of their daughter selling sex toys, her mother referring to them as “those Devil tools,” which is why Kim needs to store her samples in my closet.

“Great.” Cass picks up the camera. “And you know what? Don’t listen to me. You go for your dream. My couch is there for you if you need it.”

CHAPTER 7

- LOGAN -

"Oooh, pretty." My niece is toying with the overlay of the wedding invitation I received from Annapolis. It's laser cut paper that looks like elegant lace, fastened by a blush pink bow that only my niece can fully appreciate.

I'm more of an e-invitation kind of guy.

"Is this from a princess?" she asks. At her age, everything is princesses and fairy tales and happy endings. I hope she enjoys this stage while it lasts. Because, damn it all, it won't.

I open the bow for her. "No. It's just a wedding invitation," I say bringing disappointment to her eyes. It's for Bess's wedding, someone I only ran into a few times while I was in Annapolis, but my friend Maeve is the Maid of Honor. I'd bet my next paycheck—if I had one—that Maeve hand-picked the invitations herself.

"When I get married, I want to have invitations like these."

"Then you'll have them, honey," I tell her confidently. There's nothing too good for my brother's only child. He'll have white doves deliver the invitations if she wants it.

"Are you going?"

I wince at the thought. I hate weddings, especially going stag. But I feel a pinch of guilt for the regrets that I'm destined to send back as a reply. Maeve warned me the invitation was coming. Bess doesn't exactly have a huge family and Maeve's trying to bulk up the bride's side of the aisle.

Since my family's pretty big, three brothers and seven cousins, and about twenty SEAL brothers, I shouldn't even be able to relate to Bess's predicament. But the idea of not having them, any of them, is like a punch in the gut.

Besides, she's marrying an Army guy. A Ranger. She's going to need all the support she can get. "I might," I finally reply with a sigh as Hannah sits back down to our game of *Battleship*. Playing a board game is always a daylong event with Hannah, as she flits about the room in between moves, distracted by whatever happens to land within her line of sight.

I can imagine the struggle the poor kid is having in school and it breaks my heart.

"E4." My niece stares at me, her eyes steely and determined. She looks almost menacing from her expression, despite the pigtails popping out from the sides of her head.

I glance down at my tiny plastic ships on my board, and frown. "Hit. Submarine."

Her face lights up, like it always does. To see her smile like that, I'd gladly throw any game of *Battleship*. Fact is, though, I'm not throwing the game at all. She's whipping my ass like she always does. She's got an instinct for games that is unreal, and as soon as she is old enough, I'm taking her to Vegas.

I press my little red peg into my partially sunken sub when I hear the doorbell ring.

"He's here!" She jumps up from the table and races to the door.

I dart behind her and stop her from swinging it open. "Now remember, this dog is new to you, so let *him* approach *you,* okay? And if he doesn't seem into you, don't push it." Sounds like I'm giving her dating advice about ten years too early, but I'm not. I'm seriously worried about how this might go. My niece is my everything. She has a pretty hard time making friends at school, and the last thing I want to do is bring a dog into her world that might reject her. Or worse, bite her.

"I know, Uncle Logan. I know." Hannah's eyes roll, exasperated.

I open the door and Kosmo immediately strides toward her, sniffing. I watch them like a hawk, looking for any sign of displeasure from either of them. I know Allie is there, too, on the other end of the leash, but I can't even glance her way right now. Kosmo is almost face-high to Hannah, and I see just how vulnerable small children can be to big dogs. My heart is in my throat.

"Hi, Kosmo," Hannah says, reaching out to pet him. He licks her arm and she giggles. He immediately drops down to the ground and rolls on his back for a belly rub.

"That's a good sign."

Only now do I glance up at Allie, who isn't even looking at me. She's watching the two of them, too, and I'm grateful for it. She's dressed up again, like she was that night I met her.

"Hi, Allie," I reach out my hand awkwardly to shake hers. Considering the first night we met, I'm not really sure how to greet this woman. "This is my niece, Hannah."

Allie holds her hand out to Hannah and my niece takes it in her wrong hand and gives it an enthusiastic shake.

Hannah returns to rubbing Kosmo's belly and he is basking in the attention. "Oh, you're a nice doggie. Can he come off the leash?"

"Sure." Allie shuts the door behind her and detaches Kosmo's leash.

I sit on the ground with my niece, confident now this is a good match for all of us. "How are you doing, bud?" I scratch his belly lightly and his back legs quiver, telling me I found a sweet spot.

"Um, I have some paperwork and a few of his toys in the car." Allie tosses her head in the direction of the door.

"Want me to get them?"

"No, that's okay."

Allie slips out, and my eyes can't help following her. She's in a torso-hugging peach t-shirt and a short skirt that is made of some kind of jersey material. She looks like she's headed to a picnic. Her brown hair is swooped up into a high ponytail, revealing a dark mole at the base of her neck. And for the life of me, I have the distinct urge to kiss it.

I give myself a shake as the door shuts behind her and look at my niece, who is still petting Kosmo. "So, do you like him?"

"I love him," she says, dipping her head low to the ground and embracing him while he lies prone on his back. If there were ever a position that a dog might growl at a child, this would be it, essentially trapped against the ground. But Kosmo is savoring the attention.

"Just keep your face away from his, hon," I remind her. I can't help being a little cautious. Since I was always out rescuing strays as a kid, I was bit by my fair share. It's not something I want to happen to Hannah. But the more I'm seeing them together, the less I worry. And I worry plenty about this little girl.

When Allie comes in, we move to the kitchen table so that I can sign some paperwork and write her a check for the adoption fee. When she glances upward at me as I hand her the check, I swear I think I see a few unshed tears in her eyes.

"Thanks," she says. "I know he's found a really good home here." She glances toward the couch which Kosmo has already decided is his. My niece is still petting him, and fur is flying everywhere.

Pressing her lips together as she watches the two of them, she gives a nod as though to reassure herself.

"How long have you had Kosmo?" I find myself asking. I hadn't really considered her feelings in all of this. How hard would that be, to rescue a dog from the shelter and then have to hand him over to someone else for the rest of his life?

"Six months. A little longer than most my dogs because he was a lot harder to rehome."

"Well, I'll take good care of him."

"I'm sure you will." Her face frowns, and she bites her bottom lip. "And will you let me know how his surgery goes?"

"Of course."

"Thanks. And if there's anything he needs. Really—even if you need a dog sitter while he's recovering, because you probably will want someone around then."

"I'll clear my schedule so I can be with him when he needs me. My hours are pretty much my own. But I will definitely call you if I need anything," I add simply because I think she needs to hear it.

She nods as she reaches for the signed paperwork. For some reason, I don't want her to leave. I want to find out more about her and this passion for rescuing dogs she has.

"We were going to order Chinese tonight. Hannah loves egg rolls. You can join us, if you'd like."

"Oh, no. That's okay. Thanks, though."

"Really, it would be great. That way Kosmo doesn't feel abandoned, you know?"

Biting her lip, she seems to hesitate, her eyes transfixed on Hannah and Kosmo snuggling on the couch like the two had been raised together. Her eyes then dart to me and I feel this strange shooting sensation in my heart when her gaze locks on mine. There's something about her, and I can't quite put my finger on it. Like she reminds me of someone I knew in another life, if I believed that sort of bullshit.

But for the record, I don't.

I decide to push. "So, what do you like? Are you more a General Tso's chicken or shrimp fried rice kind of girl?"

A smile touches her lips. "General Tso's chicken. Extra spicy."

I'm wondering if there was any flirtation in what she just said. I'm really hoping there is. Because even though Hannah is here tonight, I've got plenty of other nights this week when I wasn't planning on sharing company with anyone but my new dog. And as I look at Allie, I can't help remembering how she tasted.

"You got it." I pull up the menu on my laptop and order enough food for a feast. Hannah likes taking a couple bites out of everything, and I think it's good that she wants to sample all that life has to offer, so I don't make her hold herself back when she orders eight different entrées. Trouble is, I always end up with about a week's worth of meals for leftovers.

While we wait for the food to be delivered, we move to the backyard, where Kosmo is involved in a slow game of fetch with Hannah. He runs out of energy quicker than most dogs, but I was expecting that. And Hannah seems pretty content petting him for five minutes in between each throw.

"Your niece is precious, Logan."

"She is. Can't say I had anything to do with it, but yes, she is."

"Does she visit you often?"

"Whenever I can convince her dad to let her come over. Ryan's divorced, and only gets her on the weekends. So he has a pretty rough time parting with her. But we all get together at my parents' house a couple Sundays a month for dinner. Kosmo will love it there. Lots of table scraps." I glance at Allie briefly as we sit on the back step of the porch. "So what got you into the dog rescue business?"

"My dad—" she begins, then hesitates, seeming to change direction. "When I graduated from college last year, I went to the pound to get a dog and found out it was a high-kill shelter just because there weren't enough people adopting dogs. So I decided to foster, rather than adopt. I got a few other people to do it with me, and the rest is history, I guess."

She sends me a meek smile, and I'm trying to register what she just said. Something about fostering and a high-kill shelter. But my head is still reeling from the words, "When I graduated from college last year..."

"You just graduated last year?" I can't help myself.

She nods.

Shit. "So you're 23?"

"24, actually. I skipped a semester when—"

Again, she cuts herself off. I think I've never met a woman who liked talking about herself less.

"—I needed a break," she finishes evasively.

Holy crap. "You look..." I catch myself before saying it, thank God, because no woman wants to be told she looks a lot older.

"Older," she finishes for me. She nods. "Yeah, I know. I get that a lot."

I'm still trying to wrap my head around the fact that I nearly picked up a kid practically fresh out of college in a bar. Seriously, after my last catastrophe, that's not my style. 24 is way too young for a cynical former Navy SEAL with more baggage than a 757 bound for Miami during Spring Break.

"So…" I pull my eyes from hers, keeping my hormones in check. 24, I remind myself. I go for women closer to my age. The kind with issues. That way I won't look like such a hot mess by comparison. "Your sales job must not make you travel much, then."

She stares at me, looking slightly baffled.

"Sales. You had told me you were in sales."

"Oh, yeah. That's actually why I love my job. I never have to drive further than an hour or so. And I get to be home a lot."

"What do you sell?"

She nearly chokes on the soda she is sipping as she looks at me, wide-eyed. Her cheeks blush as my niece heads in our direction with a wet dog toy in her hand.

"Um—it's probably a little too graphic for present company, if you know what I mean," she mumbles vaguely as Hannah closes in, with Kosmo only inches behind.

I nod, guessing it's some kind of medical equipment like catheters or scalpels, and too gory to be described in front of a seven-year-old. There are a few companies based outside of Dayton like that and, outside of JLS Heartland, they tend to be the bigger employers.

"And that's just a side job," she continues. "My main job is working for a small nonprofit."

"Dog-related?"

She laughs. "Not really. It's actually an organization that promotes the vegan lifestyle."

I pause, taking in this information. "But you're not—"

"Vegan? No. I tried it for a few days once and failed miserably."

I sigh, relieved that I'm not taking her down the dark path by ordering General Tso's chicken for her tonight. "I was going to say, I'm pretty sure you ate a steak at the hotel restaurant."

"Best steak I've had in a long while."

She must not get out much, because the steaks there are way below par. If she weren't so young, I'd invite her to a place I know in Dayton that serves a really good steak.

But she is young, I remind myself.

Hannah hands her the wet dog toy. "Want to try? Kosmo can catch it before it even hits the ground. I trained him."

"I saw that. You're really a good dog trainer, Hannah. So, how do I get him to do this exactly? I don't think I'll be as good at it as you," Allie says.

I love that she makes Hannah feel good about herself. I'm not sure what goes on in that school my niece attends, but it seems to be chiseling away at her self-esteem.

Watching her with my niece I feel somewhat vindicated that I misjudged Allie's age. It's not the way she looks. She *looks* 24. But something in her eyes seems almost... tired. Like she's seen just enough to be a little more burned-out on life than others her age.

No, I'd guess her age to be around 28. 28 is doable for me. There's a world of difference between 24 and 28 in my book. At 24, I was a fresh-faced, newly promoted Lieutenant JG looking to charge through life without thinking twice. Four years later, I had made it through my first two SEAL missions and was well on my way to becoming the sardonic pain-in-the-ass I am today.

After Hannah retreats to the other side of the yard as Kosmo sniffs something intriguing along the fence line, Allie looks over at me, her gaze wandering appreciatively over my pecs. She glances away briefly before asking, "So why aren't you in the Navy anymore? Your commander said you were pretty amazing when I called him for a reference. Got a silver medal, or something."

I laugh. "Silver Star."

She blushes again, and I hate how attractive she looks when the pink rushes to her cheeks. "Sorry. I'm not really up on the whole military thing," she says.

"That's all right. But I thought you said your dad was a vet?"

"Veterinarian," she corrects, and I'm realizing just how little she really talked about herself at dinner that night. I must have monopolized the conversation.

"So anyway, why'd you get out?" she asks.

I stretch my legs and watch Hannah in the distance, keeping my voice low. I never like her hearing this sort of thing. "I was shot in my shoulder pretty bad. Wouldn't have stopped me from staying in, but it's my dominant shoulder, so I have a harder time with an assault rifle." I skip mentioning the fact that I had a solid six months during which I couldn't sleep more than an hour at a time. Or the fact that the eerie silence of nighttime in Newton's Creek brings my blood pressure up at least twenty points.

Her brow pinches with concern. "I'm sorry. There wasn't someplace else they could use you?"

"Oh, sure. I could have stayed in the Navy or even commanded with an injury like mine. But I can't be a SEAL. And that's all I ever wanted to be."

"That's terrible."

I hate people's pity, but there doesn't seem to be pity in her eyes. Only understanding. So I don't mind. Giving a shrug, I say, "It worked out fine. My family's going through some stuff right now, and I think it's better for me to be here now, anyway. How about you? Why are you juggling two jobs when you should be rescuing dogs full-time?"

"You do what you gotta do," she replies with a grin. "And there's not a lot of money in the dog rescuing business."

I crack a smile, liking that she doesn't inundate me with the details of her life. It's refreshing. Anytime I meet women these days, I feel like they are trying the 30-second speed-dating tactic. I'll be standing in the produce aisle and a long-locked stranger is suddenly telling me her decades of back-story and all her life goals. Which of course, isn't really what I want to hear since I don't know what my life goals are anymore. Just get through my plumbing inspection with the County so I can put up my drywall in #3, I guess.

Certainly not the goals I once had in my life.

When the doorbell rings, I go inside to get the food. It feels good to have a reason to pull my eyes from her. Looking at Allie is somehow calming and unsettling at the same time. And it confuses the shit out of me.

Hannah washes her hands before I even have to remind her. Apparently her mother did something right, because she sure didn't pick that up from her dad. Plopping herself down in a seat at the table next to Allie, she fires off, "Do you believe in fairies?"

My gut clenches up. It's a pretty innocent question, but Allie has no idea that there's no right answer at this point. Say yes, and she'll repeat it to the kids at school and get teased, and say no, and she'll be heartbroken.

Allie looks thoughtful. "I'm not sure. I've never seen a fairy, so I don't really know they exist. But I think it's more fun to believe, than not to believe, don't you?"

"Yeah. Yeah, it is." Hannah nods sagely. "Do you want to try my egg roll?" she offers Allie.

I breathe a sigh of relief and sit on the other side of Hannah. "Wow. You never offer me any egg roll."

"Silly. I know you don't like egg rolls."

She's actually wrong. I love egg rolls. I could eat twenty of them at one sitting, but I'm having a hard enough time keeping myself in shape since separating from the Navy. I've got workout equipment in my basement, but my routine is a far cry from the seven days a week of PT I used to do. So I'm stuck eating my chicken and broccoli and pretending that crunchy vegetables don't make my lip curl up.

God, I miss the Navy.

Allie's cheeks are bursting with color as she eats her General Tso's chicken. I asked for it extra hot, as she had requested. "Too hot for you?"

She finishes chewing and replies, "It's never too hot for me."

I can't miss the double entendre, and despite the fact that my niece is two feet away, I'm wondering if I see a flicker of suggestion in Allie's eyes.

Allie probably talks to Hannah more than she does to me during the meal, and I have to admit, I enjoy watching her do it. She shows enthusiasm for everything Hannah says, and doesn't even bat an eyelash when the little girl changes topics two or three times in a long-winded sentence. Allie has loads of patience, and I imagine that's why she's so good with dogs.

"So, are you headed to the pound to pick up another dog tomorrow?" I ask as I stack up the plates from the table. Hannah has crashed on the couch next to the warm body of my new chocolate Lab mix, and I'm betting she'll be covered in hair when her father picks her up in a few minutes.

I glance at Allie when a reply doesn't come.

"I'm not sure," she finally says. I know enough about her already to know that she doesn't want to give me details.

That seems to be her mantra. And normally, I'd respect it. But this time...

"Why wouldn't you?" I dare to ask.

"I'm..." Her voice trails almost as if she is still in the process of making a decision about something. "I'm actually selling my condo."

"Really?"

"Yeah." She gives a nod, though it seems more directed at herself than at me. "Yeah, I am. I talked to a real estate agent the other day and the value has really skyrocketed."

That's pretty unusual in this town, and I hope the agent wasn't blowing sun up her skirt. "Property around here doesn't normally appreciate very quickly," I warn her.

"Well, my condo did because the commuter bus started picking up just a few blocks from me. According to my agent, the place will sell in a week. More people from Dayton and Cincinnati are coming to live here now that there's an alternative to driving."

Oh, well, that makes sense. "Are you buying something else?"

Her cheeks puff out as she expels a slow, ample breath. "I'm hoping to. I'm bidding on a foreclosure. I'm going to live on a friend's couch till then," she states with a laugh. "The only bad thing is, I can't take on any more dogs until I see if I get this foreclosure or not. And that's killing me. There are so many dogs there right now who are running out of time."

"Any idea when you will hear back from the bank?" I ask, knowing the answer, but just making sure she knows it, too. I don't want her real estate agent leading her on, especially when Allie will be sleeping on someone's couch till she closes on something new.

"Could be days or months. You never know with foreclosures." She shrugs. "I don't mind. It will all be worth it if I get it." Her eyes drift away from mine, and I can see she's imagining it, whatever it is. "I could keep a lot more dogs in this new place than my condo. I'm so tired of going into the pound and feeling like I'm choosing who is going to live and who is going to die."

Her words slice through me, flooding my senses with memories that I try to keep locked up deep inside.

Yeah, I know how she feels.

"Do you mind noise?" I hear myself asking her, even though I'm not really sure if the voice is coming from me.

She laughs. "I sure better not. The place I'll be staying is a real party building, I've heard."

"No, I mean construction noise."

Shrugging, her eyebrows arch in question.

I press my lips together a moment. "I just about finished with one of the townhomes, but can't sell it until all five of them are complete. It wouldn't get the best price with all the noise and mess. But if you and the dogs don't mind it, you're welcome to it. It would just be sitting vacant, anyway. You couldn't put any pictures up or anything, since I just painted it and I'd rather not do it over again. And if you could just try to keep the hardwoods in okay shape, you're welcome to have a few dogs there."

As soon as the words rush out of my mouth, I nearly regret them. I can already foresee having to refinish the floors before trying to sell the place in a few months. But the thought of her feeling like she's depriving some dogs of their second chance at life kills me.

Besides, whether she knows it or not, there's a good chance she won't get her foreclosure. And I don't want her thinking about the lives that were lost while she took a chance at it.

To my relief, she shakes her head. "Thanks. But I really can't afford to pay rent right now. Even short term. I've sunk every dime I have into my offer."

"No, no. I wouldn't charge you to stay there. Like I said, the noise will be pretty bad and it will be empty, anyway."

"Really?" She seems aghast.

"Really." I stand when I hear a knock on the door. Kosmo lumbers off the couch and barks, waking Hannah.

Swinging open the door, I see my brother on the other side. His eyes immediately fall to Kosmo.

"Hey, boy!" he says, bending over him and giving him an enthusiastic head rub. Ryan glances up at me. "So, you got him?"

"He's all mine now," I answer, feeling a swell of pride. I know it's ridiculous, but I've wanted a dog for so long. Being deployed as often as I was, it just wasn't a good idea till now.

"Daddy!" Hannah cries out, her voice still sleepy. She races toward him and my brother is enclosed in her slender arms.

I don't normally feel any jealousy toward my brother, not for the 6,000 square foot home he lives in by himself when Hannah's not with him. Not for the hot tub or infinity edge pool he has in the backyard. Not for the souped-up man cave just off the foyer that has a TV I couldn't even fit in my townhome.

But when Hannah embraces him with so much love it could fill a house and bust the doors open, I feel a pang of jealousy. He claims he wasted three years of his life with the wrong woman. But look at what he has to show for it.

"Hi. You must be Hannah's dad." Allie has come up from behind me and extends her hand to Ryan. She's already holding her stack of paperwork in her other hand and her purse is slung over her shoulder.

Ryan flashes her a smile, and I bristle seeing his eyes give her an appraising glance up and down. "Ryan Sheridan." He takes her hand. "Logan's younger brother." He stresses the word *younger* as if it is supposed to matter—like if she wanted the younger version of me, then she knows where to turn. It annoys the hell out of me.

"Allie Donovan."

"Allie runs the rescue organization," I tell him.

"Good for you. Thank you for saving this big guy." Ryan stoops to pet Kosmo again, purely for her benefit, I'm sure.

"My pleasure." She turns to me. "Well, I better be going. Will you let me know how your pre-op appointment goes at the vet next week?"

"I will," I respond, grateful to have a reason to call her. I'm not sure why.

"And if you have any questions—"

"I'll text you."

She nods. "Good." She bends over to pet Kosmo. "You be a good boy, Kosmo." Her head is close to his and her voice cracks. This must be harder than hell on her.

Hannah embraces her around the waist. "Bye. Thanks for Kosmo."

"Don't forget my offer. And good luck on the bidding process," I add.

"Thanks." She touches my forearm lightly, almost as though she would have given me a hug if my brother wasn't standing there.

Damn you, Ryan.

"See ya." Her eyes linger on mine a beat or two, before she descends the short staircase and walks to her car.

"I'll pack up my backpack," Hannah says, charging back inside.

Ryan's still watching Allie as she pulls away. "She's cute. Single?"

I glare at him. "Yes."

"Wow."

"Wow what?"

"You know there's only about a dozen single women in this town, right?"

"Yeah, but don't get any ideas. She's too young for you."

"How old?"

"24."

"On what planet is that too young for me to date? I was *married* at 24."

"And see how that turned out?" I raise an eyebrow. "Seriously, she's off limits, bro."

"You've got a thing for her."

"Maybe. She's—" Sweet. Kind. Responsible. Cute. And a hell of a kisser. But I don't say any of that. "Too young. Ryan, she's fresh out of college. I remember what I was like at that age."

"Not the jaded asshole you are now, right?"

I shrug. He's not too far from the truth.

"All the more reason to date a younger woman. Who the hell needs someone who's jaded? You're 32. She's 24. 'Half plus seven' is the rule, you know, and she falls within the range."

My eyes shoot upward at that formula, which I'm certain was created by a bunch of desperate old men looking for a way to justify dating much younger women. "A guy like me doesn't fall within the ramifications of that formula." Or any formula, I'm tempted to add.

"Well, if you're not going for her, then I will."

I look inside my door to make sure Hannah isn't within sight, and fist his shirt close to his neck. "Still think you will?" I ask, my eyes searing into him. It's done in jest, the way my brothers and I always roughhouse. But there's a trace of me that's really thinking about punching him for wanting to date Allie.

As I release him, he backs off laughing. "Ha! I *knew* you had a thing for her."

Hannah trots back onto the front porch with Kosmo jogging along behind her.

"Will you be at Grandma and Grandpa's this Sunday?" she asks, grabbing my hands and proceeding to climb up me like a tree the way she has since the day she took her first steps.

"I will."

She smacks a kiss on my cheek. "Thanks for saving Kosmo. I love him sooooo much." She draws out the word "so" to last at least five seconds.

"And I love you sooooo much," I say, drawing out the word twice as long as I give her a squeeze.

CHAPTER 8

~ ALLIE ~

My life has generally moved at the pace of one of those slow-moving vehicles I always get stuck behind in a no passing zone when I'm late for something. So it's no wonder that my hands are shaking as I sign the documents in front of me.

In the past eight hours, I've vacated my condo, signed it over to a couple who commutes to Dayton, and right now I'm making an offer on the foreclosure that could change my life forever.

I'm not sure if I'm nervous, excited, or terrified.

Kim is waiting downstairs in a rented van with all my worldly possessions, including my newest fosters: a German shepherd, a hyperactive Welsh corgi, and a Siberian husky who sheds enough fur to stuff a pillow every thirty minutes. I keep this in mind as I scan the fine print of my offer, trying to read as quickly as possible so I don't jeopardize a friendship that I can't imagine living without.

My condo sold as quickly as my real estate agent said it would. I had two offers in the first week and one was slightly over asking price. I was doing my happy dance till this morning when a thick lump of sadness settled into my throat as I signed the closing papers.

That little one-bedroom was my last gift from my father. Not literally, but I still think of it that way. When my mother remarried a year after my dad's death, she decided to give me a chunk of money from his estate. I think it was a guilt gift, since she must have known how I disapproved of her marrying again so quickly.

It's not that I dislike her husband—my stepdad, though I never call him that. I just felt like she swept Dad's memory under the rug so quickly and that hurts. I don't want to forget him.

So I bought the condo here in his hometown with the money my mom gave me. I know he would have loved knowing I settled here in Newton's Creek. And if he could look down on me right now, signing these papers to hopefully open a rescue kennel, I know he'd be smiling.

My heart is pounding as I walk outside to see Kim's exasperated expression awaiting me in the front seat of the van. It's hot, but she can only have the windows half open because the corgi has made it apparent she'd have no qualms about jumping out of the car and leading us on a chase. The little short-legged dog could probably outrun a greyhound, paws-down.

"Sorry it took so long." I shoot her an apologetic look as I slide into the passenger seat without letting the dogs escape. I had wanted to unpack the van at Logan's before going to the real estate office, but the closing ran a little later than expected, and I really wanted to get my offer into the bank before the end of the business day.

"No problem," she says not so convincingly, putting the

van in reverse. Suddenly tapping the brakes, she pauses to pick some fur out of her eyes and then pulls out of the parking lot, shaking her head.

The drive to Logan's townhomes is brief, but we barely say a word. I know she doesn't like the idea of me moving next door to him for free. "Nothing is free," Kim told me when I mentioned his offer. "There are always strings attached."

What's funny is that half of me is hoping for those strings. He hasn't even seemed slightly interested in me since that night we met, and I certainly can't blame him. I came across as some kind of freak the way I deserted him that night, and then a complete bitch to follow-up the next day.

If I were smart, I'd push from my mind any trace of hope that I might get to touch those washboard abs again.

But if I were smart, I wouldn't have just sold a perfectly decent condo on the off-chance of snagging a dilapidated kennel.

Logan steps out of his front door just as our wheels hit the noisy gravel leading up to the townhomes.

"Good God," Kim mutters at the sight of him in his t-shirt. He's dirty in the sexiest way possible, his tight shirt covered in sweat and some kind of grit, and a fresh tan glowing on his shredded arms.

He lopes over to our car window. "Just pull to the side of the building, if you don't mind," he says pointing. "I'm in the middle of putting pavers in the walkway. I'll help you unload everything."

"The pavers look great," I notice as I step onto a completed portion of a tidy path leading up to his door.

"You like them?"

"Love them." I glance at Kim who looks a little pale as she steps out of the van. I can't blame her. We just don't see many men who look like they've stepped off the cover of *Men's Fitness*. "Do you remember Kim from the adoption event?"

"Of course." He extends his hand. "I'm Logan. Thanks for all the work you do for the dogs."

"Mmhm," Kim murmurs, seemingly incapable of forming full sentences just yet. I know how she feels.

"I wish you'd have let me help you load the van," he tells me as I hook up the dogs to the leashes. "I was free all day."

My gaze moves from him, to the new pavers, and back to him. "Doesn't look like you were very free today. Besides, I really don't have much stuff." It's true. My furniture is pretty spare. I never got around to buying "Big Girl" furniture after college.

"Want to let the dogs run out back while we unload?" he asks.

My heart picks up its pace at the word "we." I love how he just assumes he will help. "Sounds great. But Kim and I can really do it on our own."

I feel her eyes burrowing into my side from the glare I see in my peripheral vision.

"We'd love your help," she quickly corrects me.

I step into the house to lead the dogs to the fenced-in backyard that overlooks Newton's Creek. A smile inches upward on my face, looking at the crisply painted walls and crown molding. A fireplace similar to the one I saw in Logan's house is on the front wall. This townhome doesn't have all the built-in bookshelves that Logan's had, but I sure can't complain. I've never lived in a place so elegantly adorned. The house I grew up in was okay, but a cookie cutter 1970s split foyer that had only been updated once in the early 80s can't really stand up to a renovation like this.

I take the dogs through to the kitchen and can't resist running my hand across the granite countertop. My eyes soak in the sight of stainless steel appliances, even though I'm not much of a cook.

As I set the dogs free from their leashes in the newly sodded backyard, I say a silent prayer they won't dig any holes.

I don't care what Kim says. Living here is like a gift, and I still feel a pang of guilt for not paying him.

Still... he offered. And I'd be a fool to refuse. As Cass told me, if the whole deal goes south, I can always pack up my meager belongings, throw my mattress on her floor, and live with her.

Logan enters carrying my writing desk. It's not huge, but I still love the sight of his muscles bulging as he carries it. Carefully he moves it through the doorway without marring the new trim along the wall.

"Do you want this upstairs?"

"No. Right there is fine." I can't see the point in getting too settled here. Hopefully, I'll be moving out in a month or two. Maybe even less if I get lucky and the bank doesn't move at a snail's pace.

Logan heads back into the van and within seconds he's in the doorway again with a box. "This one is marked 'samples,'" he says. "Where do you want it?"

A surge of heat touches my cheeks as I see this man with his burly arms wrapped around every type of sex toy in my line. I'm tempted to tell him I want it upstairs in the bedroom along with him, naked. "In the coat closet," I say forcefully instead.

Cass walks in behind him. "Hey, hon. Thought I'd stop by after shift and help you unpack." She does a double-take at the sight of Logan holding my samples box. "Well, you're just about every fantasy I've ever had right now," she says, batting the false eyelashes she must have left on from her work shift.

Her makeup is heavier than usual and she still has sparkles in her hair from her Buckeye Princess costume.

Logan looks flummoxed. “Pardon me?”

She’s still grinning from ear to ear. “If you can handle the contents of that box as easily as the box itself, I’ll make myself free tonight and every night for the next three months.”

I expel a breath, rushing to take the box from Logan before the bottom drops out of it and fifty-five vibrators scatter on the ground.

“Watch it, Cass,” I warn. Clearly she assumes that I’ve told him about my second job. Call me a private person, but I really don’t like sharing that information with men even though Cass insists it could only help my nonexistent sex life.

Logan gives a shake of his head, refusing to give up the box, and instead moves it to the coat closet himself. He’s returning the playful smile that Cass is shooting him, and I’m insanely jealous. “I have no idea what you mean, but I’m pretty sure I’d enjoy whatever it is that’s going through your head right now,” he counters back to her.

She tosses her head back and laughs, her platinum blonde hair flowing over her shoulders like she’s in slow motion. My hair, thin as it is, wouldn’t move like that if I used a gallon of those hair products I see on infomercials at 4 a.m.

“Those boxes,” Cass begins. “That’s where Allie keeps her secret stash. Maybe if you’re lucky, she’ll share.”

His supremely remarkable ass is pointed in our direction as he bends to put it in the closet. So he’s not looking long enough for me to go over to my so-called friend and smack her on her skinny, sparkly arm. “Shut *up*, Cass.”

Her eyes widen and I see she’s still clueless that I haven’t told him. *Hello?* She knows me. She should know better.

As Logan turns, his one eyebrow is raised slightly. "Do I dare even ask?"

Of course I *have* to tell him now because he is probably picturing illegal drugs or something in that box.

I dart a look at Cass. "Cass, go. Make yourself useful. There's a box outside with your name on it." I inhale. "Logan, those are just my samples for work."

"Oh." He gives a nod and starts to leave. It bothers me because I really don't want him thinking that I'm lying to him, especially since he's been so nice to me. "Aren't you going to ask what I sell?"

He turns. "Your business. Not mine."

"Yeah, but I don't want you thinking I've got something illegal in that box. The way Cass was talking—"

His laughter cuts me off.

"What's so funny?"

"Allie, you really don't strike me as the type to do anything illegal."

I should be relieved by that statement, but somehow I'm insulted. Do I really look that boring? I catch a glimpse of myself in the reflection of the living room window.

Yeah, I really do.

I shrug. "Okay, if you really don't care."

One eye narrows slightly as half his mouth eases up into a smirk. "Well, since you clearly want me to know, I was picturing you selling medical equipment before. But the way your friend there was joking..."

I can't resist a snort as I cut him off. "Medical equipment," I repeat. "I have to tell Kim and Cass that one."

"I guessed wrong, then?"

"Uh, yeah." I step over to the box. "I work for a multi-level marketing company. I sell my stuff at parties that other people host. I get a chunk of whatever I sell, plus if I can get anyone to sign up as a rep, I get a chunk of everything they sell till forever."

He nods, obviously familiar with the idea. "Oh. I had a girlfriend who used to host a lot of those kinds of parties selling all sorts of crap." He winces slightly. "No offense."

"No offense taken."

He laughs. "So what is it you sell, anyway? Makeup? Jewelry?"

Frowning, I pop open the box and hand him a BestMan Classic Model #8800. Some things are better seen than said.

"Sex toys," he says, staring at the vibrator in his hand before a laugh escapes him.

Cass walks in again, this time carrying a box labeled "bathroom," and sees Logan armed and ready. "Should I leave you two alone?" she asks with a grin.

I glare at her. "Upstairs bathroom," I tell her as I read the box, and she saunters up the staircase giggling. My eyes then meet Logan's which are filled with laughter.

"Alexandra, you are full of surprises, aren't you?"

I take my sample from him and put it back in the box. "Yep. So go ahead, get in all your digs. Laugh at my expense. There's not a joke I haven't heard, believe me."

"I'm not going to laugh," he says, and I angle him a look. "Anymore. I won't laugh *anymore*."

"Yeah, well, I'm laughing all the way to the bank. I make more doing this than with my assistant job, and there just aren't a ton of jobs out here in the middle of nowhere. Do you know how much I have to fork over in vet bills for all my fosters?"

His eyes are locked on mine with an expression I'm not really familiar with. Is it… admiration?

"Good for you, Allie," he replies with a grin.

I look at him, suspicious.

"What? I'm serious. Good for you," he reiterates. "You know what you need, and you find a way to get it."

"Thanks," I say, for lack of knowing what else to say. His response wasn't exactly what I was expecting. Then again, nothing about Logan is ever what I'm expecting.

CHAPTER 9

- LOGAN -

I step into the crisp spring air and into the stillness of the night. Allie didn't leave her front porch light on this evening and I see her car is gone. So I flick on my own light so that she won't be welcomed home by the darkness when she returns.

She must be at one of those parties tonight, I imagine with a slight grin. I hadn't pegged her for the kind of girl who had ever even wrapped her fingers around a vibrator, and she *sells* them?

I step quietly past her door so that I don't get her latest dogs fired up. The German shepherd and husky seem pretty docile, but that corgi is a spitfire. I've never seen so much energy and muscle packed into a tiny frame.

It's the first night of having a neighbor for me since Annapolis, and I have to admit, I like it. With the windows open to let the cool spring air in, I could hear her friends talking up a storm all evening till the three of them left at about nineteen hundred hours.

Background noise like their chatter soothes me, and till she came along, I was regretting buying this stretch of townhomes so far off the road. I still do, a little.

I turn the key in #3 and flick on the lights. No matter that I don't like it here. These townhomes will be complete by fall if all continues to go on schedule. And I'll be free to move on to something else.

Someplace else. But where?

My heart tugs me toward San Diego. But I'm not ready to face the demons of my past. Even now, as the thought passes quickly, my throat burns enough that I'm pulling two antacids from the pill box stashed in my cargo shorts.

No, not San Diego, I decide as I pour some cream paint into a roller tray and load up my brush.

I'll stay here, where I can at least keep an eye on my family for a while longer. At least till Dad and Mom face reality and settle him into a good memory care facility so that my mother isn't spending her every waking hour worrying he'll wander off and forget where the hell he is going.

Or am I using my family as an excuse?

I'm gratefully pulled off this dangerous road of thought when I hear a knock at the door. "Come in," I shout, knowing it must be Allie. No one else would show up here this late at night.

"Hey. You're up late," she notices.

Her hair is down around her shoulders and I think she's wearing the same outfit that she wore the night we met. I recognize the silk blouse and my fingers can still remember the feel of it against her skin as I held her. She steps inside and her heels click against the floor. Heels on her look as sexy as sin simply because she doesn't seem the type to wear them usually. So looking at her in heels is like looking at a tree all covered in Christmas lights. Something special. A treat. A feast for the eyes.

And too damn young for me to feast upon, I remind myself.

"So are you," I respond. "Party tonight?"

She smiles at me, as though we share a special secret, and I'm assuming there are probably only a handful of other guys who know her alter ego as a sex toy salesperson.

"A good one," she answers, glancing around the room. "I made a ton of sales." She reaches for one of the rollers on the ground. "Can I help?"

"You're all dressed up."

She dips her roller into the pan. "Believe me when I tell you that there is nothing in my wardrobe worth saving."

I glance her up and down in her outfit and feel quite differently. Sure, it doesn't look like it came off a mannequin in some exclusive boutique store, but she wears it well.

"Besides, I'll be careful," she adds.

"Shouldn't you be in bed?" Damned if my cock doesn't twitch at the thought of her in bed.

"Shouldn't you?" she counters, easing alongside of me and putting her roller to the wall. "I'm too fired up right now to sleep, anyway. These women were particularly chatty tonight."

I shrug, giving in, but hoping she doesn't get anything on that blouse. I have a strange sentimentality for it. "So what constitutes a good crowd at one of these parties of yours?" I ask.

"Pretty broad range. But they need expendable income. So they are usually a little older than I am."

"Married or single?" I find I'm curiously fascinated by this.

"Usually married."

"And looking for a way to liven things up in the bedroom?"

She shakes her head. "Actually, not really. I think most of them are just looking for a reason to get together with their friends, have a few drinks and a few laughs. I'd bet at least half of the things I sell to them go unused. They just wanted to have a reason to vent."

She stoops over to get more paint and I can't help noticing how the black material on her skirt frames some really remarkable curves.

"Think about it," she continues. "I provide an atmosphere where women actually get to talk to each other about men and sex in a completely unique way. You can't even imagine the stories I hear." She laughs suddenly. "Believe me, I walk out of those parties wondering what the hell I've been missing."

A laugh escapes me and I glance her way to see a blush creeping up her neck. Obviously, she hadn't intended to let that thought slip out. "Things a little slow in that arena?"

Raising her eyebrows, she looks at me, cocking her head slightly and looking delectable enough to eat. "Logan, I live in freaking Newton's Creek. Of course things are a little slow in that arena."

I frown slightly, suddenly worried she might head back to Bergin's. My protective side flares up. "Well, promise you'll be a little more careful about picking up men in bars. There's no way you should have followed me up to my room."

She sputters, incredulous. "Are you serious?"

"Dead serious. I could have been an axe murderer."

Her laughter somehow makes half the blood in my brain drift toward my groin.

"That's exactly what Kim said."

"Yeah, well, Kim's right," I advise her. "As I was on the receiving end of it, I wasn't going to complain that night, believe me. But now that I know you better, if you're going to try that on a man again, promise you'll talk to me first."

She turns her face toward mine and her eyelids are heavy, seductive. "I promise you'll be the first to know."

Oh, shit. That's not how I meant it. "So I can talk you out of it," I clarify.

Biting her bottom lip, she turns her face toward the wall again. "I made that much of an ass of myself, did I?"

"What do you mean?"

She shakes her head. "Nothing." She puts her roller back in the pan. "I better get to sleep."

I grasp her hand as she starts to step away. "Wait. I have a feeling I said something wrong, and I'd really like to know what."

"You said nothing wrong. You were being honest. I acted like an idiot that night, and it was certainly enough to be a permanent turn-off for any guy. I really understand. And I appreciate this big brother attitude you've got toward me, but it's somehow insulting after we kissed like we did." Her sigh is tight, as though her throat is clenched.

"Hold on. The fact that I'm pulling a big brother attitude has nothing to do with the way you bolted on me that night. And it has everything to do with the fact that you're 24. That's just way too young for me."

She scrunches up her face and looks at me. "You said you're 32, right?"

"Right."

Staring at me, her big eyes look baffled. "Okay. Yeah. Eight years difference. That's too much for you?"

"People are like cars. You drive them too hard, too fast, they get a lot of wear-and-tear. I've depreciated a lot more than my 32-year-old counterparts, Allie."

I hear her scoff, like she thinks I'm not being serious. "I'm jaded, Allie," I add, trying for simpler terms.

She still looks at me like I'm insane, but I refuse to give her details. If I tell her about my 24-year-old ex-girlfriend in Annapolis, I'd have to tell her how she'd freak out every time I woke up screaming in the night, or asked me to please not mention the fact that I was seeing a shrink to any of her friends. Then Allie would likely say that Vanessa was a bitch, and I honestly don't feel that way. It was just more than she could handle.

Hell, it was more than *I* could handle, too. I didn't like the night terrors and the cold sweats and the shrink visits any more than she did.

Even though I'm a lot better now, the women I've dated recently have been a little older, and less starry-eyed and idealistic than the 24-year-old standing next to me. That suits me well.

Yet, I'll admit, not one of them makes my heart pound like Allie is doing right now.

"Okay," she finally says quietly. "That's probably for the best anyway, seeing as you live next door and you're giving me the townhome for free. I might start thinking I need to pay you back in some way." She cracks an adorable smile.

I'm not sure if it was intentional, but her words have me thinking of several ways I'd love her to pay me back, and they'd probably have me sleeping a lot more soundly at night than I am right now. I force a laugh. "Right. No strings attached on the townhome."

I almost think I hear her mutter "damn" under her breath. But with her rattling the paint tin to load up her roller again, I'm not sure if I imagined it.

CHAPTER 10

~ ALLIE ~

I seriously like him, I keep thinking over the next several days as I'm making every excuse I can to spend time with him. I know he has no interest in me, but I can't seem to resist being around him anyway.

I tell myself that it's because he's been so generous in letting me stay, that I really should help him any chance I can. But that's only partly true. The fact is, just painting late into the night or helping him install crown molding during my lunch breaks is more satisfying than the best sex I've ever had.

Besides that, I'm really learning a lot, and everything I learn I figure I can use fixing up my kennel.

If I get the foreclosure.

That's a big *if*.

I ache slightly as I walk up the two flights of stairs to Cass's apartment. I helped Logan paint the crown molding last night and it's murder on my upper back and neck. I can think of at least a hundred ways I'd like to get my muscles sore with that man, and painting molding is way down on the list. But I'll take what I can get.

I knock on Cass's door. She swings it open, looking frazzled in her sparkly princess makeup with one eye looking a lot smaller than the other eye.

"You're missing an eyelash," I inform her.

"I know. Damn thing fell on the floor and Skylar ate it," she retorts, giving a toss of her head in the direction of her latest foster, a Shetland sheepdog. "I'm already running late for work and now I have to go to the drug store to get more eyelashes looking like some kind of crack whore."

I glance her up and down. She isn't too far from the truth about that. The heavy makeup and big hair looks fine when she has her forty-pound princess dress on. But in her cutaway shorts and t-shirt, she does look like she's in a questionable line of work.

"Want me to run over there and get some?" I offer.

"I'll never make it in time. It's on the way. I'll be fine." She disappears into her bathroom. "Leash is on the kitchen table and the extra keys are next to it."

"Thanks," I call into her, only then noticing her roommate passed out on the couch. I stare at her for a few beats, more to make sure that she's still breathing than anything else. And then I thank God for Logan so that I don't have to stay here till I find out about the foreclosure.

Logan. Again, my mind wanders happily in his direction as I shut and lock the door behind me, with Skylar tugging at her leash.

So, Logan thinks I'm too young for him. The very thought elicits another chuckle from me as I load Skylar into my small hatchback with my three fosters.

Too young? Since I was twelve or thirteen, I've been told I

was too mature. That I should loosen up and have more fun. Not take life so seriously. Act my age.

This is the first time anyone's ever said I was too young for them.

Not that I've dated many thirty-somethings. There was one once who took me to dinner a couple times in Dayton. He seemed really nice till the third dinner he forgot to take off his wedding band before meeting me at the restaurant. That sort of made me cut things short.

Other women might be annoyed by Logan's blow-off, but I'm not. I've been told I'm cute, but even as recently as last month, a guy I was attracted to at an adoption event ended up dating Cass. Who could blame him? Look at her. Then look at me. Unless a guy is attracted to my wider, better-for-birthing hips, of course he'd go for my rail thin model friend. I didn't even lose an ounce of self-esteem over that one.

So I can handle having an attractive, but off-limits man living next door, especially one who is big-hearted enough to let my dogs and me stay there for free.

But only if I get to ogle him when he wears a tight t-shirt.

I pull into a space right in front of Sally Sweet's and see Kim already setting up lawn chairs. A tray with two coffee cups is resting on the concrete at her feet and my smile forms at the sight of it.

I love Kim. I love coffee. And the fact that Kim brings me coffee makes me devoted to my bestie till the day I die.

"Am I late?" I ask.

Her eyes look sad. "No. I had to bolt out of the house early. My mom was in a mood and if I stuck around, I think she would have come up with an excuse to not babysit."

"What's wrong, hon? You look totally depressed."

"I am depressed." She takes two of the dogs off my hands. "Do you know what it's like trying to be a mom to your son when you're living with your own mom who still treats you like you're sixteen years old?"

I have no clue what that would be like. I'm still at the stage in my life when I can't even imagine myself as a mother. I have a hard enough time with my dogs. "I'm sorry. Did she say something bitchy?"

She rolls her eyes. "She always says something bitchy. And then Dad just stands there and shakes his head at me like I'm the most disappointing thing in his life. I swear to God, Allie, I have to get out of there."

I sit down and sip my coffee contemplatively. "How much money have you saved up?"

"Not enough for a down payment on anything yet." Kim is the manager of a flower shop just off Anders Street. And even though she's manager, there's not a ton of money rolling in.

"What if you pulled Connor out of pre-K?"

"I have to put him somewhere while I work. Daycare is just as expensive."

"Maybe you could move in with me for a couple months? There's tons of space in that townhouse and Logan seems to have a sweet spot for kids. He has a niece he really adores."

I see something in Kim's eyes soften, probably from hearing about a single man who actually likes kids. I know she is convinced they don't exist, and after the way Connor's dad bolted on Kim when she said she was pregnant, I guess I can understand why she'd think that. "Thanks. But it's useless to move there for a couple months and then just have to move again."

I lean back, watching the slow traffic. "I wonder what Logan is going to sell those townhomes for when he's done with them."

She shakes her head. "A lot more than I can afford. I guarantee it. What I need is a better job. But all the better paying jobs won't allow me to pick up Connor at 3:00."

"Yeah, but with a better paying job, you'd be able to afford aftercare."

"And how many better paying jobs are there around here? None. If I commuted all the way to the city, I'd be on the road over two hours a day. Even you said you applied to the corporations close-by and they all rejected you."

"But that was me, not you."

"Yeah, well, I've sent them all résumés, but I'm trapped till I hear back anything."

My heart breaks for her. I don't know how single moms do it. I drape my arm around her. "Well, I've got two parties booked this week, and I'd love to unload one on you."

Her features brightening, she looks at me. "Really?"

"Really." Why not? Foreclosure or not, she can use the income more than I can.

CHAPTER 11

- LOGAN -

My hammock swings low, nearly touching the grass as I settle in under the canopy of stars. It must have stretched from the rain, and I'll hook it up higher on the chain next time I'm standing. But that won't be for another six hours, if I get my way.

I haven't slept out here since last fall. I'd be crazy to sleep outside in the middle of an Ohio winter, and I already feel crazy enough with my heart hammering in my chest at the sound of silence. I had put the hammock out here, outside my fenced-in backyard, down near the creek where the babbling water offers some kind of noise.

The crickets are especially loud tonight, and I'm grateful. I can barely hear the owl hoot over their constant singing.

It's just what I need—a kind of natural chaos. Unpredictable. From the skittering sound of a field mouse running alongside my hammock to the sound of a fish flopping in the water, there is just enough noise to distract my brain from the shouts and gunfire of that night seven thousand miles away.

It's been more than two years, and countless hours talking to a psych. But the images still come to me on nights like this, when silence looms and I'm waiting for the stillness to be shattered by the explosion of an IED followed by enemy fire the same as it had that night.

And then the choices I made in those moments wrap themselves around my heart like a vise and squeeze till I'm breathless.

If I didn't have Allie living next door, I'd start working on #4 right now, pulling off the 1970s wood paneling and demolishing the timeworn kitchen cabinets. Even though I warned her that I'd be a noisy neighbor, I feel no need to torment her at this late hour.

She works hard during the day and needs her sleep. Every spare minute she has from her two jobs, she's been showing up in #3 ready to paint. I feel guilty, but love the company just as much as the help. And she seems so eager to learn this stuff. Watching her fire off a nail gun for the first time was like watching Hannah open up her Christmas presents from Santa. Her eyes were full of excitement.

It's hard for me to not get turned on by a woman with a nail gun.

But she's just 24. I was an idiot at 24, full of ideals and something that I thought was courage but was really just ignorance. I didn't know what the world could hold for a person. Not like I do now.

I hope she keeps that idealism and doesn't have it killed like mine was.

The crackling sound of tires on gravel carries over the wind and my ears perk up. It's Allie—I can tell because the muffler sounds like it's seen better days—and I'm momentarily irked that I've been laying out here to keep quiet when I could have been working on #4.

I give myself a shake as I hear her dogs bark briefly when she enters her townhome. I hope they don't get Kosmo started up next door. He looked to be in the middle of an enviably sound sleep when I left him on my bed a few minutes ago.

I worry about Allie, out late all the time, juggling two jobs and still up at the crack to walk her dogs every morning. I worry about her, I tell myself, because it's part of that brotherly attitude I'm trying to adopt with her.

But if I were really her brother I wouldn't be checking out her ass every time she stoops over to unleash her dogs.

In my peripheral vision, I see a few of her lights flick on, and she lets her dogs out in the backyard. It somehow warms me to have her nearby. Living in Annapolis, I became accustomed to having neighbors within shouting distance.

Minutes later, I hear her back door open again and watch her dogs jog back into her house. I see her silhouette coming out into her backyard. I can't quite make out what she's doing until she opens up her fence and starts approaching me.

"Hey," I say.

She jumps in response. "You scared me. I saw you when I let the dogs out and thought you had fallen asleep out here." She extends her hands. "I brought you a blanket."

My heart melts in a way that is completely unexpected. That's probably the most thoughtful thing a woman has done for me, outside of my mom. "Thanks. That's really nice of you."

"What are you doing out here?"

"Just love to sleep under the stars," The words fall from my lips so easily, even though it's not the whole story. I do love sleeping under the stars. But that's hell-and-gone from why I'm out here.

"Really?"

"Sure. Stay out here a few minutes and you can sometimes see the Milky Way."

She glances upward. "I don't see it."

"You have to let your eyes adjust. Here." I scoot over on the hammock. "Room enough for two." It's the God's truth. You could fit a family of four on this hammock, if you were hell-bent on doing it. So I shouldn't even feel the faintest electric charge in my heart at the prospect of her lying next to me.

I shouldn't. But I do.

"Okay," she answers, choosing to stay on the outer side of the blanket. Good call, Allie.

"Your eyes will adjust completely after forty-five minutes."

"I've never seen the Milky Way."

"And you've lived in the Milky Way your whole life. That's unacceptable."

She smiles. "Nah, I'm not really from the Milky Way. Moved here when I was eight. I'm an Andromeda girl."

"Oh, well, that explains a lot." I chuckle.

"So you must like camping, I'll bet."

"Love it. My brothers and I had a tent that we'd spontaneously put up in the backyard any clear night that came along. I used to wake them up at midnight sometimes, when the stars were out, and we'd race out the back door without even thinking twice. Used to drive my mom nuts, the back door slamming shut in the middle of the night and the dogs barking. You never did that as a kid?"

"Spontaneity has never been my thing."

"No?"

"No," she answers firmly. "Come on, think about it. Last

time I tried to be spontaneous, you were stuck with two orders of dessert."

"Ahh. The lava cake."

"Mmm. You ordered lava cake? Had I know that, I might have gotten the nerve to stick it out."

"So was I your first?"

"Excuse me?"

"Your first act of spontaneity."

Frowning, her chest rises and falls in a deep breath. "No. I went to New York City once on a whim with my boyfriend and some friends from college."

"Oh, hey, that sounds hopeful. You can't *not* have fun in New York. Well, unless you got mugged. Tell me that didn't happen."

There's a long pause, just long enough for me to look over at her and see her eyes glistening under the starlight. Glistening too much.

"It was Thanksgiving. I was supposed to go home for the holiday, you know? I had promised my parents I would. But everyone got this crazy idea of driving to New York for the parade. My parents were fine with it when I called to tell them I wasn't coming." She pulls a corner of the blanket over to her hands, and toys with the edge of it. "My dad died of an aneurism that weekend."

"Oh, Allie. I'm so sorry."

"I keep thinking that if I had just gone home, I would have noticed something. Maybe I would have had him go to the ER. My dad and I were like this," she says, raising her hand and crossing two fingers. "I knew what was on his mind before he did sometimes. It was almost eerie, my mom used to say. Maybe I would have known and could have gotten him help more quickly. Maybe I could have saved him."

As she brushes her hand against her cheek, my heart cracks at the sight of the tears, now streaked across her fingers. Without thinking, I take her hand in mine, and am not fully prepared for the charge of emotion that swells inside of me when I feel her cool fingers encompassed in my warm ones. "Allie, I'm no doctor and don't know much about aneurisms, but if there were any signs that you could have noticed, your dad would have gotten to the ER on his own. Was your mother with him?"

She nods. "But she wasn't as connected to Dad as I was. Mom used to say I was his clone." She smiles, but I can tell it's forced.

A flood of advice is welling up behind my lips. Useless catch phrases and customary advice from PTSD specialists and shrinks, and even some of my brothers in the SEALs who didn't bear the weight of that deadly mission on their shoulders quite as squarely as I did. But none of their well-meaning words will help her. I know that for a fact.

"I was worried about you tonight," I say instead.

"Huh?" she answers.

"You. Driving home late on this narrow country road. If something happened to you, it would be my fault."

"No, it wouldn't."

"Yes. It absolutely would. I offered this place to you. And if you got hurt or worse, then it would be my fault."

"Oh, I get it. You're telling me that I can't take responsibility for everything."

"Yep, exactly. You can't control all the bad things that can happen in life any more than the good things. And even though it doesn't take the hurt away, it's the truth. What if a meteor tore out of the sky right now, and killed you? My fault. I was the reason you're lying out here."

"What if Kosmo decides he hates you and clenches his thick jaw right over your jugular while you're sleeping?" Her eyes glimmer mischievously and I'm glad to see it.

"Totally your fault. You handed over the dog to me." I

smile back. "Imagine all the dog bites and fur allergies you've caused in your life. It's a wonder you can sleep at night." I move to my side slightly, trying to keep my arms from wrapping around her protectively. "But also think of all the smiles you've brought, all the love and the laughter, all the lives you've saved." What I'm saying is borderline sappy, but I think it's what she needs to hear.

She sighs. "Okay, you win."

"I'll tell you what," I begin, barely letting the words form in my brain before escaping me. "I'll help you be more spontaneous and you can help me be less jaded."

"Deal," she extends her right hand to shake mine, and only then do I realize I'm still holding her left one.

My breath catches at the feel of holding both her hands in mine, and I glance back up at the stars to distract myself. I pause. "So why do you even live out here, anyway? There aren't many new grad jobs. You could do a lot better in Cincinnati or Dayton or Columbus. Or hell, you've got no obligations holding you down. You could move anywhere."

She shrugs, and the movement causes her shoulder to nestle in closer to my body. The feeling is making my heart beat a little faster, especially now that I'm thinking Allie isn't as starry-eyed as I think she should still be at 24.

"My dad grew up here, and it just seemed like a good idea at the time," she responds. "I don't know. It makes no sense, but I just missed him and wanted to feel closer to him." Giving a shiver, she pulls the end of the light blanket over herself. "So why are you here, Logan?"

My lips press together, as I prepare to actually share something of myself. I'm not very good at it, but I can't help feeling like she's given me a little piece of her world tonight, and I really should do the same. "My dad got diagnosed with vascular dementia."

"What's that?"

"It's a little similar to Alzheimer's. Essentially, he's losing his memory. Eventually, he won't even know who I am anymore."

"I'm so sorry, Logan."

"It's okay. He's actually doing really well right now. But when it first happened, I thought I'd be needed out here more. I've been away for a long time. Might be good to help out for a change." I frown, thinking how little help I've been since I arrived. My mom is getting by fine with my dad without any help from me. Staring up at the stars right now, I'm not really sure why I'm here anymore.

"So, do you plan to head to San Diego when you're done with the townhomes?"

Her words make my insides knot. "Why would I do that?"

"Well, you had told me once that San Diego is home for you. I just figured if your family is doing all right, you'd head there."

My blood pressure is inching upwards and I feel that familiar squeeze in my chest. "I might," I answer her, knowing that's exactly what I want to do, but exactly what I *can't* do.

I hate how weak it makes me feel to have survived countless missions only to cower behind the excuse of my family now. But facing an enemy armed with AK-47s is a lot easier than what I'm avoiding in San Diego.

"See the Milky Way yet?" I ask, anxious to change the subject.

She looks up. "Oh, wow. I can. How is it that I haven't seen this before?"

"If you're any closer into a city, you don't stand a chance of seeing it. But out here, if the air isn't humid and there's no moon, you have a chance on some nights." I grin at the look of wonder on her face, seeing that her first lesson in spontaneity was a success.

"It's pretty amazing."

"When I was on missions or in training, a lot of the time we'd be in the middle of nowhere and the Milky Way would be stretched across the sky so boldly there was no missing it. A lot sharper than it is out here. I don't know how anyone could look at that and not be blown away by the sight of it." I glance over at the feel of her eyes on me. "What?"

Her eyes dance in the low light. "You better watch talk like that. You don't sound that jaded to me."

Swallowing a laugh, I turn my face back to the stars, feeling sleep tug at me beneath the warm blanket she stretched over me.

24, I remind myself. *24.*

CHAPTER 12

~ ALLIE ~

I should be exhausted, and my back should ache. I hadn't intended to actually fall asleep on the hammock with him last night, but the warmth of his body next to mine and the stars above us drew me into a deep slumber.

Waking up alone, I discover a note saying he went to pick up donuts and coffee at Pop's.

I'm in lust. A man who can lure me under the stars and listen—actually *listen* to me—and then pick up donuts and coffee the morning after is like a dream come true.

Struggling to lift myself out of the low-hanging hammock, I plant my two feet on the ground, and gaze out at the brook in my view. This section of Newton's Creek really is beautiful, and I feel lucky every day I walk my dogs along its cool, clear water.

If a few mountains popped up along the horizon to replace the struggling farms, I'd picture this creek slicing its way through Montana or someplace else far west. The water tumbles over the rocks, and small boulders create an unintentional pathway across. I wonder what's on the other side of the creek, and am sorely tempted to try to balance my way across it.

Logan looks as out of place here in Newton's Creek as this brook does. Sure, there are jokes that men grow tall as the corn out here, and the farmers and others who make their living off the land do get broad-shouldered and tan. But there is an essence to Logan that sets him apart—an air of command that my heart seems to lap up like a tasty, cherry-flavored aphrodisiac.

He's not meant to be here though, landlocked in Ohio. I can see the pull of the sea keeping his heart firmly anchored somewhere like San Diego.

My phone buzzes in my pocket and I pull it out, seeing my mother's picture pop up on my display. I tap it and hold it to my ear. "Hi, Mom."

"Hi, honey," she answers. "I'm so glad you picked up. Is everything okay?"

"Of course. Why?"

"Well, I left a message last night and you didn't call me back after you were done with your party."

I swallow a laugh. I swear my mom thinks these sex toy parties are orgies or something. I can't seem to convince her it's just a bunch of soccer moms drinking cheap Chardonnay and telling tales.

"Sorry, Mom. I was going to call you when I got home, but—" I cut myself off, thinking it wouldn't be a good idea to tell her that I spent the night squished up against a hot former Navy SEAL under the stars. "—I was just so tired."

"That's all right. I'm a little worried about you right now, though. Living in that townhome rent-free. If you need money for a place—"

"I'm fine, Mom," I interrupt. "Really. Logan is a great guy."

I stand, arching my back to stretch, and head in to let my dogs out while I spend the next five minutes convincing my mother that I'm perfectly safe.

I jump in the shower, deciding to skip washing my hair today. It's kind of liberating, knowing Logan's not interested in me. At least I don't have to bother with makeup anymore before I walk the dogs.

I check my phone again for new emails and texts, still hoping I might have missed some word from my real estate agent. I can't resist.

Setting down my phone on my dresser I spot the four slips of paper tossed carelessly alongside my jewelry box. A smile creeps up my face as I lift them, grazing the paper across my chin as I think.

I wonder…

"What are you doing today?" I ask Logan.

A tempting bag of donuts is in his grasp and one hand is raised to knock on my door. But I had opened it before he even had the chance.

His eyes widen at my direct tone. "Umm, eating donuts with you."

"Great. We're going to Buckeye Land."

"Excuse me?"

"We're going to Buckeye Land." Okay, I wasn't expecting much of a response. It's not like he's a five-year-old fairy princess fan. I guess a little convincing is necessary. "You're teaching me to be more spontaneous, right? Well, I'm teaching you to be less jaded. And what better place than Buckeye Land to do it? Come on. My friend Cass works there and she got me a family-four-pack for free. We can invite your niece and brother."

The mention of Hannah does the trick and he is on his phone within seconds calling his brother. We make arrangements to meet them there in an hour, just long enough for me to down my coffee and a donut while he takes a shower next door. The thought of Logan in the shower nearly sends me into a second shower myself—a cold one—and I go against my earlier resolve by putting on make-up and squeezing into my cutest shorts—the ones Cass says make my legs look muscular.

A few minutes later, I gawk at the sight of him walking Kosmo along the stream. Kosmo is thriving in his new home. Logan said the vet has made arrangements for surgery next week and it's all I can do to not offer to go with him, even though he has to drive three hours to a specialized vet hospital in Akron to get it done.

After Kosmo has worn out, which doesn't take long in his present condition, Logan returns to his home and I meet him out on the front walkway. "I can drive," I offer.

Glancing over at my car briefly, he only says, "No. I like driving." I can't blame him. My car isn't a sight to behold and it smells even worse than it looks.

He walks past his truck and opens the passenger side door of his BMW convertible. I slide in, loving the feel of the leather against my thighs.

"Is this new?" I ask. I've seen it parked out here, but haven't actually seen him drive it yet.

"Not very. I bought it when I got back from my last mission a couple years ago. The truck's new. I kind of needed that when I started renovating. This one's pretty useless on a trip home from Home Depot."

I love the way he turns the car on by just pressing a button, and marvel at the rear and side view cameras as he backs out of his driveway. I don't know much about cars. But I know what I like.

I like this.

Given my calling in life rescuing dogs, I don't imagine a leather-seated BMW convertible is in my future any time soon, so I soak in the luxury while I can as we talk during the drive north.

"I can't believe I'm going to Buckeye Land," he mutters.

"I know. Roller coasters. Cotton candy. Tilt-a-Whirl. And if you're lucky and stand in line long enough, you'll get to meet the beautiful Buckeye Princess. Aren't you a lucky boy?" I counter sarcastically, and give him a playful pat on the thigh.

He shoots me a look and I know there's no way he would have agreed to go to Buckeye Land if he didn't have a niece he adores. Truth is, I'm actually excited to go. The roller-coasters are more geared toward the elementary school set than for adults, but I love any rides.

In my stomach, I feel a little flutter from the thrill of being spontaneous.

I could get used to this feeling.

CHAPTER 13

- LOGAN -

"She's cute, Logan." My brother's eyes follow Allie and Hannah as they filter into the line to meet the Buckeye Princess. "I like her. So, you're dating her now, I take it?"

"No," I respond quickly. Almost too quickly. "I told you. Too young."

"Great. I'll ask her out then."

"Like hell you will." Hadn't we settled this already?

"Why can't I? If you're not interested in her."

"If she's too young for me, why the hell isn't she too young for you?"

"Because some of us don't live by your absurd rules, Logan. I look at her and I see a smart, fun, capable woman who's cute as hell and really good with my daughter. I'd be a damn fool to not chase after her."

I see the same thing he does, but I don't jump to the same conclusion. And I hate that he's right. There's nothing wrong about the age difference when it's my brother. He hasn't seen what I've seen, done what I've done. He's worked hard at JLS Heartland, but there's no mistaking that he comes from a life of privilege. She'd be good for him and Hannah. But I'm not about to tell him that.

"I don't want Allie to get her heart broken by you. She's been through a lot. And your track record hasn't been that great with women."

"Only because the women I date never take a shine to Hannah. If they don't see her for the jewel she is, to hell with them."

I tend to agree, and I've heard it from him plenty. Hannah is sweet as pie, but can be a little hard to handle sometimes—impulsive, dramatic, and headstrong.

I can't imagine where the headstrong part of her comes from.

A lot of people don't really "get" Hannah like Allie seems to. I watch them from a distance in the crowd as they play *Rock, Paper, Scissors* in line. Allie tosses her head back, laughing when she either wins or loses; I can't tell. They're both smiling broad enough that it warms my heart even from this distance.

No wonder my brother wants her.

But so do I. I just don't want to admit it because it breaks every vow I made to myself after my last relationship.

"You can date anyone you like," I finally say, pulling my eyes from the sight of them. "Just not Allie."

"Hell with that. If you're not going to date her, then I am. What the hell's *with* you these days?"

"What the hell is with you, Ryan? You're the acting CEO of a multi-billion dollar company. You think you can't find someone else to date?"

"I need someone *right*. I need someone *now*." His words seem weighty and he bites back a curse.

I can tell there's more to his statement than him just wanting to get laid. I take a slow sip of my drink and set it down in front of me. "What's the sudden rush?"

He shakes his head and reaches for his drink, looking like he's wishing for something a lot stronger. "Adriana is getting married."

I suppress a scowl at the sound of his ex-wife's name. At first, I can't imagine why he cares. But then I start wondering about the man she's suddenly bringing into my precious niece's life. "Who's the lucky guy?" I ask, my tone dripping with sarcasm.

"Some orthodontist. I've never met him."

"Are you going to?"

"Probably not. She says it's not my business."

"It is too your business if he's going to be allowed around Hannah."

Inhaling deeply, his shoulders rise and fall as his gaze drifts off in the direction of his daughter. "He won't be around her much. She wants me to take Hannah."

A feeling of elation creeps up in me, and I try to hammer it down because obviously there's more to this than he's telling me. "That's great. I mean, isn't it?"

"Maybe. Could be. Adriana says she wants to start fresh. Have a family with this guy. She feels like Hannah would be in the way."

"Are you sh—" I stop myself, remembering we're in a family environment. "Are you kidding me?" I shake my head. "She didn't tell Hannah that, did she?"

"No. And I'm pissed off that I actually had to specify to her not to. She says she's tired of dealing with the schools, the doctors, all the complaints from the teachers. Told me it's my turn to try to figure my daughter out."

I know Hannah's been in and out of the doctor a lot trying to find the right medicine for her ADHD. They all seem to cause her some pretty bad side effects. The pills might work wonders for some kids, but they definitely weren't doing the trick for Hannah.

My eyes narrow. "So she pops out one kid, decides she's not perfect enough, and decides to get rid of her and try again? Bitch," I utter the last word quietly, even though I doubt anyone can hear us. "When are you going to tell Hannah?"

"Not until the legal paperwork is done. I keep thinking Adriana will change her mind."

"I hope not. I'd sleep a lot better with Hannah at your place than at Adriana's with some new guy playing 'Dad.' It's not like Adriana has the best judgment when it comes to men. No offense."

He nods, unoffended. "It's not that easy, though. I'm taking over so much work for Dad at the company. My hours are crap. I can't remember the last time I made it home before 9:00. Plus, all the traveling. And if dealing with the schools and the doctors takes as much time as Adriana says, I really don't know how I'm going to do it."

I feel the pinch of guilt for not helping him at JLS. "You have family to support you," I offer, knowing I'd much rather be picking up Hannah every day from school than trapped behind a desk at JLS.

"Yeah, well, what I need is a wife."

I scoff. "That's the last thing you need. Look what's happening with your last wife. What you need is a nanny."

"Maybe." He presses his lips together, his gaze following Allie and Hannah as their line curves and they disappear. His eyes narrow suddenly and meet mine. "I'll give you a month to figure it out with Allie, Logan. After that, I'm asking her out. If she says no, then fine. But you've can't stop me from asking."

I bite my tongue. I don't have a damn thing to use against

him for ammunition. If I'm not interested in Allie, then maybe she would be good for him.

But the thing is, I'm damn interested.

Standing, I scrunch my empty cup in my fist and toss it into the recycle bin. "Looks like they're getting close to the front of the line. Maybe we should get their hot dogs." I step away from him without looking back. I don't want him to see how defeated I feel.

"Do you have a party tonight?" I reach for Allie's hand as I help her out of my car. She seems flustered by the gesture, a blush touching her cheeks as my fingers wrap around hers.

"Nope," she answers, her eyes barely able to meet mine. Her hair is tousled, probably from riding the Buckeye Brawler one too many times, and I fight the urge to pull it out of the ponytail and watch it fall around her shoulders. What is this woman doing to me?

"How about we let the dogs out for a bit and then grab dinner?"

Her eyes widen. "You mean go out?"

"Unless you'd rather eat in."

"Umm, I'm kind of on a budget right now. How about we make dinner instead?"

I try to keep myself from rolling my eyes. What kind of a guy does she think I am? "I'm buying, Allie. I wouldn't have asked if I weren't."

Shaking her head, she reaches into her purse for her key. "Oh, no, that's not right. It's enough you're letting me live here rent-free."

As she digs in her purse, her eyes glance upwards to me. Most of her makeup washed away during the day after getting drenched on the log ride, and I'm stunned by how gorgeous her eyes are without any of that paint to muck up the sight of them.

If she looks at me like that any longer, I'll be offering to do a lot more than just buy her dinner.

"Of course it's right," I finally respond, pulling my eyes from hers as she opens her door. "You got us in for free, remember? Least I can do." I see the hesitation. "Come on. Let's go to that new place on Anders Street."

"Francesca's? The one with the Zagat rating?" She seems intrigued.

"Yeah. I haven't had a chance to try it. How about it?"

"Okay," she finally says. "Just give me a few minutes to change."

When she shuts the door behind herself, I can't help but appreciate the fact that she can get ready for dinner in a few minutes. Most women I've dated tend to take forever to get ready. For me, the only thing that needs to get ready to eat is my mouth.

That said, I probably should change too, I decide as I look down at my t-shirt and shorts. Francesca's seems like a pretty casual place despite the great reviews, but my mother would scold me if I took a woman out to dinner wearing a shirt that has a chocolate ice cream smear on it.

I'm greeted by Kosmo at the door and it always makes me smile. "How you doing, boy?" I ask, giving him a good petting before I lead him to the backyard. While he hangs out there, I charge upstairs to change into a polo shirt and some khakis.

I brush my teeth at the feel of cotton candy and frozen cheesecake on a stick coating the inside of my mouth. It has nothing to do with the prospect of kissing Allie again. Nothing.

Really.

But as I swish the mouthwash in my mouth, I'm wondering if I'm feeding myself a load of crap.

Kissing Allie again is all I've been able to think about today. Every time I see her lush lips curve upward in a smile, I can remember what it felt like to have her mouth against mine. Then when Ryan dared to say he was interested in her? Well, I just about went territorial alpha wolf on him.

For a guy who swore she was too young for me, I'm having a damn hard time remembering that. As I pull my polo shirt over my head, my phone buzzes in my pocket. I glance at the display and see a text from Maeve come in.

"Where's your RSVP saying you'll come to the wedding?" she wrote.

I frown, typing, *"I sent it last week. Didn't you get it?"*

"I got one from you saying you can't come. I'm still waiting for the one that says you can."

I expel a breath. There is no saying "no" to Maeve.

Another text comes in. *"Come on. Bess really needs more peeps. And there will be lots of single women there. LOL"*

"All the more reason to not go," I text back.

"Sigh," she writes, *"Just think about it more, K? You can't tell me you wouldn't like a weekend back on the coast. Check us out."* She attaches a photo of her and Jack in the tandem kayak I gave them last year rowing somewhere alongside a sandy beach, probably near Little Creek, where Jack is stationed now.

I feel a tug at my heart at the sight of blue water stretching out to the horizon.

"I'll think about it," I write and turn off my phone before I can see her reply.

I knock on Allie's door about fifteen minutes later and my breath catches at the sight of her in a tank dress, tight-fitting at the bodice and flaring out just above her knees in a way that catches the breeze even as she steps out onto the small stoop outside her doorway.

"You look great," I say, unable to resist.

She glances over her shoulder as she locks her door, completely unaware how seductive her stance is right now. "Thanks. So do you."

Opening the car door for her, I'm met with an eyeful of leg as she slides into the passenger seat. God, she's got incredible legs. Not long, but curvy and strong from all those walks she takes with her dogs.

24, I remind myself as I get in the car.

I have to remind myself because she's just not 24 like Vanessa was. In fact, it suddenly seems insulting to Allie to even compare her to my ex-girlfriend. Vanessa had made it to her 24th year unscathed by life, completely oblivious that sometimes there might be some bumps in the road, and that some people, even though they look strong and invulnerable, might actually have a few chinks in their armor.

Allie's not like that, I'm realizing. She doesn't seem like the type of woman to scare away at the first sign of imperfection in a man.

Holding the door open for her, I smell a hint of cherry as she walks by me. She always smells like something sweet. Chocolate, cherry, vanilla, honey. Always something mouth-watering.

Conversation flows easily on the way to Anders Street, as it always does when I'm around her. When we arrive, we settle into a window seat and watch the light foot traffic in downtown Newton's Creek. It's a sleepy town by comparison to any others I've lived in. But it does have its own brand of charm.

"So, have you heard anything about that foreclosure?" I ask her, closing my menu after deciding on the salmon for my entrée.

She smiles. "Anxious for me to move out?"

"Hardly. I'm actually getting pretty used to having

someone next door now. Especially now that I've seen your painting skills." I send her a wink.

"I haven't heard anything yet. And God knows I've been touching base with my real estate agent so often I think she's considered filing a restraining order."

"Figures. Banks are slow to move. I take it the house is vacant now?"

"Oh, it's not a house."

My eyebrows hike up an inch. "Not a house. Well, what is it?"

"It's an old boarding kennel. It went out of business a while back and has just been sitting around abandoned."

"A kennel?"

Her smile is exuberant. "You can see why I wanted to jump on it now, huh?"

I can see why she would have run away from it, actually. If it's been abandoned for a while it will come with a hotbed of problems. And where does she plan to live in this kennel?

She must have read my mind. "There's an office inside and a small kitchen. I figured I could turn that into my living quarters for a while."

"Sounds a little sparse."

She shrugs. "Can't be worse than dorm life."

Actually, it can be worse, I want to tell her. I've fixed up enough homes during my down time in the military to know first-hand. "Did you get it inspected?"

Nodding, she glances up from her menu and orders after the waitress approaches. I order too, hoping that I'll still get more details from her after our server leaves.

"It's got a lot of problems. But Nancy helped me get a nonprofit loan to fix it up. 3200 square feet all on one level. It'll house 35 dogs," she volunteers.

"How much is the loan for?"

I nearly cough when she tells me the figure, barely

enough to cover a modest kitchen renovation. She must see my hesitation because she quickly adds, "I'll just fix it up room by room. The roof needs replacing first, then..."

She continues talking, but my mind is crunching numbers. With 3200 square feet on one level, that new roof she mentioned is going to eat up her entire loan. And since she seems pretty smart, I'm betting she knows it.

What she doesn't know is that there's no way I'm letting her leave my townhome till that place is deemed safe to live in.

"Sounds like a good plan," I force out of my mouth. "A nonprofit loan," I say, taking a sip of my beer as soon as the waitress sets it in front of me. "Nancy sounds like a handy kind of boss to have."

"She is. She's been through all this before, you know, when she started her nonprofit. I've learned so much from her. I'd actually like to go back to school one day and get my Masters in Nonprofit Management."

"That's great." Looking at her, I see such ambition. She has a mission and is focused on it. It's how I used to be. It's what I miss most about myself since I left the SEALs.

But most of all, as I look at her right now, I can't quite feel that brotherly feeling I've been trying out when it comes to her. I feel attraction. Even worse, I feel respect. Women I respect are sexier than hell to me.

"So what about you, Logan? What are your plans for the future?"

It is a completely natural question considering the way our conversation has been headed. But she couldn't have asked me anything that could make me more uncomfortable right now. I take another sip of my beer. "Just to get these townhomes fixed up and move on to another project."

"Do you have your eye on anything?"

Just you, I feel the urge to say, a harmless flirtation to change the subject. But I think of something more to the point. "There's an old kennel that might need some help."

She laughs.

"I'm dead serious, Allie. I'll do it for a lot less than anyone else. I've got nothing better to do with my time."

Shaking her head, she reaches for her wine. "Sure you do. Like maybe moving on to a project that can pay you what you're worth. You really do incredible work. How is it that you know so much about renovation when you've been in the Navy?"

"My family's worked in construction for three generations now."

Her mouth tilts to the side as she considers. "I've met your brother and I can't really picture him hauling a bunch of 2 x 4s off a truck. He just doesn't seem the type."

I laugh, a little louder than I should in the quiet restaurant. "And what type do you think he is?"

"I picture him sitting behind a fancy desk in a slick office with a pretty assistant who runs to get him coffee every morning."

"You nailed him completely. But he definitely gets his own coffee. He's the acting CEO of JLS Heartland."

"Seriously? That's that big development company that puts up cookie cutter mansions with no backyards, right?"

Ouch. Glad my family's not around to hear that. "Yes, that's the one."

"No kidding. I actually applied for a job there when I first moved here. Got turned down."

"You'll have to yell at Ryan about that."

"Never. It turned out for the best. It's a lot easier taking on my dogs with a job that isn't standard nine to five."

"Well, seriously, talk to him about it. He could probably find you something that's more flexible."

She shakes her head. "I could never leave Nancy. She's

been a great boss. And it's really giving me the insight into running a nonprofit that I need. I write all her direct mail pieces and grant proposals. I even write her speeches sometimes."

My mouth hitches upward. "Yeah, but if you made more at JLS, you could stop selling sex toys at night."

Her eyes narrow, but she's still smiling. "Maybe I like that job, Logan. It's nice giving these poor neglected women some way to satisfy themselves." Her voice is low and she's leaning slightly over the table toward me, giving me a glance at some cleavage that has my temperature heating up a notch.

Pulling her head back again, she giggles behind her glass of wine as it touches her lips. "Seriously, though, it's actually fun. I essentially get paid to go to parties and hear about everyone else's sordid sex lives."

"My last girlfriend got invited to one once. They're really popular these days, I guess."

She waggles her eyebrows. "And I'm riding that wave all the way to the bank."

Our conversation quiets as the waitress brings our meals.

"So, did she buy anything?" Allie asks when we're alone again.

I've bitten into my salmon and it's everything the reviews have promised. As the flavor saturates my taste buds, I'm trying to remember what we were talking about. "Who?"

"Your girlfriend. Did she buy anything at the party?"

"I have no idea."

She seems almost confused by my answer.

"What?" I ask her.

Giving an awkward shrug, she slices into her filet. "I thought men always liked it when women pulled out their toys."

"What gave you that idea?"

"Oh, please. Everyone knows that's a fact."

I lower my chin. "Any woman sleeping with me won't need a toy to supplement the experience." I get some pleasure from the blush that I see creeping up her neck.

"Really?" she sputters.

"Really. Toys might be fine when a woman is alone, but when a man is there, he shouldn't need a crutch. It's a sign of laziness."

"You think?"

"I know." I smile.

"Interesting," she ponders. "I never thought of it that way. You know, having you as a friend might give me the insight into men I need."

"You've never had a male friend?"

Her brow furrows slightly, considering. "Not really."

"Well, you do now." Impulsively, I reach for her hand, and am struck by the charge that shoots from my fingertips straight to my dick.

Friend, huh? Who am I kidding? Quickly, I set her hand back down and change the topic to something safer. "And as your friend, you'll have some help getting that place in shape if you get it. Can I take a look at it? We can stop by tonight before the sun sets."

It's worse than I thought.

Peering into the window of the old kennel, I smack my hand against my ear as the high-pitched buzz of a mosquito draws close to it.

I'm getting eaten alive out here. The lot obviously hasn't been maintained at all since the owner left and the structure itself is a shambles.

I lean back a bit on my heels thoughtfully, trying to tug out some of the optimism that I must have buried in me somewhere. I look over at Allie, who is biting her fingernails nervously as I peruse the place.

With some hard work, it could probably be everything Allie is hoping for.

With a *lot* of hard work.

Through the window, I spot an office in the front, and a small kitchenette with beat-down appliances.

I step over an overgrown hydrangea to get back to what was once the walkway. It's covered in moss and dirt, and still moist from heavy rains yesterday, making me slip a little as I take a few steps toward the street. My eyes fall to the sign that once greeted visitors:

Newton's Creek Boarding Kennel

R.I.P., I can't help adding the tagline in my head. This place has definitely seen brighter days.

I walk through the shrubbery toward another window.

"Should we really be snooping around like this?" Allie calls over my shoulder, and I hear a slap of her hand against skin, probably swatting a mosquito.

"Hell, yeah, if you're planning on buying the place."

"But I've seen it all."

"Can't hurt to keep looking. Listen. If you're dating a guy, do you decide to marry him after a couple dates?"

"No."

"Then why would you commit to buying a place until you've looked it over for a good long time?"

"For your information, I've looked plenty at this place. I've driven by it at least four times a week since they put the sign in front of it."

I peek into the window and see long rows of kennels, each a pretty good size, even for the huge German shepherd Allie has now in her care.

Without thinking, I find myself nodding at the vision I now share with her. I can see why she wants this place.

Anyone else would just plow it down and start fresh. Maybe build a house or even a small development of homes on this lot. There aren't too many opportunities to actually buy a kennel like this. Even though it's run-down, it has pretty good bones. I turn my back to the building and check out the lot. "How many acres does it come with?"

"Just two. But there are farms on either side, so it's not like I'll have neighbors complaining about the dogs barking." She turns away from me and points. "I picture fencing off a couple areas over there so that the dogs can play outside a bit."

"That'd work."

"So you don't think I'm crazy?"

I approach her, trying to focus on what she's saying. It's a challenge because somehow seeing her all excited like this has got my blood stirring.

"Crazy like a fox," I reply. She turns to me, and she's almost too close for comfort. Her eyes shimmer with emotion, and I'm not sure why, but the sight of it makes my hand edge across her chin and brush a lock of her hair behind her ear.

"Thanks for saying that. I know Cass and Kim think I'm nuts. Selling my condo and locking up every dime I have in an offer for this place." Her voice is breathless, and I'm way too conscious of the way her chest rises and falls with every breath.

"I think it's a great idea, Allie. Don't let the world get you jaded."

"Like you?"

"Like me." Watching the way the setting sun reflects on her features, I lean into her, and swear I just meant to brush my lips against her cheek. A simple kiss. A kiss from a friend. To show support.

Tell that to my cock that is suddenly perking up below my zipper.

Then I catch a whiff of her sweet breath so close to my lips and I can smell the chocolate mousse she ordered for dessert. And I want a taste. I desperately want a taste.

I feel her sharp intake of breath as my lips touch hers. Chastely at first—I can barely feel her warmth against my mouth. Her soft whimper in response rouses my hunger, smothering any control left in my body.

She draws another breath as my mouth covers hers, and I'm lost to her, my instincts taking over. Her full lips part and I trace along the ridge of her teeth, till my tongue meets hers. Her body is melting and I wrap my arms around her instinctively, wanting to protect her from falling.

But who will protect her from me?

Reason escapes me as her tongue entangles with mine, the movements both hesitant and suggestive. I feel my body harden in response, pressing against her, pinning her against the wide trunk of an oak. Her warm hands move to my shoulders, sliding upward to my neck until her fingers are tunneling into my hair. It's only now that I realize my skin has been starved for her touch, and now that I have it, I want more.

The pads of her fingertips kneading into my scalp send shockwaves through me. And every cell of my body responds, silently demanding her caress.

Our breathing is jagged, and our mouths are searching, exploring each other as though this moment was inevitable. With her breasts pressed against me, I can feel her heart pounding behind her ribcage and its rapid-fire beat is as desperate as my own.

I want to lose myself in her right now. In all her hopes and plans and dreams. If I could just fuse my body with hers,

I'd be able to silence the voices that haunt me, even for a little while.

Which is every reason I shouldn't be with her right now.

My breath catches suddenly and I pull back from her. I stare at her for a moment, panicked at the depth of feelings that are stirring me. "Shit, Allie. I'm sorry."

She's breathless, frustration in her eyes. "Why? Why on earth would you be sorry?"

"I told you I wasn't what you needed, and then I go and do this."

"Actually that's not what you said."

"What?"

"Last week. That's not what you said. If you had said that you weren't what I needed, then I'd have told you that you don't know *what* I need."

I stare at her a moment, noticing the green flecks in her eyes. From far away, they seem brown, but standing this close to her, with her body still leaning against the overgrown foliage of an oak, they definitely look green. I force myself to step away from her, and it's likely the hardest thing I've done since I left the Navy.

"What do you need?" I dare to ask.

"I need you to start treating me like an adult. Dammit, Logan. My whole life I've been told I'm too mature for my years. Devin even dumped me for it."

"Devin?"

"My last boyfriend. He thought I was no fun. Too serious. 'Stop acting like you're forty,' he'd say, even though it was only weeks after I buried my dad. And now here you are, treating me like I just celebrated my sweet sixteen. It's insulting."

I nod. "You're right. I'm sorry." My shoulders sag as the sunset dips below the horizon. "You never told me that. About your ex."

Her cheeks bunch up in a grimace. "Yeah, well, we all have our stories to tell, I guess. So, what is it you need, Logan?"

"Huh?"

"I told you mine. You tell me yours."

What do I need? My breath stills at her words and I struggle to find a response. I can still taste her on my lips and there's a tightness in my groin right now that is telling me exactly what I need right now.

I need that woman who invited herself up to my hotel room—someone I don't have any depth of feelings toward. Someone I can lose myself inside, who can pull me from the chaos in my head, even if it's just for one night.

But I do have feelings for her now. And I know that when she sees a beautiful sunset, I'm picturing the darkness that will soon follow.

She sure doesn't belong in the hell I live in.

Her green eyes are still on me as I step back another foot from her. "Your friendship," I say lamely. "I need your friendship."

Her eyes have something in them that I hadn't expected. Understanding.

She reaches her hand out toward me. "Then that's what you'll have," she says with a smile. I take her hand in mine and feel that same familiar charge between us. It's not unexpected anymore. I always know it will be there when I touch her. And that scares the hell out of me.

CHAPTER 14

~ ALLIE ~

I lie awake in my bed, only hearing the heavy breathing of dogs in the room. One sleeps at my side in the bed, while the other two sleep right next to me on the floor, so close I have to remind myself not to step on them if I get up in the middle of the night in the darkness. I'm not even sure which one is in bed with me until I reach out and feel the short hair of a corgi beneath my fingertips. I should have figured she'd be the one up here. Even though she is the smallest, she is by far the bossiest of the bunch.

Corgis aren't little dogs. They are big dogs with short legs.

At the feel of her wet nose nuzzling my cheek, I rise.

The house is quiet, but it usually is. Even though Logan said he'd be doing some noisy work at night, the only thing I've seen him do at night is paint. I know he's holding back because he doesn't want to wake me.

I wonder how many other ways he's holding back when it comes to me.

He's out of town tonight, and the stretch of townhomes feels a little too empty with him gone. Kosmo is getting his heart surgery and Logan felt more comfortable staying close to the vet hospital in a hotel rather than having to drive three hours to constantly check on him.

But I wonder, just a little, if he needed to get away from me.

After that kiss, things pretty much went back to usual between us. He even let me help tile the bathroom, and I have to say, working that wet saw was a bit of a thrill.

I couldn't let there be anything awkward, not after the pain I saw in his eyes. I don't know what secrets he has, but I know they are too painful to deal with for him. And if he only wants a friendship from me, then by God, I'll honor that.

There's no hiding that I want more from him, though. Desperately. Enough that I nearly had to dust off my vibrator that I have stashed in my drawer. But the hum of modern technology in my vag would only depress me at this point. It's Logan I want, not a battery-operated substitute.

What slays me is that it's not even his looks that I find most attractive anymore. How could I be stuck on superficial when the guy is letting me stay here for free with my three rescued dogs? He actually listens and doesn't think I'm crazy for my wild aspirations. He is an absolute dream uncle to his little niece. Toss in that undeniable SEAL presence he's got, and it's enough to make any girl go crazy for him, even if it wasn't all wrapped up in such a handsome package of muscle-sculpted flesh.

He's staying in Akron tonight—a place with a hell of a lot more single women than Newton's Creek. And as much as I shouldn't even be imagining this, I can't help thinking he's probably not sleeping alone tonight. He might have headed out for a drink, same as he did at Bergin's that night, and had a ready-female follow him back to his hotel room.

I know. I was once that girl.

I wonder now, sometimes, what would have happened if I had stayed that night.

We would have had mind-blowing sex. Then we'd have run into each other the next day at the adoption event. Maybe if I hadn't run off on him, he wouldn't see me as the naïve young woman he seems to see me as now.

We could have stood a chance.

Or, on the down side, he might have seen me as the skanky girl who followed him to his room too easily and not have wanted to extend things. *Easy* is pretty easy to find when a guy looks like Logan.

In that case, I probably wouldn't have had the offer to stay here rent-free, and the three dogs lounging in my room would have made their journey across the Rainbow Bridge compliments of the County.

Being a good girl, in this case, may not have been the best move for my libido, but it was definitely the best move for my dogs.

The upside of being Logan's friend is that I am still in his life. Truth is, I really enjoy spending time with him. He's spontaneous in a way that I'm not. When he pulled off a heap of cotton candy and affixed it to his face like a beard just to get a laugh out of Hannah at Buckeye Land a few days ago, my sides nearly split laughing.

Most guys who look like him *like* looking like a Greek god, and would never muck up their face with pink cotton candy. They're too busy admiring themselves in the mirror.

I reach for my phone, considering leaving him a text asking about Kosmo. I'm sure he turns off the sound when he goes to sleep. Maybe a text from me in the morning might remind him I'm alive even if he wakes up with someone else in his bed.

I open my messaging app and see a text from Logan sent at 11:30 after I had gone to sleep. *Damn.* I should have left my phone on. I turn on the sound again.

"Just got off the phone with the vet," it says. *"Kosmo took a bit of a turn. Had a reaction to the anesthesia. I might be here a little while longer."*

Crap. I bite my lip as I start typing.

"Logan, I'm so sorry! Are you okay?" I hit send.

Only seconds later, a call comes in and I recognize the number. "Logan?"

"Hey. What are you doing up this late?"

"It was too quiet around here."

"You miss me." He's saying it sarcastically, but it couldn't be closer to the truth.

"Maybe I do. It's pretty lonely out here in the woods without you. Did you hear anything new from the vet since you wrote?"

"Not a word. I'll head in there first thing in the morning. I'll text you as soon as I know anything."

"Or call. You can always call." I have to admit, I feel better just hearing his voice. "So, why aren't you sleeping, Logan?"

"Hate the quiet. I got a room right by the elevator and the vending machines hoping I'd get some noise, but I seriously don't think there's another soul on my floor. Lonely as hell in this bed without someone drooling on the pillow next to me."

"Aw, is that an invitation?" I kid.

"Kosmo. I was talking about Kosmo drooling." He laughs. "It really makes me wonder how the hell I managed in Annapolis without a dog."

"Was it noisier there?"

"Yeah, a little. I was right on the Academy campus, but with the windows open I could still hear some city noises."

"And I can't imagine you slept alone much," I say teasingly.

"Yeah, Vanessa was over a lot while we were together."

Vanessa. It's the first time I've heard him mention a name.

"Did that help?" I ask. "Having someone around?"

"It did, actually. Even though…" He stops short, which he doesn't do often.

"Even though what?"

"Nah. Nothing."

"What, Logan? I'm always dumping all my problems on you, why can't you dump a little on me?"

There's a long pause.

"I slept a lot worse back in Annapolis. It was kind of hard on Vanessa. She ended up leaving because of it. It was so soon after I got back from… well, it was pretty hard being around me at night. I have PTSD. Do you know what that is?"

Post Traumatic Stress Disorder. I may not have any family in the military, but I know something about it just from reading news articles. "Yeah, I know. Logan, I had no idea."

"I'm a lot better now. Most the time I can make it through the night. Just sometimes it gets too quiet and I go a little nuts."

It suddenly makes sense to me, why he'd like to work at night, why I'd find him sleeping on a hammock by a babbling brook in the middle of the night.

And why he'd think I was too young and naïve for a guy like him.

Why do I get the feeling Vanessa was about my age?

"Well, call me if you get that way. I snore. You can put me

on speaker phone and have all the noise you would ever want." I seriously can't believe I just told him that.

"I know," he answers.

My eyes widen. "You know I snore?"

"I can hear you sometimes through the wall. You're pretty loud."

I touch the wall, wondering if I'll ever be able to sleep again knowing he's on the other side of it. "I'm mortified."

"Don't be. I've slept a lot better since you moved in. I might have to ask you to stay after the renovation is complete just so I can keep sleeping so well. I was hoping Kosmo would be a loud dog. We had a beagle once who sounded severely asthmatic. Do you think I can put in a request now for a second dog, maybe one who sounds like Darth Vader?"

"I'll keep my eyes open for one."

I hear him sigh on the other end. "You should get back to bed," he says.

"I was up already, remember?"

"What's keeping *you* up?"

Thoughts of you, I want to say. I miss his presence here, and I know that even if friendship is all I ever get from him, that would be enough.

But I might be upgrading my vibrator to a newer model.

"I was thinking about you," I slip, quickly catching myself by adding, "and Kosmo. I'm so sorry he's not doing well."

"He'll be all right. I'll probably be here another night though."

"Do you need anything?'

Like me, naked with a big bow on my head, maybe?

"No, thanks."

I frown, grateful he can't read my mind.

Even after we hang up the phone at 2 a.m., I still can't sleep. The idea of him unable to sleep in a quiet hotel room by himself has lodged a knot in my throat.

It's all I can do to make it through my work day, and it is a busy one for a change. Nancy is in Los Angeles having a field day at a vegan conference and she's got me editing her speech last minute.

I'm tapping away at my keyboard, but my mind is a hundred miles away. Well, 195 miles away to be exact, since I looked up the hotel information Logan left me on a mapping app on my iPhone.

My phone vibrates on my desk. A predictable warmth spreads over my skin as I see it's from Logan, and I feel relieved to read that Kosmo will be able to come home tomorrow morning.

But even as I enjoy the relief of knowing one of my rescues will be all right, I feel an urge that I can't quite put my finger on… at least not until Cass shows up at my door to pick up the samples from our newest line for a party tonight.

"Hey," I call from my doorway as she pulls up. The sight of my car parked next to hers has me realizing just how desperately I want to drive to Logan right now.

He needs noise to help him sleep?

I can be noise.

"Hey. Got my vibrators ready?" Cass shouts back.

I roll my eyes, glancing down the walkway. Even though I know I'm the only one living here right now, sometimes Logan has an electrician or plumber coming and going as they bring #4 up to speed. But no one is in sight.

"Yep," I reply. "Three new ones to show off. And a whole new summer line of scented lubricants. They're only available till August 31. It's part of their *Weekend at the Beach* line."

"Yippee," she says with marked sarcasm. I can tell Cass

hates doing these parties, but she makes a killing at them, so obviously she's good at faking it.

I lead her into the house and open my closet.

"Ahh, the closet of treasures." There's a smirk on her face. "So, do you have any parties scheduled tonight?"

"Nope. I've hit a dry spell."

Concerned, she looks at me. "Do you need the money? I can pass tonight's off on you, if you'd like. Should be an okay crowd. The woman attended a party I gave a month ago and wanted to host one herself to get a Model 62-Magnum for free."

I nod, glad to hear the company's monthly special is creating some buzz. "No, I'll be all right."

"Just going to hang around?"

"Yeah. Guess so." My voice trails slightly.

"What's that look?"

"What look?"

"That 'I've got someplace I'd rather be' look. Are you thinking of knocking on your hot neighbor's door, and asking if you can borrow a cup of sugar?"

I snort. "No. He's not even home. He's in Akron while Kosmo gets his surgery done there."

"He staying the night?"

"Two nights, actually. Kosmo had a reaction to the anesthesia and had to stay longer than expected."

"Aww, that's sweet. All by his lonesome."

I can tell from the pout on Cass's lips that she's thinking the same thing I am.

Her grin is wide. "Need a dog sitter tonight, dear friend? I can swing by my place and pick up Skylar and camp out here for the night." She shakes her head. "I'll be jealous of you for at least a week, but I'll get over it."

"It's not like that, really," I inform her, because it isn't.

Getting laid really isn't my motive tonight. (Okay, it's my fantasy. Not my motive.)

But Logan told me about his PTSD in confidence, and I'm not about to tell anyone else, least of all Cass who tends to let things slip more easily than she should.

"Sure it's like that." Her eyes flash knowingly.

"I couldn't." I'm shaking my head as my small voice repeats weakly, "I couldn't."

"Sure you could, kid. What's the worst thing that could happen?"

"He opens his door and has some hot blonde there sitting on his hotel bed."

Cass shrugs. "I might put up with a threesome for a guy as hot as Logan."

I laugh, smacking her on the arm.

"Come on, Allie. Didn't you tell me he was trying to get you to be more spontaneous?"

I stare toward the front door, knowing my car is beckoning me on the other side. What would I do in this situation if it were Cass or Kim sitting in a hotel room with PTSD, unable to sleep? I'd haul my ass to Akron with a bottle of wine and a deck of cards to kill the hours.

Why should I be any different with Logan?

I nod slowly. "Okay, I'll go."

Cass enthusiastically claps her hands in glee. "I'm totally psyched. And not because you're getting laid, but because I get to spend a night away from my psycho roommate."

Laughing, I reach into the kitchen drawer for the extra key Logan gave me and hand it to her. "You're sure you don't mind?"

"Not a bit. Now run upstairs and pack. I'll be here by eleven tonight to let out the dogs. I promise." She leans in and air kisses me on both cheeks—something I'm betting she picked up in New York, because it's not something we generally do in Ohio.

As she darts out my door with her boxes of samples, I realize there's no turning back.

And Lord knows, I have no plans of turning back anyway.

CHAPTER 15

- LOGAN -

Exhaustion eats away at me as I plug in my cell phone to charge it and set it on the marred nightstand. The furniture in this hotel room could really use some updating, but I'm not one to complain. Compared to some of the places I've slept in my life, this is a five-star luxury resort.

Of course, I haven't actually slept much here yet, just laid on the stiff king-size mattress, staring into the darkness and listening to the hum of the digital clock that's probably been sitting on that nightstand since the late 1980s.

The only thing that is updated in the room is a flat screen TV on the wall, and I'm grateful for it since I spent plenty of last night watching yesterdays' stock ticker scroll by and Cindy Crawford trying to get me to buy facial crème on an infomercial.

The TV should have lulled me to sleep, but it's a trick that rarely works for me. My brain tunes out the chatter and replaces it with haunting memories.

I'm trying to focus on the good news of the day. I get to bring Kosmo home tomorrow morning. I miss my townhome, my hammock out back, and strangely enough, I really miss the little brunette who has moved in next door. It's so easy to like Allie.

I pick up the flyer I found in the hotel lobby and look up a pizza place on Yelp to see if there are any good reviews. It's bad enough being stuck here for another night, but there's no need to be eating sub-par pizza.

I hear a knock at the door and don't even stand up before shouting, "Who is it?" Probably some kind of turn-down service, but I'm surprised by that since last night I got in pretty late and didn't find any little chocolate mints waiting for me on my pillow.

"Allie," the voice on the other side of the door says. Immediately, my brain thinks the worst. It's so damn predictable with me. Too many years in the SEALs on 24-7 recall were spent waiting for the other shoe to drop. I dart to the door and open it.

She's struggling, juggling three bags of Chinese food, a six-pack of Sam Adams, and a bottle of Chardonnay. And there's a deck of cards peeking out of the front pocket of her jeans.

"What are you doing here?"

She grins up at me, looking tentative and tempting at the same time. "Being spontaneous."

Stepping to the side to let her in, her usual sweet scent is mixed with the familiar aroma of General Tso's chicken, egg rolls, and chicken and broccoli. My mouth waters, more from the sight of her rather than from the smell of dinner. "You drove three hours just to bring me dinner?"

"Well, actually, I have my overnight bag in the car. I

thought I'd sleep on your couch and snore for you. Make sure you got some sleep. I didn't like the idea of you being here by yourself right now."

My jaw goes slack. Honestly, that's the nicest thing a woman's ever done for me. And if my dick wasn't as tired as the rest of me, it would probably be standing at full attention. But as it is, I just pull her toward me instinctively and let her softness meld into my frame. "That's really nice of you, Allie."

We just hold each other for a moment, and it's surprisingly soothing.

When I finally let her go, even though I really don't want to, she says, "So I brought dinner, drinks, and even some cards if you're really desperate to kill some time tonight and the snoring doesn't lull you to sleep."

If I wasn't so exhausted, I think there are about fifty things I'd rather do with her than play cards to kill time. And none of them are clothed.

"You really didn't have to do this," I tell her.

Batting her hand through the air, she blows me off. "'Course I did. You do plenty for me. It's about time I did something for you." Pulling out the containers from plastic bags, she fills the small hotel desk with food. "I got you chicken and broccoli like last time. And I got egg rolls because I couldn't help noticing your mouth watering every time Hannah took a bite out of hers. You really shouldn't deprive yourself like that."

I grin at her know-it-all expression and realize that egg rolls aren't the only thing I've been depriving myself of lately. "You notice everything, don't you?"

"I have been told I'm an acute observer."

I don't know about acute. But she sure is cute. "I owe you dinner for this one."

Stabbing a piece of chicken with a plastic fork, she gazes

up at me. "Do not. You just bought me dinner the other night."

"That was payback for the day at Buckeye Land."

She laughs. "Like you really wanted to go to Buckeye Land."

"I'll admit, I didn't. But watching Hannah have so much fun made it one of the best days I've had recently." Of course, it hadn't been just Hannah I had enjoyed watching that day. It was Allie.

"So did I succeed?"

"Succeed?"

"In making you less jaded. Remember? That was the deal. You make me more spontaneous, which obviously you did since I just drove three hours to eat Chinese with you. And I make you less jaded."

I stare at her thoughtfully. I really want to say that she did. I know that's what she wants to hear. But I'm still the same guy I was the day before I met her. If I were different, I would have slept like a baby last night. It's just not in me to lie to her.

"I think I'm still a work-in-progress," I confess.

She surprises me with a flash of a smile. "Good. Because if you didn't need me anymore, then I might have to find someplace else to live. And I'm still officially homeless."

I'm glad to not have disappointed her. However I choose to define Allie in my life, I can't dodge the fact that she really does matter to me. "Any news from your real estate agent yet?"

"Nope, and I know she's sick of me texting her. I just can't resist, you know? I keep thinking a response from the bank might be waiting in her email and she just overlooked it."

"I don't blame you. I'd be the same way. That place is your dream."

Her eyes are locked on mine as though I'm the only person who really understands the significance of that kennel. And maybe I am. I see it the same way she does—as a chance to really make a difference.

I've always had a mission to focus on. And without the SEALs, I'm grateful to latch onto someone else's mission just for a small taste of what I once used to feel to the core.

Watching the faraway look she has in her eyes right now as she munches on a spice-laden chunk of meat, I worry a little about what might happen if she doesn't get that foreclosure. The place is an eyesore, and pretty far off any main roads. But someone else might take an interest in it, someone with a lot more money than her. I don't feel comfortable asking her what she offered on the place. My dad brought me up to believe that money, religion, and politics were cards you held close to your chest. But I'm guessing she couldn't make a full-price offer.

I could have sweetened the pot, I consider. Money isn't exactly lacking in my family and thanks to the money my grandfather settled on me after his death, I don't have to wait in line to get it.

"You know, I'm not sure what you bid on the place, but if you need some money to bulk up your offer a bit, I've got some funds that aren't tied up in anything right now."

Her jaw drops about an inch. "Are you out of your mind? You've got five townhomes you're trying to flip, Logan."

"I can afford to invest in something worthwhile."

Laughing, she wads up a napkin and tosses it my way. I think she's being playful till she touches her finger to my chin to wipe a few pieces of rice off my five o'clock shadow. The feel of her skin on mine, even briefly, sends the faintest blip of awareness to my fatigued groin.

"You're in serious need of help if you think dumping your

money into a flailing nonprofit like mine is a worthwhile investment," she retorts.

She's ignoring my offer, and I let her. Being raised in my family, I can recognize stubborn pride when I see it. "You think it's a worthwhile investment," I point out. "Why shouldn't I?"

Shaking her head, her smile is still wide on her face. "Because for me, it comes from here." She knocks her chest with her fist. "When I walked into that dog pound for the first time, well, it was like my dad was talking directly to me. He always made a place in our home for any abandoned animals. Our house was crawling with secondhand dogs."

I smile. "And what did his voice tell you?"

"Well, I was looking at all these dogs, trying to find the one that needed me the most, and I heard him whisper, 'One is not enough.' So I tapped on the worker's shoulder as she's taking out the poodle I had decided on, and I said, 'I think I'd like more, please.' She honest-to-God looked at me like I was nuts and said, 'You want more? I got more,' and handed me two more that were slated to get euthanized later that day. She didn't want to see them die any more than I did. Then that night I called my boss and asked her how she set up her nonprofit."

"When did you find out about the foreclosure?"

"Kim actually told me about that. She drives by it every day taking her son to pre-K. It was out of business before I even knew her, but when it started to fall into disrepair, she started eyeballing it for me, waiting for a 'for sale' sign to go up. It was on the market for a while at a price way too high for me. But when no one bought it, it turned into a foreclosure."

"Seems like it was meant to be."

"I'd like to think so." She leans back in the weathered desk chair and sets down her fork. "So what about you, Logan? I'm always talking about my silly dreams. What kind of things are floating around in that serious looking head of yours?"

I take a moment to bite into my egg roll and my mouth absolutely waters as the fried goodness seeps into my mouth. As I chew, I think about what to say and realize I'm coming up dry. "I haven't got a clue what I'm doing actually, Allie. Being a SEAL was everything to me. When my dad got sick, I let myself get caught up in the initial drama of it, you know. I can say I was trying to be supportive and helpful to my family, but I wonder if I was just using it all as a distraction from the fact that I don't really know what the hell I'm going to do for the rest of my life." In those few sentences, it was the most honest I've ever been with a woman. It was the most honest I had ever been with myself.

"Well, back when you were a SEAL, had you thought about what you'd do when you got out of the Navy? I mean, you can't stay in forever, I'm guessing, right?"

"Yeah. I guess I thought I'd settle down in San Diego. Buy a nice sailboat. I figured I'd have a family by the time I retire, you know, have a couple kids that I can totally mess up the way my dad did for me." I laugh.

"Your dad did a great job with you." She gives me a playful pat on my thigh and the proximity of her hand to my crotch in that instant puts my hormones on high alert.

Shrugging as I pop the last bite of my egg roll into my mouth, I lean back in the stiff chair I had pulled up to the side of the desk, aching to stretch out on the bed. "He did a hell of a job with my brothers. The jury is still out on me."

"How can you say that? You were a Navy SEAL. You protected our country. You got the Silver Star."

"So, I *was* something great. Now I'm just some guy trying

to flip a few townhomes." I move to the bed, unable to suppress my need to get horizontal. "My brothers, however…"

Wiping her mouth on a napkin, she moves to stretch out alongside me. "I don't care if your brothers are freaking millionaires, they can't top your achievements."

My brothers *are* freaking millionaires, I want to tell her. So am I, technically, though it's something I don't care to admit, even as I sip a Sam Adams and feel more relaxed than I have in days. Truth be told, JLS Heartland has kicked my family right into the status of billionaire, though my mother will never admit it and I tend to share her quiet view.

It's only now that I realize how little Allie might know about me, unless she has been punching my name into a search engine. I know she's aware that Ryan is acting CEO of JLS, but I doubt she's pondered how a thirty-one-year old got to such a lofty position.

She's just 24, I remember. Thirty-something probably sounds like the end of the road to her.

Some days it sure seems that way to me.

"Want your fortune cookie?" she asks, turning on her side.

"I think I'd rather not."

"You're no fun," she pouts. "I'll read yours." Eagerly, she cracks open the cookie. "'Be careful of the company you keep at night.'" She reads, her eyes lighting up.

"Does not. Give me that." I pull it from her grasp. "Careful of the brunette next door. She brings disaster,'" I pretend to read. I feign a gasp. "My God, it's what I've been thinking all along."

She snorts, pulling it from my hand. "Liar. It says, 'Tomorrow is a new day.' Yeah, totally lame, huh? Fortune cookie messages are so vanilla these days. I swear the companies are afraid to put something scary in there for fear they'll get sued."

"Let me see yours." I get up to retrieve it from the desk and immediately want to get back in a lying position. I'm that tired. I've gone without sleep before in the field without any problems. But the rush of adrenaline keeps me going. Right now, even the fact that an appealing woman is stretched out on my bed isn't enough to combat the lure of sleep.

Cracking open the cookie, the message falls to the bed as I crash alongside her again. She pulls it off the timeworn bedspread.

"'Yesterday is forgotten,'" she reads, and her face curls up in revulsion. "These totally suck. I want my money back."

My laugh is low and weak as my eyelids start to droop. Downing the last of my Sam Adams, I roll to my side. "I'm beat."

"You look it."

"I'll sleep on the love seat," I offer.

"It doesn't pull out into a bed?"

"Nope."

"You'll never fit. I'll take it, or… I promise to not accost you if I can share the bed with you." Her eyes are filled with laughter.

"You sure you don't mind?"

"Not a bit. You'll hear me snoring better that way, anyway."

"Your snores will be a gift from God to me, Allie." I pull off my t-shirt. She averts her eyes as I drop my jeans and slip under the covers. The sheets feel cool and crisp to me tonight, not itchy and stiff like they did last night. I guess I'm not a guy who can sleep alone very easily.

A part of me worries I'll wake up with a nightmare. I don't want to scare the living shit out of her like I did

Vanessa. Yet somehow, watching Allie quietly pick up the leftover Chinese and put it in the mini-fridge, I can't even begin to compare my ex-girlfriend to her. Allie is cut from a completely different cloth. And it's a cloth I'd like to wrap myself up in, I realize as my brain sinks into sleep.

Some other time. Maybe.

CHAPTER 16

- LOGAN -

When I wake up, my arm is resting on Allie's shoulder and I'm sporting morning wood. Not cool. Not good at all, especially since I really should pull away from her, but everything in me wants to lie this close to her a little longer.

The snore that escapes her is anything but ladylike, and for me, it worked better than a prescription sleep aid, the kind that's highly addictive with plenty of nasty side effects.

But there just aren't any adverse side effects when it comes to Allie. No drama. No pretense. Hell, rarely even any makeup, I think with a smile looking at her now with her face only inches from mine.

She is what she is. And what she is, is perfect for me.

I wish I were perfect for her.

Her lashes are longer than most women's, and I'll bet her friends envy her for that. I see these women wearing their trendy false eyelashes these days, and they've got nothing on

Allie's real ones. Her cheeks are full; I'd even call them plump, though never to her face because I doubt she'd like that. Yet they give her face a softness that I just want to touch. Her hair flows down her neck falling to the top of the nightshirt that she must have changed into after I fell asleep. I'm almost embarrassed by how quickly I drifted off and how hard I slept.

And speaking of hard…

I press my lips together in a frown, forcing myself out of the bed to get my body back under control.

I slip into the shower and the cool stream of water brings me instant relief till it eventually warms up to a better temperature. A film of Kosmo's fur and saliva washes down the drain. Half of the day yesterday, I sat with him at the hospital, since they allowed me to pet him and keep him company. I got plenty of appreciative licks for it. Apparently, he's like me. He doesn't like to sleep alone either.

Anxious to pick him up, I rush to brush my teeth and shave, hoping the hum of my electric shaver doesn't wake Allie in the next room. I flick off the power momentarily, and hear her unmistakable snore coming through the bathroom door. Smiling, I turn the shaver back on. The girl sleeps like the dead. I envy the hell out of her for that.

By the time I emerge from the bathroom fully clothed and ready for the day, the snoring has abated and I see Allie stirring slightly, moving from her side to her back. Her breasts rise and fall under the sheets, and the sight of it makes my jeans feel a lot tighter in the crotch.

"Hey," she murmurs as her eyes open and rise to mine.

"Morning. How did you sleep?"

Smiling, she moves back to her side, revealing a hint of stunning cleavage as her breasts press together between her arm and the mattress. "I think the bigger question is, how did *you* sleep?"

"Like a log. I owe you more than you know."

"Stop it. You owe me nothing." She rises from the bed, and I can finally see a nightshirt that reads, "I sleep with dogs." The oversized shirt has no shape to it, but it's about the sexiest thing I've seen in a long time. "Mind if I jump in the shower?" she asks.

"Go right ahead," I reply, grabbing my phone off the charger and checking for messages. "The vet hospital opens at 8:30."

"Great. I won't be long."

After we're ready and packed, her car follows mine as we drive to the hospital, and Kosmo is ready for us when we arrive. He looks so vulnerable, still heavily drugged, with his chest shaved and a fresh incision healing up near his heart.

When he sees Allie with me, his tail wags, but he doesn't rise. Allie immediately gets down on the floor with him and presses kisses to his cheeks. Lucky dog.

I go over the post-op instructions with the nurse, sign the paperwork, and make a follow-up appointment for three months from now to make sure that the surgery was a success. He still has trouble walking, so I gather him up in my arms and lay him down in the back seat of my truck on a blanket that he likes to sleep on from home. I've never been so grateful I bought a four-seater truck as I am right now.

Allie is waiting for me, leaning up against her car as I settle him in. Approaching her, my heart is filled with something more than gratitude. For the first time since being on the Teams, I feel like someone has my back.

"Thanks again for coming, Allie."

"No problem. I'll follow you home."

"How about I follow you?" I suggest. Truth be told, I'm not sure how many miles her ancient car has left, and if she ends up on the side of the road, I don't want to miss it.

"You think you can keep up?" She winks as she slides into her car.

"I'll try my best." I slam her door and wait to make sure she locks it. Climbing into my truck, I glance behind me at Kosmo, who looks like he had one too many. "We'll be home in a few hours, boy."

I try to keep my truck at a close distance to hers, and even when I lose sight of her, I can tell she's close by because of the drone of her muffler. Her car really needs some work. No, I correct myself as I look at the rusty rear end of it. Her car needs a grave.

It's just old enough that I'm not certain whether she even has airbags, and if she does, I can't imagine they are very good. She definitely doesn't have a back-up camera, and with her being around dogs, one might come in handy.

I heave a sigh as I hear her engine sputter when she presses her foot to the accelerator to pass someone. Frowning, I talk to Kosmo just because he's a pretty captive audience right now. "She needs a new car, boy. Don't you think?"

I nod at his silence. Silence, after all, means tacit agreement. "Yeah, I agree, boy."

The angle of the sunlight on Allie's car showcases the streaks of dog slobber covering her windows.

No, what she needs is an SUV or a van. Something that she can transport dogs more easily in. I've seen her pile three or four dogs into her car and it's a little like watching clowns at a circus piling into an old VW Beetle.

I wonder how much she'd protest if I bought her something more suitable. If I tell her it's for her dogs, I might get her to accept it.

The drive is long, just long enough for me to make plans to head to a dealer on Monday morning and take a look at some options. She's got a nonprofit. I can donate anything I want to a nonprofit, can't I?

I'm surprisingly happy when I pull alongside Allie in front of the townhomes. "You're home, Kosmo," I tell him, glancing behind me to see his eyes are half shut.

Allie greets me at my car door, extending her hand. "Want me to open the door for you guys?"

I nod, handing her my key, and stoop to lift Kosmo. He seems to shun my help, though, and stumbles out of the truck on his own, half wagging his tail as he approaches the front door. He staggers straight to my leather couch and looks at it with longing, unable to make the jump up on his own.

I bend over and lift him onto the couch. "You're home now, boy." I scratch his neck lightly and kiss his cheek. "Now get some rest."

Allie is standing by the door. "He seems happy to be home, huh?"

"Yep." Me, too, I realize. "I better grab my mail. Want me to get yours?"

She nods. "I'll get a bowl of water for Kosmo in the living room in case he's thirsty."

"Good idea. Thanks," I say over my shoulder. It's almost noon, but the birds are still in high form, singing their hearts out. I can hear the creek babbling behind the backyard and imagine yesterday's rainfall is making it flow a little harder than usual. The gravel crunches beneath my feet as I feel remarkably content after a good eight hours of sleep. I crack a smile. More like ten hours, I realize, doing the math. I certainly wasn't much company for Allie last night.

And Allie was the best company I could have asked for.

I grab a couple envelopes out of Allie's box first, all junk mail from the look of it. In my own, the usual stack of bills greets me. And a card.

My heart seizes up as I see the return address.

I don't hear the birdsong any longer and the cheerful

babbling of the brook has been replaced with a loud, droning sound from the surge of blood flowing to my head. I know what the envelope is. Instinctively, I know.

Walking back into the house, Allie says something to me, but I don't know what. I'm not even sure if I shut the door behind me, and only with the knowledge that I don't want my dog wandering off, do I force myself to check it.

I set the mail down on the counter and lift the card. The handwriting is neat, probably Clare's, each letter proudly created with a calligraphy pen. There are no tears on the envelope. Now isn't a time for tears.

Now is not the time for rage, either, but it's what I feel building inside of me.

"What's that?" I hear Allie ask me, but I can't even come up with an answer. I open it, seeing the words on the card. Even though I already know what they'll say, each one cuts into me like a knife.

"It's a graduation announcement," she answers herself, since apparently, I seem unable to.

My hands are shaking as I flip it over and a wallet-sized photograph falls to the counter from behind it. It's small and posed, like most high school senior photos. And God, the kid looks just like Torres.

I can see him now, ducking behind the Humvee, his leg shot up and his hands covered in blood as he struggles to stop the bleeding from Crosby's neck. But there's no panic in his eyes. There was never any panic in his eyes. Nor in mine; it was what we were trained for. No panic, even as I made the call that would end his life.

"Who is that?"

Her voice seems so faraway to me now, and I feel like I have to crawl through a tunnel back to her world to answer her. "Son of one of my brothers in the SEALs."

A silence hangs between us for a moment, and I feel

myself sinking again into a memory till her voice tugs me back. "And his dad died?"

I'm surprised she figured out that much, and I almost glance at her except that I can't pull my eyes from the photo of a young man who is graduating without a dad because of me.

"My fault," I say, and I'm shocked to hear the words fall from my lips. It took six months with a shrink before I could say that to him, and I never was able to admit it to anyone outside of his office on base.

I wait for her questions, but they don't come. Instead I feel myself talking again. "We were on a mission and got hit by an IED followed by some heavy fire. We had two men down, and I was pinned behind a Humvee with them. One was bleeding pretty bad, shot in the neck. It didn't look good. Torres was shot in the leg. We had another Humvee coming up behind us and needed to get to them, but the vehicle couldn't make it to where ours had fallen off the side of the road."

My palms are wet, caught up in emotions as this kid's picture slices my soul open and raw emotion pours out of me. "I had to get them to safety. But I'd have to do it one at a time. Crosby was worse, so when our backup started firing to cover me, I grabbed him and ran. I had thought I could make it back to Torres in time, but I was too late. He was shot in the head."

"You couldn't save them both."

I snap back to reality, the colors and contrast of the world suddenly so sharp to my eyes that they burn. "I couldn't save either one of them. Crosby died only minutes after I pulled him away from the Humvee. There was nothing I could have done to save him. I could have saved Torres. If I had taken him first, he would have lived. And this kid," my hand is shaking as I wave the photo in Allie's direction, "would have his dad at his graduation rather than in a fucking casket."

I wish she'd leave, and I want to tell her that. But I can't. All I can do right now is feel the two hands that she's planted at either side of my face as she looks into my eyes. "You couldn't have known Torres was going to get shot again. Anyone else would have taken the other man first, too. He was in the most trouble. You couldn't have known what was going to happen. If you had taken Torres first, you'd be feeling guilty about Crosby because you wouldn't have known that he was going to die anyway."

"Yeah, no shit, Allie. But at least this kid would still have a father. It's about him, not me. Who gives a shit how I feel?"

"I do!" Her eyes are harsh now, unlike the sweet girl who rescues dogs in her spare time. I don't want to see the anger in her. This is why I can't be with her. There's blood on my hands and I can't wipe it clean, no matter how many shrinks I see.

I grasp her hands, probably too firmly, and pull them off my face. Her gentle touch burns me right now. I don't deserve her compassion. She should save it for Torres's kid. He's the one in pain right now. He and his mom.

I feel the rage burning inside me—rage I feel at the world, not at Allie. But she's the only one around and if she's smart, she'll get the fuck out of here now. "You want to know why I'm up at night?" My voice sears my throat as the words escape me. "That's why, Allie. That's why I can't be with someone like you. Your world is different than mine."

"We live in the same world, Logan."

"We don't. Yours is full of a future. Mine is still sinking in the past."

"So stop it. It's not what Torres would want. Or Crosby."

My eyes narrow on her and I can't help the anger I feel toward her optimism. "Save your dogs, Allie. Don't try to save me. I'm not worth it." My tone is biting and I hope it's enough to drive her away. I don't care right now if I hurt her feelings. I'll hurt her more if I drag her into the nightmare I live in each day.

Grabbing my neck, there's a fire in her eyes that I've never seen before as she pulls my face down to hers.

"Fuck what you say, Logan. *I* think you are worth it," she says, and then presses her lips to mine fiercely.

My body feels like it's been torched as I spin her around, pinning her against my counter. "What do you think you're doing?"

Her teeth scrape against my chin as she moves her mouth downward. "Bringing you back to my world." Her breasts are pressing against my chest and I can feel her nipples harden against me. My fingers drop the photograph and find their way up to her head, tunneling through her hair and grasping the back of her neck like I'm holding onto her for dear life.

I start to protest, but she's pulling off her t-shirt and I'm seeing skin that I need desperately to taste. My lips drop to her delicate collarbone as I cup her breasts with my hands.

I shouldn't do this. I know I shouldn't. But I also know that I desperately need to sink myself into her just to feel human again.

CHAPTER 17

~ ALLIE ~

My breath is ragged as he slips his hands beneath my bra, and I'm covered in goosebumps from the feeling of his calloused fingers swiping against my taut nipples.

I know this is the wrong way to get what I want from him, and I can already imagine the regret I'll feel afterward. But right now, I've never felt more powerful than when I saw that lost look in his eyes replaced by desire.

Never have I felt more like a woman than at that moment, and it's got me in heady stupor, my veins coursing blood to my hormone-soaked brain. I reach down to feel the throbbing beneath the zipper of his jeans and he pulls my hand away. I'm struck by disappointment, till he reaches beneath my legs to lift me up.

I savor the taste of him as he carries me upstairs and lowers me onto the bed. Standing above me, his eyes are full of heat, and I know not to expect a sweet, gentle bout of sex from him right now. If I wanted that, I should have initiated it some other time, back in that hotel room maybe. Not at a time when the demons of his past have filled him with fury.

He pulls off his shirt and I nearly gasp at the sight of him. I've seen his muscles before, but it's an entirely different experience knowing that I'll get to touch them, feel them sliding against me skin-to-skin. I pull off my shorts and toss them to the side of his bed and he does the same with his jeans.

I reach for the erection that is tenting out from his briefs and he lowers his mouth to mine while I touch him. Teeth graze against my tongue and I hear a moan that is more like a growl when I slip my hand beneath the thin fabric and feel the supple, tight skin throbbing over such hardness.

His mouth is moving to my breast, leaving a damp trail of kisses along my neck. Freeing himself from his briefs, I feel his cock pressing against me, urging for entry. Arching my back, I ache for more pressure, and he senses my needs as his hand moves to my panties. I should be embarrassed by how wet he's made me, but I can't feel anything but pleasure as he slips two fingers past the fabric and enters me.

I cry out from pleasure instantly, my body bucking beneath him, urging him deeper, wanting more contact. My muscles quiver as his fingers open slightly, spreading me more. I come hard and completely, and my pelvis is still rocking as his mouth moves lower on my body and I feel his hot breath above the thin cotton.

He peels me free of the cloth and his voice is thick with command. "Open your legs."

I can't think to deny him. I'd do anything at this point to keep these sensations going. His lips meet my clit and my vision glazes over from the feel of his tongue circling around my center as his fingers move inside of me. I feel myself climbing up again, soaring toward a climax that is still just outside of my reach, till one of his fingers delves deeper, arching just so that it hits my most sensitive depths and I come hard against his mouth.

"More," I say as he climbs off of me, and I am relieved when I see him pull a condom from his nightstand drawer. I honest-to-God might have forgotten, desperate as I am to feel him inside me. He sheaths himself quickly and I take a long look at his form above me. "You're huge," I utter softly, and feel the heat of embarrassment sting my cheeks realizing I said it out loud. But it's true, he's long and thick and it seems in perfect proportion to his body.

My words seem to arouse him more, as he plunders my mouth again so thoroughly my lips feel bruised.

There's emotion in his eyes, and I don't know how to define it. Harsher than lust, fiercer than need—almost an urgency steeped in anger. It scares me, and has my heart picking up speed as he spreads my legs, but also makes me moist with desire.

"Say you want this, Allie."

I feel a spike of terror flare through me that he's become just rational enough to stop. And I don't want him to. I need him inside me like I need my next breath.

"I want this. I want this." I repeat it over and over, even as he slides himself inside of me. He's barely nudging into me at first, and it's not what I need. My fingers rake against his back, and I pinch them into his skin as I pull him closer, urging him deeper.

His head gives a single shake as he resists. "I could hurt you," he says, and I know his words have more meaning than just this one joining of our bodies, but I don't care.

"Hurt me," I say, grabbing his ass and pulling him closer. He responds by entering me with a single thrust, so deep that it does hurt, a spellbinding pain that I want to feel again even as he slowly pulls out. My body yields to him as he thrusts again, pounding into me, jarring against my womb and rocking my body against the sheets that are slick with my sweat.

I've never felt a man this deep inside me and it's shattering me. My breathing is staggered and I'm certain my heart is skipping a beat or two, trying to recover from the shock of his entry. My channel spasms around him as I soar through a climax that has me seeing stars in the back of my skull. I cry out his name and I feel my eyes tearing up, moist like the rest of me.

"Are you okay, baby?" He's staring at me and I can tell the rage is subsiding, before I'm ready to see it go.

"I'm okay. It feels good, Logan. Don't stop. Please, don't stop."

He brushes a lock of hair off my face, and I see a trace of tenderness in his eyes. Then more, as he kisses my jaw up to my ear and whispers, "You're so gorgeous when you come."

I feel his tongue tracing along the outer edge of my ear as he starts to move inside me again, slower this time, but just as deep. His hand moves down my leg and he slides my thigh higher on his hip. My other thigh follows, till my ass is arching upward with my legs wrapped around him. The angle is a little different now, and I can feel his cock touch my G spot on his next thrust. My eyes widen, and he smiles in response. "That's it, baby." His words coax me up a spiral again, chasing pleasure, as I feel another orgasm in my reach. I've never had sex like this and every cell in my body seems overly receptive to his touch. I'm exhausted, and feel like there's no way I can have another, but the need is so great.

My eyes lower from his face to his abs, to the tight V of muscles that leads to where we are joined together and the sight of him inside me just about pushes me over the edge.

One of my hands moves from his back to his rippled chest and I feel the muscles moving underneath his skin and he slides in and out of me. I rest my hand at his heart and can feel its rapid beat beneath my fingers. The rhythm of it soothes me, even as the feel of him pressing inside me has every muscle in my body tingling and contracting.

His eyes are locked on mine as his muscled arms hold him up from my body so that I'm not crushed, allowing me to take in the sight of his remarkable form joined with mine.

I want to feel him shatter the same way I did. I need to feel that—to know that the power I briefly possessed when I tempted him into this is still mine. "Let me feel it," I urge him. "I want to feel you come, Logan. Now." I try to make my voice demanding, but it's not as powerful as his was. But from the flare of passion I see in his eyes, I'm thinking I might have won. He pulls one of my legs upward so that my calf is over his shoulder. Then the other. I'm totally vulnerable to him now, my body so open to his length that when he thrusts inside of me I cry out intensely. His body stills at the sound of my gasps.

"Don't stop," I demand, and revel in the look of desire in his eyes as he takes me. I'm drunk off the sight of him pounding into me. I know I shouldn't get such a thrill from the look of his body, but I can't help it. I've never had this before, and I might never have it again, and even that doesn't dampen this feeling of wantonness that grips me as he thrusts inside of me. His body glistens from sweat, accentuating the shape of him and driving me upwards again into the heavens as a burning heat pools at my center, building, building…

My body aches beneath him, muscles I didn't even know I had cry out, yet still the fire builds inside me with every thrust. Till I finally feel myself come again, screaming out his name shamelessly, my entry gripping him tighter with each spasm, till he joins me in release with a final thrust.

His chest heaving, he gently moves my legs back down to the bed. My body seems to protest as he pulls himself from me.

"Did I hurt you?"'

I want to lie and tell him he didn't. But I remember he said he never lies, and I want to honor that. "In the most extraordinary way." I smile as I say it, and I hope he takes my meaning.

His lips brush against my face—my cheek first, then my nose, then my lips, resting there for a moment or two before he slips from the bed. "I'll be right back."

The bed is damp and cold without him and I long to beg him to come back. But I can't assume that he wants more of me. I offered myself to him as a distraction from his pain. And if the pain is gone, I might not be what he needs anymore. The thought of that terrifies me.

I hear him in the bathroom, moving around. The sound of water running. He might be showering, wiping himself clean of the mistake he just made with me.

Oh, God, I hope it wasn't a mistake. It would devastate me. Even if I never get to have sex with him again, it hurts even more to think he might not want to be my friend anymore.

I'm wallowing in my own thoughts, negativity spiraling out of control as it always does with me in unfamiliar situations. And this is completely unfamiliar. I feel tears dampen my eyes, maybe from fear or shame or just an overwhelming feeling of loneliness at the thought of losing him, when he comes back to the bed.

"Hey, what's wrong?"

Damn, he notices everything.

"Nothing, I—" I want to tell him that I'm not used to these situations and it scares me. I want to tell him… but I can't.

"You don't have regrets, do you?" He lies down next to me, pulling me to my side and resting his hand on my waist. His touch is so tender, it slays me inside, letting him deeper into my soul.

"No. No, definitely not. I—I'm not really…" My voice wavers. "I've only had one sex partner in my life. I'm not really good at these things."

There's shock in his eyes, and there's no denying it. I know my average is damn low since my friends tease me about it regularly. And I remind myself that just because I haven't had a lot of sex in my life, doesn't change the act itself. It's still just sex, and I shouldn't act like it's a big deal.

But it *feels* like a big deal right now, with nesting hormones surging through my veins uncontrollably and me just inexperienced enough to not be able to control it. I don't remember feeling quite this way with Devin, even my first time. And that means that in the span of just a few weeks, this man has crept closer to my soul than someone I supposedly loved for over a year before he dumped me on my ass.

I can still remember the pain of that rejection at a time when I needed him most. And if Logan means more to me than Devin did, then I'm even more vulnerable.

I feel the fear inside me, making me shiver as he pulls my naked body closer to his. He takes my hand and gives a playful tug.

"Come on," he urges as he stands, his hand still joined to mine. "I thought a hot bath might be in order."

My heart does a little happy dance as he takes me into the bathroom and I see the steam rising from the soaker tub. I remember the first time I saw this tub, and the thought of him in it with me has fueled my fantasies on more than a few occasions. So the prospect of actually fulfilling the fantasy has me just about passed out on the floor.

"You like baths, right?" he asks, dipping his foot into the tub and leading me to join him.

"I love them. My condo only had a stand-up shower."

He tsk-tsks a little with a laugh. "That's a sin." He slides down the back of the tub and moves me so that I am sitting facing away from him, cradled between his legs. They are powerful, like the rest of him. His calves are as thick as my thighs—and I'm no toothpick—and corded with muscles that make me suspect he's run a few marathons in his life.

Reaching for the bar of soap, he touches his lips to my neck. I feel his erection coming to life behind me and it sends my heart racing again. Sliding the soap across my chest, my nipples pucker at the sensation. Then he rubs the soap in between his hands to a nice lather and sets the bar to the side. His hands caress me, up my arms to my neck, down my back, and again to my breasts. I inhale sharply as his touch journeys down my belly, and one hand toys with my soft curls while the other softly slides along my opening. I part my legs more, aching to have the feel of his flesh inside me again, but he whispers, "Not now, beautiful. Rest now. I worked you too hard." I can feel his low chuckle vibrate against my back.

His fingers continue their sultry massage, circling and teasing, but never penetrating my folds. "Please," I beg, unable to hold back.

"Shhh," he murmurs as one hand moves to my chest, cupping a breast and squeezing a nipple just to the point it almost hurts, but not quite. His mouth plunders my neck, sucking on me, grazing his teeth against me, and then his tongue forges a path down my shoulder.

He reaches to pop the plug from the drain, still letting the fresh, hot bathwater flow from the faucet. "Rinse cycle," he says, and I feel him smiling against the skin of my upper back as he kisses me.

Between my legs his fingers play with me again, making all my muscles as taut as a violin's strings. He circles my clit, and then lightly traces the outline of the folds that are still tender from his entry. Reaching my center again, I moan, low and desperate. "Oh, Logan."

"That's right, baby. Feel it."

The fresh, hot water that is making my skin sizzle is nothing compared to the heat I feel in my veins as my core seizes up. I feel the blood flow pooling at my center, throbbing, aching.

"Let go," he urges me, as my pelvis arches against his hand.

"Inside me," I beg. "I need you inside me."

"Not now, baby. Later," he tells me and I pray it's a promise he'll keep.

He circles and circles the hard nub of my sex, dipping down to caress the tender folds just before I'm about to come. It's like he's teasing me, prolonging the orgasm till I split into two. "No, no," I beg him as his finger moves away again, at that moment when my climax is just within reach.

"Don't rush it. Enjoy it."

Enjoy it? I'm dying inside, a heady, agonizing, completely thrilling death. His other hand massages me, moving from one breast to the other as my hips continue to press forward, aching for a firmer touch.

"Please, Logan. Please," I don't even realize I'm shouting till I hear a slight echo of my voice against the tiled walls.

"Now, baby," he says, bringing his finger back up to my clit, and squeezing it gently as he circles it. I cry out, loud, the air expelling from my lungs, my body vibrating, encircled in his hold. I thrust against his palm, throwing my head back against his shoulder and pressing my chest toward his other hand. I pulse against him, throbbing like a heartbeat, over and over till the waves finally slow and I'm able to breath again.

No, this is nothing like anything I've ever experienced in my life.

And I might die without it.

CHAPTER 18

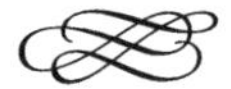

- LOGAN -

I walk back down the stairs to the living room and gaze at the mass of fur slumbering on my couch. Kosmo is out like a light, the pain killers obviously doing the trick. Standing in the middle of the room, I gaze up the staircase to where I left Allie to get dressed.

It hadn't felt right leaving her side, but I really did want to check on Kosmo. And catch my breath. I really need to catch my breath.

I sit down beside Kosmo and lightly touch his fur. I don't want to wake him, but somehow I need a little reassurance.

I was her second lover? That terrifies me. Makes me feel like I should have listened to my instincts where she was concerned. Stayed away. Far, far away.

But it also makes me glad as hell that I didn't sleep with her that night in the hotel. I saw tears in her eyes after we had sex. I can't imagine how a one-night-stand would have torn her apart.

I rise from the sofa and head to the kitchen, seeing the photograph of Torres's son on the counter. It doesn't cripple me now like it did before. The shock of looking at him, seeing his dad's eyes staring back at me, had dragged out the demons in my soul.

And unleashed them on Allie. *Oh, God, what have I done?*

Fuck that. What's done is done. But what do I do now?

I hear the stairs creak behind me, and when I look at her, it's like all the answers come flooding to my senses. I've never considered myself an overly emotional guy. But somehow when I'm with her, I feel warmth in a part of me I had thought was long dead.

I love my family, and they held in their grasp the small part of my heart that still insisted on beating in my chest. The rest I thought was necrotic—dead tissue that would never be resuscitated.

As Allie moves closer to me, that's the part of me that comes alive.

She glances down at the photo that I must have picked up at some point. I don't recall.

"He's a handsome kid," she says.

I nod.

"Have you ever met him?"

I nod again, and take a few moments before I answer. "A couple times. I visited him with my SEAL brothers from the Team shortly after we returned from the mission. And we were at the funeral." I shake my head slowly, remembering. "You've never seen anything till you've seen a military funeral when it involves kids, Allie. It brings pain to a whole new level. His son, Lucas, was fifteen when it happened, young enough to not really be consoled by that flag we drape on a casket as though that's supposed to take away some of the pain."

"It doesn't?" Her question doesn't seem like a question. More like something she's just saying to keep me talking.

"No, it doesn't."

"Did Crosby have kids?"

I shake my head. "Single. His parents and sister were at the funeral and a legion of family." I crack a smile. "Funny, meeting all of them after I've listened to Crosby talking shit about them for two years. I wished I could have told him that he was right—his Aunt Lois really does smell like mothballs and his Uncle Lou has interminable gas." I laugh, and it somehow eases the pain to bring up a good memory.

I slip the photo and the card back into the envelope. "My SEAL brothers and I promised ourselves we'd keep tabs on Torres's kid as time went on. I've failed at that."

Even though I'm not looking at her, I can feel her eyes on me.

She takes my hand. "Is that why you've stayed away?"

"Hmm?"

"From San Diego. You said yourself that your family is doing well without you. So why did you decide to stay here if you still call San Diego home?"

My eyes meet hers and I realize I can't hold anything from her. She seems to have found the pathway to all my secrets, to my very soul, if I have one. "Yeah. I'm a coward."

"You're not a coward."

"Hell, yeah, I am. A band of terrorists could burst through that door and my heart rate wouldn't even speed up, but I can't find the balls to just look at this kid in the eyes knowing what my choice cost him and his mom." I pause, pressing my palms to the cool granite. "I send checks on the holidays and birthdays, though, if that counts for anything."

She smiles. "It probably counts for a lot." She takes the

announcement from me. "Was that your last mission with the SEALs?"

"Second to last. My last one got me the Silver Star." There's bitterness in my tone and I don't hide it. "Torres should have gotten that. He should have been with us." I shake my head, freeing myself from the clutches of memory, and stalk toward the fridge. "Are you hungry? I'd like to think I made you work up an appetite."

She shakes her head. "I really should check on my dogs next door. Cass dog-sat last night, but I'm not sure what time she left for work this morning."

"I'll go with you."

"You don't have to."

"I want to."

We step into the sunshine and I realize I don't even know what time it is. I didn't think to put my watch back on after the bath. I feel a rumbling in my stomach that tells me it's past lunch, though it could be later than that.

Slipping her key into her lock, she turns to me. "You don't have to… stick around, you know. I'm sure you have work to do."

"I don't have anything more important than you right now."

Her eyes sparkle at my remark and I see her shoulders lift and fall in a sigh. I know she's feeling uneasy about this, and it's the last thing I want. I don't know where this is going, but I can't ignore that everything has changed between us.

"My family is having their usual Sunday dinner next week. Want to come?" I don't want her to think that this was a one-time-thing, and it's the best way I can think of to show her.

"Oh, that's not necessary."

"I know it's not necessary, but I'd like it if you came. You already know Ryan, and Hannah would love to see you again."

"Okay, thanks," she answers. There's a light pink hue to her cheeks as she turns the knob and we step inside.

And we see her two friends sitting on her futon drinking coffee, both with meaningful looks in their eyes.

"Helloooo," Cass croons.

"Cass," Allie gasps. "I thought you'd be at work by now."

She shrugs. "I called in sick. I don't get a chance to hang out in luxury without a drunken roommate passed out on my couch very often. Thought I'd enjoy it while it lasted. Kim swung by on her way to pick up Connor from pre-K."

Kim's eyes are like daggers on me. She hates me, I can tell. I could sense it if I were twenty miles away from her. "Hey," she greets us, her voice an octave lower than it usually is.

"I didn't see your cars," Allie says.

"We parked along the side in case Logan was still working on the pavers and needed the space." A grin sweeps across her face as she looks at me. "But I guess you're probably too tired for that now, huh?" Cass snorts as she raises her coffee cup to her mouth darting her eyes from Allie to me to Allie and back to me again.

Shit. I really need to put more insulation in these walls or something.

"Oh, no," I hear Allie murmur next to me.

"Yeah. Funny. It was a peaceful morning till the neighbors started up. All that screaming." Shaking her head, Cass raises her eyebrows at that last word, focusing her gaze on Allie.

Allie's shoulders slump forward and she looks at me, mortified. I can't help laughing. There's not much that embarrasses me, and if these women think I can make Allie scream like that, then that's nothing for me to be ashamed of.

Allie sputters, "You didn't—"

"Hear the show? Oh, yes, every minute of it. And Kim here showed up in time for the second act."

Cass cracks me up with her directness. I like Allie's friends. Even Kim, because there is something to be said for a woman who can stare down a former Navy SEAL like she is now.

"I need some coffee," Allie mutters, suddenly eyeing the coffeemaker in the kitchen. She looks at me. "You want some?"

"No, I'll just head back to my place and keep an eye on Kosmo. Dinner tonight?"

She brightens at the suggestion. "'Kay."

I lean in and kiss her chastely. I think Cass would love to see a show from me right now, but Kim looks like she's going to pull out a .357 Magnum and blow me into the next life.

I watch Allie walk toward the kitchen and give a nod to her friends. "Ladies." I turn my back and hear someone rise from the futon.

Kim opens the door for me and her eyes meet mine, dark and fiery. "If you hurt her, I will dismember you."

I try not to crack a smile, because the threat just seems out of character from a woman who looks like your stereotypical carpool mom. But she seems dead serious.

Still waters run deep.

"Understood," I acknowledge, giving her a nod.

CHAPTER 19

~ ALLIE ~

Beep-Beep. Beep-Beep.

One eye flings open and then the other.

I haven't needed my alarm to wake up since I bought it, so I'm surprised to hear what it sounds like. The high-pitched beeping is annoying, but effective, considering I'm reaching toward my clock now to turn it off even though every muscle in my body is begging to stay completely still.

This must be the way triathletes feel the morning after a competition, even though the only exercise I did was in bed with Logan.

My entire body breaks out in a blush at the recollection. I've never been so thoroughly and completely seduced by a man in my life, and I'm definitely liking the sensation. My vibrator will be collecting dust if this continues.

I figured it would be smart to sleep away from him tonight. I have a conference call with Nancy this morning and she's in… shit, I have no idea where she is. Besides that, Logan's plumbers are going to show up at the crack of dawn to finish the plumbing in #4. I don't want to tiptoe out of Logan's in his borrowed t-shirt and have them get the wrong idea. No, wait. I guess they'd get the *right* idea, but it's not one I want to share.

I slip on my yoga pants and the bunny slippers Kim got me for my birthday and step to the closet. It's a walk-in closet and my scant wardrobe looks a little lonely in it. If I were staying, I might consider buying more clothes just to fill it up.

But I'm not staying. And this little fling I'm having with Logan is just a fantasy that I'll wake up from eventually. That kills me because there's no denying I'm falling for the guy. Completely, utterly falling into a four-letter word that I don't dare say out loud.

I slip on a blue washable silk shirt that has seen one too many gentle cycles but looks okay through the small camera of my iPhone. It's incongruous with my yoga pants, but it's my usual mismatched conference call wardrobe. Business on top, bedtime on the bottom.

After letting the dogs out, I pour my coffee, noticing the plumbing trucks out front through the window. I squint my eyes to see if Logan is walking around outside with them. I'm hungry for the sight of him, and it's only been eight hours since I left his townhome in the dark of night. My heart does a little flip when I catch a glimpse of him climbing into his truck. I don't know where he's headed, but I'm wishing I was with him.

I lean against the counter, recalling our weekend together, each memory making me feel more vulnerable. We drove around the countryside with the top down, and even ventured into Dayton to pick up a couple pounds of Esther Price. (Because if I'm going to watch my waistline expand, I'll do it eating the sea salt caramels that I'm certain are paving the streets of heaven.) And at night, he had me wrapped up in so many positions, I was certain I'd end up in the ER. But there must be some special hormone excreted during sex that makes the body a lot more bendable.

We walked around town and he told me all of his stories of growing up here. So many of the memories he has here remind me of the stories my dad used to share with me.

He knows a lot about this town for someone who was so anxious to leave it when he became an officer in the Navy. And even though it breaks my heart, I know that he'll leave again. Every time he looks at our little creek, I know he's envisioning deeper water, the kind he'd be looking at every day in San Diego.

He'll only be mine for a while. But I'm determined to enjoy it.

I pull open my laptop and look at Nancy's schedule. Cincinnati, I notice. So she's actually home this week, which means she'll be keeping me busy. When she's not travelling, she's trying to get more reasons to travel.

My phone chirps and I switch on Skype. "Hi, Nancy! How was your weekend?"

And so begins every conference call I've ever had with Nancy. Ten minutes chatting about personal stuff (I avoid the topic of Logan because if she got a whiff of what happened, I'd be on the phone an extra hour) and thirty minutes for business.

I make my calls and edit some letters and a speech for Nancy for the next several hours before I think to check my party schedule for the week. Frowning, I see I have three bookings. Good for the bank account, but bad for my sex life which, now that I actually *have* a sex life, cuts like a knife.

I'm not sure how I'll manage to sit through hours of

talking about vibrators when I could be having sex with a real, live man. It's not a position I've been in before.

Like so many positions I've found myself in this weekend, I recall, cracking a smile.

After showering and changing around lunchtime, I glance out the window again, looking for Logan's truck. He's still MIA, and I'm going into withdrawal.

I start back up on Nancy's speech until my heart leaps when I hear Logan's truck door slam outside. I don't know how I know it's his. All truck doors make the same sound when they slam, and there are plenty parked in front of his townhomes this morning. But call me crazy, when he slams a door, it just sounds sexier.

Glancing in the bathroom mirror to make sure I don't have something stuck in between my teeth or dangling from my nose, I head over to the door prepared to fake an interest in how much progress they're making in #4. I don't care if he sees through it. I just need to get an ounce of his presence before I can finish off my workday.

It's hot outside, hinting of summer. Mother Nature seems to be giving us a tease this time around because the air is thick with humidity and the temperature has me longing to step back into the AC.

He's already in the townhome by the time I'm outside and since there's too much activity in there to hear my knock at the door, I enter #4 anyway. The workers don't even acknowledge me. They seem so consumed by their work. But Logan smiles broadly when he sees me, and it fills every nook and cranny of my heart.

"Morning," he says.

"Afternoon," I correct him.

He glances at his watch and his eyebrows rise. "You're right. I haven't eaten lunch yet. Been busy. How about you? Hungry?"

"I had a bagel late in the morning. But I could use something."

"How about we head into town and grab something?"

"It's a deal."

Touching the small of my back, he guides me out of the townhome.

He walks in between his truck and a brand-new SUV that must belong to one of the workers. It's shiny and unblemished, such a contrast to most of the pickups squeezed into Logan's parking area this morning.

"Something caught your eye?" he asks, noting my double-take at the car.

"No. I mean, kind of. It's a nice new car, and I bet the owner will get pissed when it gets its first scratch on some job site, you know?"

He shrugs. "The owner doesn't really hang around too many job sites."

"Oh, I figured it was one of the plumbers."

"Nope. Do you like it?"

I keep heading to his truck and toss him a look over my shoulder. "Well, sure, if you like fancy, shiny, and spacious. But you have to admit, my car has a lot more character."

He takes me by the hand and leads me back to the SUV. "Yeah, maybe. But I was thinking this is really the kind of car you need." He swings open the back door. "You could load your dogs in and out of here a lot easier." He shuts the door and moves to the back hatch.

"Logan, I really don't think you should help yourself to someone's car like this," I scold, glancing toward the townhome.

"The owner won't mind a bit. Check it out." He opens the back. "You could fit at least four small kennels in here, don't you think? Most spacious SUV I've seen, but it's not too bad on mileage because it's a hybrid. It's got all the safety features, too. Back up camera. Side view camera..."

He drones on with the list of features of this car and I have to admit, I'm getting slightly annoyed. I know my car is approaching its death bed, but it's going to have to do for a while.

"Logan, it's lovely. It's also the kind of car that's way out of my reach for the next ten years or so." It's hard to blame him for all the enthusiasm he's showing. Guys like to look at cars, so I forgive him.

"But do you like it?"

"Sure, I do. It's great. But I'm hungry. Let's get lunch."

"Okay. Mind if we take your car?"

My face droops. My car smells like dog and it will take an hour to clear the foothills of fur off the passenger seat. "I guess."

"Great. Here." He hands me something that looks like a car door opener.

"What's this?" I stare at it in my hand.

"Keyless ignition," he states matter-of-factly.

I shake my head, wondering if there is some hotline I should call to report that a former SEAL has completely lost his mind. "This isn't mine, Logan."

"Yes, it is. It's the keys to your new SUV."

My world shimmies slightly to the right and then to the left. The hammering noises coming from the townhouse seem softer, almost dreamlike. "What?" Is this his idea of a joke, or am I just dreaming? Because those are definitely the only two possibilities I can think of right now.

"I bought you a new car."

"Excuse me?"

"You need a new car, Allie."

Yes, and I need a lot of things I go without. But that's

what you do when you're in your early 20s and didn't have the foresight to major in Computer Science.

"You can't give me a car," I say.

"Of course I can. I'm donating it to your nonprofit. That way you can't complain about how I didn't ask you first."

Vertigo touches my brain and I stagger slightly, which has Logan reaching out for my arm—his gentle touch the only proof I have that I'm not in a dream.

"You bought me a car?"

"I bought you a car."

I look at him. "You can't afford to buy me a car," I tell him. For Pete's sake, he's been fixing up five townhomes with his own bare hands these past months. Is he nuts? I mean, it's the sweetest gesture anyone has ever done in the history of the world, *but is he nuts?*

"I can afford to buy you a car, Allie." He looks a little frustrated. He's shaking his head, but it seems he's shaking it more at himself than at me. "Hop in. I'll drive since you seem a little lightheaded."

Lightheaded doesn't even cover half of the emotions that I'm feeling right now. I feel like I'm taking advantage of the nicest guy on the face of the earth. Does he feel like he needs to buy me this because he's sleeping with me? My last boyfriend bought me a new hairdryer for Christmas and I had been with him for a year. That's really more what a girl like me is used to.

I'm terrified that he might be feeling remorse for what he shared with me this last weekend. I broke him down—all that talk about Torres and the war. I made him vulnerable and now he's having some kind of reaction to all that sharing.

I climb in and feel the leather seats against the skin of my thighs. Leather interior for dogs? Glancing behind me, I notice the factory-made seat covers in the back. Holy crap. He thought of everything.

"It's got heated seats, too, for the winter," another fact he throws at me to compound my guilt.

"Logan, you are so kind. I mean, you are so, so, so kind. But we have to get this back to the dealer right now. I can't let you buy me this. You've got five townhomes you just bought. And you just bought yourself a car. The payments alone on your new truck are probably more than my mortgage payments on my old condo."

He flicks on the turn signal, heading away from town, and I'm not sure where we're going. Back to the dealer, I'm hoping.

"I paid cash for my truck, Allie."

My brain tries to wrap itself around the idea of paying cash for anything these days.

"I paid cash for your car, too," he adds, turning onto the road adjacent to the highway, and driving quietly for a few minutes. His lips press together suddenly as he watches the road. "Listen, there's something I should probably tell you. I kind of assumed you had figured this out on your own. People around here usually do. But I guess, being gone as long as I was, I kind of fly below the gossip radar in Newton's Creek."

Oh, shit. He's married or something like that. Or some other huge skeleton is lurking in his closet, and this is a guilt gift. My heart is picking up speed right now and my hand slips to the armrest to give myself something to grip onto.

Damn, this leather feels soft.

He pulls to the curb of a long industrial road that leads to a massive building springing up from the surrounding farmland like Oz at the end of the yellow brick road.

And that's what JLS Heartland probably is to a lot of people in this town. Oz. Because without it, there would be a lot more unemployment around here.

"See that sign?"

"Yeah. JLS Heartland. That's where your brother works, right?" Oh, shit. They're embezzling money from the company. No, I shake my head immediately, keeping my ample imagination in check. Logan's too honest for that.

"Right. Acting CEO," he answers. "What's my name, Allie?"

"Logan." I'm right. He has lost his mind.

"My given name. Remember?"

"Jake, right?"

"Jacob Logan Sheridan, the Third."

"Okay," I say hesitantly.

"And the initials are?"

I shrug. "JLS." I glance at the sign again. "JLS?"

"Yes. That's my family's business."

"You're the JLS in JLS Heartland?"

"Well, my grandpa is, actually."

My mind is in a whirlwind. I grew up with my feet firmly planted in middle class soil. The idea of knowing someone attached to a family like this is really foreign to me.

"Don't get the wrong idea. I don't get a lot of the family money since I'm not on the payroll. But when my grandfather died, he left me a good chunk of change. He was in the service for a while, too. He probably knew I'd have to start my life over at some point. So that's how I bought the townhomes and still have enough to live comfortably on till I sell them. And that's why I have enough money that I can donate to a cause I really believe in, Allie."

My heart stirs at his words.

"I don't want you thinking that I bought you this because I'm sleeping with you either. I made the decision before that ever happened, and I'll swear to that." An easy grin sidles up his face. "I might have sprung for the leather interior because of that, though."

A small laugh escapes me.

"I just didn't want you trying to squeeze all your dogs into that tiny car anymore. It's not even safe, Allie. And I want you safe. You deserve that." He sighs. "I would have told you before I bought it, but I knew you wouldn't let me. And even if you're pissed off at me, I'll deal with that a lot better than thinking of you trying to drive that car to your next adoption event with a German shepherd crawling on your lap."

Silence prevails for a moment while I try to bring myself back to a reality that is a whole lot more plush than my fifteen-year-old hatchback. "Logan, I don't know what do say."

"Say nothing then."

"Thank you. I'm just really in shock here. I've never been given something like this before and I'm not sure what I'm supposed to do now."

"You've already done plenty. Though, if you're handing them out, I wouldn't mind one of those kisses of yours." He seems boyish beside me now, his eyes filled with mischief. I lean into him and touch my lips to his. He smells of coffee and raspberry Danish and I know he must have stopped at Pop's on the way to the dealer this morning. As his tongue urges for entry past my lips and his hand reaches up to caress my cheek, my senses are consumed by him. His fingers channel into my hair as I lean close. My heart rate picks up, right along with my breathing.

If we weren't sitting in a car in broad daylight right now, I'd be stripping down naked and seeing if those seat protectors in the back are nearly as soft as this leather.

A car honks its horn at us and I'm humiliated.

Logan rolls down his window. "Can't a guy get a little privacy here?"

It's Ryan in his convertible Jag with the top down. "Thought that was you. New car?" He eyes the SUV.

"Nah, it's Allie's. She's just letting me take it for a joy ride."

"Oh. Hey, Allie." He nods at me. "I thought maybe you were reporting in for your first day of work, Logan." Ryan gives a nod to the building looming at the center of the massive parking lot.

"Hell, no. What are you doing rolling into work at lunchtime?"

"Are you kidding? Been here since six-thirty. Just broke for lunch, not that I owe you an explanation, slacker. I better get inside. I've got a meeting in a few. You coming to dinner Sunday?"

"Yep. With Allie."

"Hey, great. Good to see you, Allie." He nods in my direction and drives off.

Logan shuts the window and angles a look at me. "So. Want to take her for a spin?"

I have chills, honest-to-God chills from the thought of driving this. "Yes." I expel a breath as I say it and I know I sound wanton. But I guess he's used to that tone from me by now.

Smiling, he opens his door to get out. "Mmm. The way you say 'yes,' it's got me hoping I'll hear more of that word tonight."

CHAPTER 20

- LOGAN -

I love watching her get ready for the day in my bathroom. I know it's strange, because I've always been one to get annoyed with the sight of tiny jars of mysterious facial creams spread out over my vanity. But I haven't gotten much time with Allie all week since she's been working so many parties. So right now, the sight of her in my bathroom putting on some kind of flesh-colored makeup, that I swear doesn't change her appearance in the slightest, just makes me smile.

She's in one of my old PT shirts, and I'm glad I didn't throw them out after separating from the Navy because she looks so damn cute in them. Flitting a look over to me, she seems to be a bundle of nerves today.

"Stop watching me," she scolds. "You're making me more nervous."

I really don't think that's possible. "There's no need to be nervous. My family's pretty easy to get along with. Besides, you already met my brother. He's definitely the only snob in the family."

She rolls her eyes. "Your brother's not a snob. He's the perfect gentleman."

I grumble low enough that she can't hear. Sure, he was a gentleman that day at Buckeye Land. Because he was eyeing Allie like she was a piece of meat. I made it pretty clear to him since then that Allie and I are an item now and there won't be any poaching. But I'm wary just the same. "Don't be fooled by him. You'll like my mom, though."

"How about your dad?"

I shrug. "He's a charmer, I hear. A good guy. He's a little short with me still sometimes."

"Because you didn't follow in his footsteps?"

"Maybe. Or maybe because I preferred getting shot at more than going into the family business," I laugh.

Her face is serious. "I've never met anyone with vascular dementia before. Is there anything I should know?"

"You probably won't even notice. He's still in the early stages. He hasn't had a spell in a couple months and none as severe as that time last year."

She nods, and her hands are shaking a bit as she shuts her compact. "How about your other brother?"

"You mean the prodigal son?" I chuckle. "I'm still not convinced Dylan's actually coming today. Just because he texted and said his flight is coming in doesn't mean something won't pull him away again from his family." I say it knowing I'm just as bad as he is. I let the Navy take me from my family for a decade, so I'm not one to cast stones in my youngest brother's direction.

Her face is scrunched up. "Why the attitude about Dylan?"

I smile. I like how direct she is with me about things. It's a sign she might be able to survive around a guy like me. "You're right. I shouldn't be that way. Dylan is… how do I say this? He was born under one of those lucky stars you hear about. Went to college on a full wrestling scholarship, which Dad certainly boasted about even though we sure never needed the money. Competed at the Olympics and took a silver, but still managed to walk away with a couple endorsements just because he's eye candy for the women."

She lets out a little snort. "If it makes you feel better, I haven't got a clue who he is. But that's just me. My life was pretty much wrapped up in my schoolbooks when I was in high school and college, and then my dogs after that."

I pull my iPhone out of my pocket and pull up one of the shaving ads Dylan did a few years ago. "He started a chain of gyms with the money from his endorsements. I think he's got eight or nine of them now."

Her mouth drops as she looks at the image on my phone. "That's your brother? Better keep Cass away from him. She'll duct tape him to her bed and keep him as her pet."

"He might actually like that, for a while anyway. He's a bit of a player."

She slides over to me and presses her chest against mine. I feel her nipples harden under my t-shirt and all the blood in my brain flows downward.

"And you're not a player?" she asks.

"I think you know I'm not. Never had time for it and never had the interest. I'd rather have one woman I can focus all my energy on."

"I'm glad to be that person for now."

I hear the "for now" that she tacked on and it makes me frown. She's got to know this isn't a fly-by-night thing for me by now. Right?

"You make it sound like you might be going someplace," I state.

"More likely, you will. I just don't think you were meant to be landlocked in central Ohio, Logan."

I frown, knowing she is right. I've been itching to be near the water again, and even considering taking Maeve and Jack up on that wedding invitation just to have an excuse to get out of town for a while. Meanwhile, Allie is Midwestern to her core. She's even trying to buy a property out here that will keep her busy for years. Where is this thing headed for us?

The thoughts roll off me. I've never been one to think too far into the future when it comes to relationships. "Well, I'm here now." I pull her closer to me and I'm sure she can feel just how much I'd like that t-shirt off her right now. It's not like we don't have the time. "We're not leaving for another hour."

"I just took a shower and did my makeup," she protests.

"You can fix yourself back up."

"We're supposed to be there at three."

"Ish. Three*ish*. We're a very *ish* kind of family."

"We can't—"

She quiets when I slide my hands beneath her t-shirt and toy with her nipples under the pads of my thumbs.

"Oh," she moans.

"Still think we shouldn't do this?"

"Maybe just a quickie."

I nudge her onto her back. "With you, I don't think I'll ever manage a quickie. I want to plunder your body thoroughly each time." I slide her panties off her and feel my pulse quicken at the sight of her dark curls. My hand explores the soft skin beneath the thatch and I get harder from the look in her eyes when I find her nub, begging to be touched. My fingers slide down to her moisture, and I slip a finger inside her. She tightens around me. I love how tight she feels even around just my finger. My cock aches to stretch her out more.

Quickie? If I let myself, I could handle a quickie with her, just focusing on my own needs, pounding myself into her till I'm finished. But I love the way she feels as she cries out, clamping up those folds around me and pulling me in deeper as she comes. I get almost as much satisfaction feeling that, as I do exploding inside of her.

I move my head to her chest and push her t-shirt up, exposing her breasts. My tongue strokes her nipple, and it gets even harder from the attention. She tastes a little like soap, fresh from the shower like she is, and her skin is as smooth as butter. Her breath quickens and I can feel her heart beating as my lips are pressed against her. I move to the other breast as my hand toys with her clit. I want to watch her come again, right now, with my face only inches from hers and in broad daylight so I can enjoy the sight. My fingers explore, picking up the moisture from her slit and moving it up to the bud beneath her curls. She purrs my name, and opens her legs more. A request. But I wait for her demand. I tease her more, sucking on her breast as I use my free hand to massage the other. I love the way her nipples respond to my touch.

Lower still, my other hand teases her with her own moisture, and she opens even wider. I slide my finger along the side of her entry, not dipping in this time. She murmurs something unintelligible, and I know what she wants.

"Say, please." I advise her.

Her eyes flicker shut. "Please." Her voice is barely a whisper and sounds almost pained as her pelvis lifts higher. I shouldn't have made her wait so long. But I have one more demand.

"Open your eyes for me, baby. I want to see them when you come."

Her eyes open and she stares at me, but I'm not even sure if she's seeing me. She seems drunk on hormones, and engrossed in need.

"Good girl," I say, plunging two fingers deep inside her and hearing her cry out immediately from the pressure. She arches her neck backward, her hips rocketing upwards, trying to pull me in even deeper. My cock is so hard as I watch her. I hadn't intended to take care of my own needs before taking her to dinner, but now there's no turning back. When her body sinks back into the sheets, I pull a condom from my nightstand and pull off my shorts. I need to be inside her now. I sheath myself, then prop myself above her. Her legs are still open, waiting for me, but I know I need to make this fast.

"Roll over," I tell her.

She does as she's told, and for that, I'm grateful. I'm breathless, unable to explain. I pull her hips upward, and wrap my arms around her so that I can lightly pinch her clit. She makes a little noise in response. "That feel good?"

"Inside me," she demands. "Now. Please."

I laugh, loving how polite she is even in her most desperate moments. I slide into her slick entry. I know I'm big for her small frame and I try to hold back. She seems to sense this, arching her back a little more to take me in.

I have to remind myself to touch her. It's not all about me, but I'm feeling selfish suddenly, with her tight around me, gripping me with the muscles inside her channel.

My fingers roam from her breasts, down her belly, to the center of her need, and she tightens up again, tighter still, around me. It's all instinct now, driving into her so hard and fast, unable to slow myself. I see her body in front of me, rocking back and forth as I take her from behind, and it only makes me want to press into her deeper.

"Harder," she says, and the word has me completely

undone. I feel her folds grip my cock like a vise as she screams out my name, letting herself succumb to a climax. I'm only a second behind her, plunging into her depths as though mating with her is the only thing that can keep me alive.

One final thrust and I fall to my side, taking her with me. I'm seeing stars, and fight the lure of sleep to recharge myself. My body is slick from sweat. It wasn't a marathon, but a short, hard sprint that's left me reeling inexplicably.

I look at her reddened skin where I was gripping her. "Oh, God, Allie, I didn't mean to take you so hard."

A tired smile creeps up to her flushed cheeks. "I only hope you mean to do it again soon."

I'm relieved at her words, yet stunned by what she has done to me. I need to have more control with her. But control is one thing I'm lacking every time she enters the room.

When she rolls onto her back, my hand moves to her breasts, stroking them, savoring the feel of her skin beneath my touch. I make a trail of kisses down her belly, down to her sex, opening her legs. "Did I make you sore, baby?"

"A little," she admits.

I dip my head between her legs and offer myself as a salve for her aches. She inhales a sharp breath as my tongue moves along the stretched tissue along her opening, and then enters gently. I love the taste of her. It's indescribable and intoxicating, and makes my blood surge south even as I struggle to recover from the last time I let myself go inside of her. She tastes like every fantasy I've had in my life and I'm addicted to it.

Addicted to her.

I open her legs more, lapping at her folds and sucking her nub tenderly, softly, the way I know she needs me to be right now. "Feel a little better?"

She doesn't answer me, just digs her fingers into my hair and holds my face to her. "More, please," she whispers.

"Are you sure you're ready?" God knows I am.

"Mmhm," she answers, gazing down at my erection as I move above her. I pull off the old condom and slip on a new one. I hate the damn things and wonder what it would feel like to slide into her without. I know I'm safe, and pretty sure she is. But I'm sure she's not on the pill, and I don't take chances.

I slide into her, determined to take it slow this time, determined to let this time be all about her. And as I feel myself sink into her, I can't help wondering whether it would be such a bad thing to get her pregnant. I get harder just at the thought of pouring inside of her, making a baby. I don't know where the thought is coming from, but it's there, and it's never been there before.

These sure as hell aren't my normal thoughts during sex. And I should be mortified, but I'm not. Instead, I'm just watching her eyes fall to half-mast as I move in and out of her and I'm feeling perfectly complete, perfectly at ease, and calmer than I've ever been in my life.

She is my world. *Right now,* I amend. Though somehow *right now* just doesn't seem to be enough.

My movements are slow and I'm certain to rub against her clit each time I'm deep inside her. Her eyes shut in response and I watch a breath fill her lungs, raising her breasts closer to me, urging my mouth to take a taste. I kiss her reverently, taking a nipple inside my mouth and letting my moisture sooth the irritated skin from where I grabbed her too hard earlier. She deserves this—tenderness. More than just a quick fuck.

"Do you know how beautiful you are?" I ask her.

Her eyes widen. I'm generally not a conversation-during-sex kind of guy, but I need to know that she sees herself the way I see her.

She shakes her head slightly. "Never really thought of myself as beautiful before. Cute, maybe. But not beautiful."

"You are. That first time I saw you in the bar. You were chatting with the bartender, laughing at something he said, and all I could think was, 'I want to make her smile like that.' It's like I had never seen anything so sincere in my life. Your eyes sparkle when you do, and the smile isn't just on your face, but in your whole body. The way you hold yourself, leaning into people as they talk as though what they're saying actually means something to you. The way your brow arches a little as you listen, and then that look of surprise when you laugh, as though it's the best damn feeling in the world and that everyone should laugh with you."

I sound like a fucking pussy, and I'm glad my brothers will never hear this. But when I feel her tighten up around my cock again, getting slicker by the second, I can tell that at least *she* appreciates what I'm saying.

"I'm glad you didn't come into my room that night. I'd never want just a one-night-stand with you, Allie. I want—" I nearly say it. I nearly say forever, but I catch myself. The last thing I want to do is make a promise to her that I can't keep.

Or could I? I'm not a SEAL anymore. I can go anywhere I want, live where I please. I have nothing pulling me away from Newton's Creek and one good thing pulling me to stay.

"What do you want?" she asks, prodding me on.

How do I answer that? How do I tell her the truth without making promises?

"More. I want more," I tell her, sliding deep inside her, slowing, even as the clock on the nightstand tells us to hurry. I won't rush this moment. I'll savor it as long as she'll let me.

CHAPTER 21

~ ALLIE ~

I've sunken into Logan's sheets and I'm not sure if I'll ever get up. Logan's showering and I already did the same—my second shower of the day and a pretty quick one, considering we're running late now for his parent's dinner. But I'm still naked on top of his bed, unable to get the strength to get dressed.

I feel the tug of sleep pull me in, till I hear the buzz of Logan's phone go off next to me on the nightstand.

I didn't intend to see the message that popped up. I'll swear to my dying day that I was just glancing that way to see what time it was. But I'm looking at it now, and it's got my stomach in knots.

"I've still got a crab cake and a flute of champagne with your name on it. You better be there."

I wouldn't think too much about the message. Really, I

wouldn't. But the tiny photo displayed next to the name "Maeve" has me instantly feeling small and homely.

She's gorgeous. Someone much more suitable for a guy like Logan.

And she's invited him to some fancy dinner.

I shake off the feelings of jealousy as he steps out of the bathroom with a smile. A smile for me. Not for Maeve.

She is probably just some old girlfriend, reaching out to him with the hopes of reconciliation. Who could blame her?

My brow creases, remembering. Wasn't that the name of his interior designer friend? So it might be completely innocent.

It might be.

I act like there's nothing wrong as I get ready for dinner. I know he sees I'm nervous, but considering I'm meeting his parents for the first time, I'm reasonably justified.

"You're late, bro." Ryan's eyes are narrow on his brother as we finally walk up the front pathway that leads to double entry doors. I'm beyond intimidated by their house. It's borderline palatial, like one of those homes I see on design shows on TV, the kind that makes you want to take your shoes off at the door and speak in hushed, reverent tones.

"I am," Logan answers.

"Nice to see you again, Allie. Hannah is out back with my dad playing badminton. She'll be so happy to see you."

I almost crack a smile at Ryan's tone. He always seems to speak as though we are in a business meeting. Even at Buckeye Land, he looked like he was sizing the place up for a hostile takeover. He would intimidate the hell out of me if I hadn't also seen the way he is with Hannah.

"I can't wait to see her, too," I reply as I see Logan's mother approach.

"Allie!" Her arms are outstretched and she envelops me in a maternal hug.

My heart feels a tug, the feel of her arms around me making me miss my mother, and I make a mental note to call her first thing in the morning.

"Welcome to our home," she says as we step inside. The soft, silver hair framing her face seems to showcase her striking blue eyes—the same eyes as I see on Logan. Her face is stunning, but not flawless by any means. She seems to have embraced her age with such dignity, and because of it, she looks all the younger and more beautiful for it.

I want to be like her when I grow up.

"Thank you so much for having me," I tell her.

"You couldn't be more welcome. I don't think I've ever known Logan to bring a girl home to us since he was sixteen. So you must be someone really special."

"Mom," I hear Logan protest as his brother laughs behind him. It's funny how a mother can turn a hardened SEAL warrior into a shame-faced little boy.

"Logan!"

Another man approaches us from the back door. I recognize Dylan from the picture Logan showed me and all I can think is how this family won the genetic lottery when it comes to looks. He's an inch or two shorter than Logan, but broader in the chest, even though I didn't think that was possible. His hair seems golden compared to Logan and Ryan's darker hair, but his eyes are the same piercing blue.

Logan gives his brother a hug. "Damn, Dylan, you get bigger every time I see you. You gain any more muscle and how will I kick your ass next time you cheat at poker?"

"It's that new equipment I got in the gyms. It's sick, Logan. You'd love it, if you'd ever get your ass to one of my gyms to try it out." He glances my way and extends his hand. "You must be Allie. Hannah's been chatting you up quite a bit in the backyard. I think she's your biggest fan."

"Second biggest fan," Logan counters, wrapping his arms

around my waist. "How about I get you a glass of wine, baby?"

I nearly have to resuscitate myself from his use of an endearment like that in front of his family. I glance over at the kitchen table and see another glass of wine and a couple bottles of beer sitting unattended. *So long as I'm not the only one drinking.* "Yes, that would be nice. Thanks." I sound a little breathless—must be because I've never been around so many handsome men in my life, and certainly never been able to go home with the hottest one of the group.

I try to not let my eyes wander around the room as I am talking to his mother about my dog rescue. But it's hard. The living room is lavish, with stunning oil paintings showcased by recessed lighting, a few sculptures displayed on built-in shelving, and a jaw-dropping stacked stone fireplace as the centerpiece of the room.

I hear a chuckle coming from the back entrance and I bite my lip as I see Logan's dad approach, being dragged by his granddaughter.

"My granddaughter says there's some kind of hero here in our house." He extends his hand to me as Hannah lunges toward me with a hug. "Jake Sheridan, Allie. Splendid to meet you."

Logan's father is strikingly handsome with the same wide jaw and sculpted cheekbones as his sons. Though his smile is genuine, I can't imagine having to face down this man in a boardroom or at a business meeting. He has the same intimidating look as Ryan, even in his polo shirt and crisp khaki-colored pants. But his voice, his stature, his air of command reminds me of Logan.

My heart is touched with sympathy for this man at the thought of him facing a diagnosis of vascular dementia. I've known him a matter of seconds, yet I can already tell that the idea of being helpless or dependent would be unacceptable to a man like him.

I try to focus on his smile as we talk, pushing back the image of his future. Logan is right. He is a charmer, listening to me talk about my dogs as though my tiny nonprofit is as significant to this town as JLS Heartland.

We eat barbeque ribs on the back porch, and I can't resist helping myself to another scoop of mashed potatoes. Logan's mother—Anna, she asked that I call her—makes them with some of the skin left on and a hint of roasted garlic bringing the flavor to a whole new level.

We play badminton for a while, and Ryan, Hannah, and I catch fireflies while Logan talks to his parents on the back porch. I can tell I'm the topic of the conversation from the way he is looking at me, and he blows me a kiss that takes my breath away.

Logan, his brothers, and I step into the living room while his parents stay with Hannah, who has dozed off on the porch swing. They talk sports and I pretend to show an interest for a while until I retreat to the kitchen to refill my drink.

As I return, I catch Ryan talking to Logan. "The papers should be signed this week," he says gravely. "So I'll tell her next weekend."

Logan nods stoically while Dylan gives Ryan a swift thump on the shoulder.

"That's good. It'll be hard. But it's good."

Ryan is nodding, but looking unconvinced. "Logan, can I have Maeve's number? I was thinking I'd do something to Hannah's room. Really make it special—like a fairy castle theme to sort of soften the blow."

"Good idea, Ryan. She'll do right by you. And can probably do it all by remote." Logan pulls out his phone. "I'm texting you her contact info." He sees me approach, and slides his hand lightly along my arm as I return to my seat next to him.

Dylan flashes a smile. "Logan, how the hell did you get so lucky? You know there are only about twelve single women in Newton's Creek, don't you?"

And just like that, the mood in the room brightens.

"They adored you," Logan says as he joins me in his truck. He touches my hand lightly and my skin sizzles with awareness. I can't wait to be alone with him.

"Do you really think so?"

"I know so."

I bite my lower lip. "Can I ask you something?"

"Shoot."

"What was Ryan talking about after Hannah fell asleep? Something about needing a designer for her room. Softening the blow of something?"

Logan nods slowly. "Hannah's mom is remarrying. She decided she doesn't want Hannah to live with them."

"Why not?"

"Tired of her, she says. Hannah is a bit of a handful. Adriana says she's tired of the complaints from the school. Teacher meetings. Doctor visits."

"What a bitch," I fire off without hesitation, and then cringe at my tone. "I mean, sorry—I don't mean to be judgmental. But she doesn't really sound like a prize of a mom."

"She's not. She says she wants to have more kids with this new guy. Start fresh."

"Holy crap."

"No kidding. Personally, I'm happy that Hannah is moving in permanently with Ryan, but it'll be hard on her, settling in. And the kid has enough self esteem problems without her mom making her feel unwelcome. But in the long run, I think it will be for the best. Ryan's scared shitless about it, though. He works killer hours, you know. Has to travel a lot to job sites in different states. Not sure how he'll juggle being a CEO and a full-time dad."

"If he needs help, I'm around a lot since I work from home."

He takes my hand and gives me a squeeze. "Thanks. That will mean a lot to him."

Frowning, I bite my lip again, working up the nerve. "Can I ask you something else?"

"'Course."

"The designer you mentioned. She's the one that decorated your place, too, right?"

"Yeah. Maeve."

"So she's a friend?"

"Good friend. You'd like her."

I'm not so sure.

"Why not?"

Oh, shit. I said that aloud?

"I mean… oh, I don't know what I mean." I sigh in defeat. I'm so insecure.

He glances over at me. "Wait a sec? Are you jealous?"

Caught. "I'm just—ugh. How do I say this? I saw a text come in from her on your phone. I didn't read it, of course. Just saw the first line or two, you know, because it pops up. Something about having a crab cake dinner with your name on it."

He laughs. Hard. So hard that the shame I'm feeling at my jealousy is getting edged out by annoyance. "Hey. I can be as jealous as the next girl. And I saw her little photo pop up by the text. She's freaking gorgeous. How am I supposed to feel?"

He's still laughing. At a stoplight, he pulls his phone out of his pocket. "Pull up the texts from Maeve."

"I'm not going to snoop in your phone."

"Do it."

I roll my eyes. I'm humiliated enough. He doesn't need to make me feel worse. I tap on the texting icon and see her photo in contacts. Her model-like features have my stomach churning as I tap on her face and pull up a recent conversation.

"Scroll up a little bit."

I do as he says, and see another photo that she sent him.

"Open that one."

I do it and—holy crap, who is that hot guy with her? They look like some kind of Hollywood couple. Her, with her perfect hair and features, and eyes that could stop traffic. And him, with his pecs poking out of his t-shirt as he rows a tandem kayak. No, they don't look like a Hollywood couple. They look like what a Hollywood couple *wishes* they looked like.

"Who's he?" I ask, still staring at the phone.

"Her husband. Love of her life. Man she was destined to marry since birth, I'm thinking. And also a fellow Sailor. We served at the Naval Academy together."

"Oh. I feel like an idiot."

"Don't. I'm actually kind of touched that you'd get jealous like that. It means you don't want me to date other women, which by the way, I have no inclination to do."

My heart goes pit-a-pat. Either that, or I've developed a heart murmur.

"Me neither," I quickly tell him.

"Good. You'd actually like Maeve. She's one of those people that everyone loves. She doesn't have friends. Everyone is family to her, you know? She's been harassing me about a wedding invitation."

"Who's getting married?"

"Her friend Bess. I met her a couple times. She's a sweet kid. Quiet. Engaged to an Army guy. I think she has a little girl."

"His kid?"

"I didn't get that impression. Anyway, she doesn't have a ton of family so Maeve's gotten pretty desperate to fill up the bride's side of the church, if you know what I mean."

"Oh, you should go then. That can be really hard. She needs support."

"You sound like Maeve. But really, I barely know Bess, and truth be known, I hate weddings. I RSVPed with a no ages ago, but Maeve's pretty insistent." He pauses. "Then again, it might be fun if I could tempt you into going with me."

I sputter. "Oh, I can't do that."

"Come on. I'd love to show you Annapolis."

"I can't leave my dogs."

"Cass will take care of them again. You can't tell me she wouldn't love to."

He's right about that. She's been begging for more opportunities to get away from her apartment.

"It's not for another week," he continues. "So check your calendar, and talk to Nancy. If Nancy can't give you a day off, I could get us a Friday night flight and have you home late Sunday."

"I have an adoption event on Saturday."

"And you have volunteers who could handle it for you."

"I probably have a party scheduled Friday night."

He raises his eyebrows. "And one of your friends could take over it, I'll bet. Didn't you say Kim is trying to earn more money? Come on, you'd love Annapolis."

I probably would love it. I'd love anyplace if I went with

him. "Okay. I'll go," I tell him, releasing a swarm of butterflies in my stomach.

Satisfied, he smiles. "So how did you like my crazy family?"

"Loved them," I reply without hesitation. Being around the Sheridans makes me long for my own family dinners before my dad died.

I really should visit my mom more often—to build up some new family memories, I guess. She's only a few hours away.

But she's not at home. Not *my* home. I walk up to her house now and see a place she bought with her new husband, not my dad. I have no memories there. They fixed up a guest room so that I can visit, but it's not *my* room, not where I drew misshapen unicorns on the walls with a permanent marker when I was six and had to stare at them for the remainder of my childhood long after I outgrew my unicorn stage. The doorways there don't have the tiny etched marks where my dad tracked my height. The rooms don't look out onto the maple tree that we planted as a sapling before I was even old enough to talk.

The house they bought is nice. But it's not home to me in the least.

"Are you okay?" Logan asks as he looks over at me at a stoplight. "You seem a world away."

"I'm fine. Sorry. I just got to missing my mom."

"Why don't you go for a visit? I can take care of your dogs."

He makes it too easy for me, and that's what I don't need right now. "I should. I know. It's just hard."

"Because your dad's not there."

I shake my head. "No, actually. It's more because some other guy is taking his place."

"He's not taking his place, Allie. No one will ever replace your father. Not to you. Not to your mother."

I shrug. "I'm not so sure. She seems pretty happy."

"And that makes you angry."

"No," I deny. I'm not that childish. Am I? "It just makes me… frustrated. Frustrated that she moved on so quickly. Did she even mourn him?"

"I'm sure she did. She was married to him for how long?"

"Almost twenty-five years."

"Twenty-five years," he repeats. "That's a long time to wake up with someone in the same bed, Allie. That's a long time to have someone to eat dinner with every night. With you gone, I can understand why her heart needed to find someone else."

I never thought about it that way. I always thought that by replacing Dad, she was showing that she didn't love him as much as I did. But maybe she loved him so much she needed someone to fill the void.

"You think?" I feel small for even thinking these thoughts.

"I'm sure."

I press my lips together in thought. I will call my mom tomorrow, if for any other reason, to tell her about the wonderful man in my life. I know she'd want to know. And I want her to know.

CHAPTER 22

- LOGAN -

Allie's bed must have been bought on clearance at the torture store. I've never felt a bumpier mattress. When I last made love to her I found myself distracted—yes, actually *distracted* by one spring that kept jutting into my knee and one into my side.

I put it on my mental register of things I'd like to get her. There are so many. It's not that I'm a snob. When I was her age, living on a Lieutenant JG's salary, I was sleeping on a foam futon in my quarters at Coronado.

But I don't want Allie to go through years like that. She's already been through enough, burying her father so suddenly and getting dumped by an asshole boyfriend right after. I want to trap that guy in a headlock and just *squeeze*.

She's dozed off on the bed beside me and I watch her eyelids flutter as though she's in the middle of a dream. Stretching my hand out toward the nightstand, I reach for my watch. I have to go next door and give Kosmo his pain meds in a little bit, but I'm having a hard time pulling myself away from Allie, even if I do feel like I'm lying on a bed of rubble.

And I've laid in plenty of piles of rubble, so I'd know. In the field, you grab sleep when you can, where you can.

Her eyes open and she gazes at me with a smile. I think about what I told her in the car the other night—how her mom probably just couldn't take the void in her life left by her husband's sudden death. And I realize just how big of a void I'd have in my life if Allie decided to leave me. We haven't been together that long. But already I feel like my soul has been completely fused with hers.

And I didn't even think I had a soul till I met her.

"I fell asleep," she mumbles.

"You did," I answer. "I wore you out." I smile as I say it, remembering how amazing it felt to be joined with her. My cock perks up at the thought, ready for seconds. Or thirds, as the case may be today.

"What time is it?"

"Nearly five." I worry I'm pulling her away from her work too much. My hours are my own. But it's not like Allie has that luxury.

"Gotta wake up," she groans, stretching out her lithe body and making me hard as a rock in the process. "I've got a party at seven."

"A party," I repeat, wishing selfishly she'd cut back on work. I hate the idea of her out late driving when she's tired. "Can't skip it, I suppose?"

"Nope. We got a new vibrator in this week. Always fun showing off the new products."

A broad smile sweeps across my face. I'd love to be a fly on the wall at one of those parties. "And how exactly do you show them off. Drop your panties?"

Her jaw drops. "You seriously don't think that, do you?"

I laugh heartily. "Of course not. Though I have noticed you wearing a skirt to these all the time. Who knows if you're wearing anything under it?"

Stroking her hand down my chest, she grins. "Want to hear my sales pitch?"

I'm tempted. "Actually, I'd rather see the product line."

Her eyes narrow at the challenge. "I'll go get my samples. But there are limits to what we can do with them."

I grab her hand, not anxious for her to leave. "Then where's the fun in that?"

She lowers her body on top of mine. "I have one of my own, if you're curious."

I raise my head up slightly, glancing over at the nightstand drawer she's eyeing. "You bet I am. I have to see the competition."

She grins, reaching over and pulling out a vibrator. "It's their basic model. None of the bells and whistles." She flicks it on and touches it to my neck raising her eyebrows. "But it gets the job done in a pinch."

I look at it. "I'm bigger," I tell her.

"No kidding. I haven't exactly had occasion to use it since you came along, and I'm not sure how I'll go back to it."

I don't like the sound of that, as if I might not be in the picture one day. "I'll just have to stick around then, won't I?" I flip her over onto her back. "Want me to use it on you?"

"I think I'd rather just have you," she says, reaching for the vibrator.

"Still," I consider, pulling it away from her, "we could get creative with it." I lower myself onto her belly. Grabbing a pillow, I lift her rear to slide it under her so that I can get a good view of the soft, pink flesh I love to sink into. "This will be a first for me, Allie. You know how I feel about using technology as a crutch."

"With a body like yours, I can't imagine you'd need to," she whimpers as I tongue her clit, making her folds moisten and swell. I flick the vibrator back on and have to suppress a laugh at the weak hum of the motor. Basic model, indeed.

I slide it inside of her, watching her body open up to the invasion. I lick her again, feeling the vibration against my tongue as I move it in and out of her. The sight of her taking something inside of her that isn't me somehow has me bristling inside, as I gaze up at her puckered nipples and watch her breathing quicken from the sensation.

So long as she's enjoying herself, I guess.

I move my mouth over her, unable to reach all the places I want to explore because of the damn vibrator. I can't taste her like I usually can, and my mouth aches to feel her fluids flowing over my tongue. She lifts her hands to the top of the bed, and I'm wishing she had a headboard she could grip right now. The sight would just about bring me to my knees.

Except that I'm already on my knees.

Sliding it in and out, I watch her pelvis rise up. I fight back the ridiculous jealousy I'm feeling for the chunk of cheap machinery, when I suddenly start to hear the hum of the motor get quieter and quieter, till it stops dead.

Her eyes widen. "What happened?'

I laugh uproariously as I flick the power button off and on and off again. "Batteries are dead. So, do you need my services, after all?" I ask, already reaching for my jeans on the floor to search my pockets for a condom.

A small whimper of frustration escapes her. "I do."

"Oh, I don't know. I was a little insulted at the sight of me being so easily replaced."

"Never."

"Tell me you didn't love it with *it* as much as you do with me." I raise my eyebrows teasingly as I slip on my condom.

"It meant nothing to me," she says, playing along.

I hover my cock above her open legs. "Beg me for it."

"Please," she murmurs.

"I'm not convinced."

"I need you," she whimpers, her body writhing beneath me, anxious to complete the climb to ecstasy that was stopped short by mechanical failure.

"To what?" I ask, my hand toying with the moist slit that beckons for my entry.

"Fuck me, dammit!" Her eyes flare, as she says it between her teeth.

I cock my head. "If you insist." Sliding into her, I feel her come undone immediately, throbbing against my length and giving me a better massage than modern technology ever could.

CHAPTER 23

~ ALLIE ~

I have exactly one dress in my wardrobe that is suitable for a wedding and Kim and Cass are staring at me in it right now, shaking their heads.

"Looks frumpy," Cass says bluntly as her eyes drift over the scooped neckline that leads to three-quarter length sleeves. At least it's red. That has to count for something.

"You're a little harsh," I comment.

"It's not really frumpy," Kim consoles me. "Just more like something you'd wear to a business dinner or something."

"I wish you could borrow something of mine," Cass pouts. I know she means well by the statement, but I don't want to be reminded that I don't have her willowy, statuesque frame. "Do you have anything for her?" she asks Kim, who is a little more my size.

"I'm a mom. What do you think?" Her expression is pretty hopeless as she gazes at me. "I've got a dress that I wore to the pre-K spring fundraiser last year, but your dress shows more skin than that one, believe me."

Cass looks thoughtful. "I know. What size shoes do you wear?"

"8," I reply.

"Think you can squeeze into a 7 ½?"

"Maybe, if I pack some aspirin."

"Perfect. I've got some heels that would really sex that dress up a bit."

"I don't want to look vampy, Cass. The wedding will be in a church, you know." I'm already excited to see it, after looking up the historic church where it will take place. It's right in downtown Annapolis, and Logan says the reception will be on a boat on the Chesapeake Bay. That's a venue that's impossible here in the distant suburbs of Dayton.

"Believe me, with that conservative neckline, you could tattoo 'Fuck me' on your forearm, and you'd still look like a soccer mom."

"Thanks," I reply dryly. I pull the dress off me and hang it back up. "Can I swing by later and pick them up?"

"I'll just bring them when I come to dog sit tomorrow."

Nancy was thrilled to give me the whole day off on Friday, practically doing backflips when I told her, and Kim took over my party this weekend. I am actually going to get a vacation—a real, honest-to-God vacation where I fly on a plane and stay in a hotel and eat out and see something other than my familiar Midwestern landscape.

It might throw me into shock.

I can't wait to see that blue horizon that is always beckoning Logan to the coastline, and to watch the sunset over the Chesapeake Bay.

Or does the sun rise over it? No matter. I'll enjoy it, either way.

"Excited?" Cass asks.

"Yes. And nervous. What if his friends hate me?"

"No one can hate you."

I press my lips together, not completely convinced. "I haven't been on a plane in years."

"And now you're doing it on someone else's credit card." Leave it to Cass to point that out. "I'm insanely jealous, you know. Free rent. New car. Trip to the coast. You're freaking Cinderella."

"Better than that. He's a SEAL. Not a prince. I'd prefer a SEAL any day," Kim chimes in.

Me, too, I'm thinking. But I only smile in reply.

"Have you thought about what you'll do after he finishes up these townhomes?"

My stomach pinches. I've thought plenty. I know he's going to sell them. And I really can't stay here while he has them on the market. My furniture does nothing to show off the features of this home, and a buyer would barely even be able to see the hardwood floors under all the fur that collects on them daily.

Slipping on my shorts, I shrug. "Hopefully, I'll hear back from the bank before then and with any luck, I'll be slumming it in my run-down kennel till I can fix it up." I'd be perfectly happy with that, too. Logan has certainly been a nice distraction from waiting around on the bank's answer. But my dream of that kennel is still in the forefront of my mind.

"Maybe you can move in with him while you fix it up?" Kim suggests.

The thought had crossed my mind. "It's too early for that." I comment. It *is* too early, I say again in my head, tugging my shirt on. Neither one of us has even said the L word yet, even though I'm thinking it 24/7.

And then some.

I don't think I've ever been as nervous as I was on that flight to Annapolis. But as we approached Baltimore-Washington International Airport, and I caught a glimpse of the stunning Chesapeake Bay, the sight of it soothed me instantaneously.

Now, with my feet firmly planted on the ground again, I can understand why Logan likes the coast so much. The waves lap against the rocks alongside us as we walk along the shoreline of the United States Naval Academy, and it's the kind of sound I could listen to all day.

I see the uniformed men and women walking around and I try to imagine Logan in a uniform here, but I can't. Despite the photographs I've seen on his wall, I have a hard time imagining him in a uniform.

We walk toward Main Street and I immediately feel at home. Annapolis might be a state capital, but it definitely has a hometown feel to it with its picturesque street lamps and historic architecture. I smile at the huge boats squeezing into a narrow inlet of water at the end of Main Street.

"That's Ego Alley," he tells me, pointing as we head in that direction.

"Ego Alley?"

"Yeah, they call it that because everyone brings their boats down here to show them off to the gawking tourists. Good for the boaters' egos, you know."

"Yeah, but how do they get them out?" I comment, wondering how a ship as big as the sailboat I'm looking at now could possibly turn around in such narrow waters.

"Sometimes with minor damage," he laughs.

I press my side against him as we sit on a bench waiting for the water taxi that will take us to the Eastport side of Annapolis where our bed-and-breakfast is. My feet ache from playing tourist, but it's a good kind of ache, and Logan promised me a foot rub when we get back to the room.

I'm dying to be alone with him, and wonder if we can order dinner in.

The water taxi arrives and Logan takes my hand in his steady grip as we step onto the small boat. We have the vessel to ourselves except for the captain, and I love snuggling next to Logan as we bounce along the waves. Glancing at him, I'm struck by how peaceful he looks right now, more at home than I've ever seen him in Newton's Creek.

"You look good out here. Out here on the water," I mention.

"It's where I belong." He says the words so easily and has no idea that they pain me deeply.

"Is that why you joined the Navy?"

He laughs unexpectedly. "No. No, actually it's not. I had barely even seen waters like this till after I came to the Academy."

"Then why did you join?"

He shrugs his shoulders dismissively. "My dad was so dead set on me taking over his business for him. But I just wanted to write my own ticket in life, not slide into a position that someone else had already prepared for me. I was young and had no clue how to break out on my own. So I decided I wanted to serve. I think I chose the Navy simply because it forced me to break free of them completely. There's not much of a Navy presence around Newton's Creek. Selfish, huh?"

"I don't think so."

"Yeah, but it's not the most romantic of reasons." He pulls me closer and whispers in my ear. "If I were a young officer trying to get lucky with you, I would have laid on the lines about wanting to protect my country and work for freedom and liberty and the American way of life."

"It would have worked." Cracking a smile, I steal a quick kiss from him. "So why the SEALs, then? That couldn't have been to break free from your family."

"No way. I did a little growing up in my first years as an officer, and I fell in love with the SEAL ideals. I wanted to make a difference. Be part of the elite. Challenge myself. But more than anything, I think I just loved being so focused on the mission. And once it's in you, it's in there for life."

He frowns slightly, and I fear I might have hit a sore spot. "I can see why you love the water," I say, changing the subject. "If I could just lift the Chesapeake Bay and drop it down next to Newton's Creek, I'd be a very happy woman."

"You really like it there?" he asks.

I'm not certain, but I almost sense disbelief in his tone. I lean back in my seat, thinking about the wide, open skies and rich farmland stretching out for miles in front of me. The peace of it. The people. The memories of my dad in every square mile. "Yeah, I do. It just seems like home to me. Being there makes me feel like I have a little piece of my family back the way it once was. I know it doesn't make much sense."

"Funny," he says quietly.

"What's funny?"

"I left Newton's Creek to get away from my family, and you went to Newton's Creek to recapture yours."

I snuggle into the crook of his shoulder, wondering how it is that I can feel more like I've found my home when I'm close to him, than even when I moved to Newton's Creek. I want to tell him, but I won't.

I probably never will.

CHAPTER 24

~ ALLIE ~

In her dropped waist gown of ivory lace and English net, Bess Foster Griffon must be the most beautiful bride I've seen in my life.

Enchanted by the romantic image, I watch her and her new husband in his Army dress blues walk beneath an arch of sabers raised by men in uniform. Some wear Navy uniforms, and some Army, Logan points out.

"We call it a sword arch, but they call it a saber arch. It's pretty much the same thing. You'll want to get your camera ready for the next moment," he adds as Bess and Tyler reach the final set of sabers and they drop in front of them, entrapping them momentarily, as the couple kisses.

Grinning, I snap a photo on my phone.

"Not for that moment," Logan corrects. "For this one."

The sabers rise and Bess gets swatted gently on her rear

with a saber by one of the saber bearers. "Welcome to the Army, Mrs. Griffon," he says and everyone applauds.

Taking a photo again, I find myself laughing and crying at the same time, and I don't even know the couple. But I'm pulling for them. Something about being here, a part of these traditions, makes me feel closer to them. I can't imagine how difficult it must be to be married to the military, but I'm betting this is a couple who will survive it.

Bess's daughter walks toward a horse-drawn carriage with Bess and Tyler following her. She looks like a little angel, dressed in the purest of whites, with her flower's girl gown cascading behind her as she piles herself into the carriage.

A second carriage picks up the wedding party and I spot Maeve and her husband among them, looking even more stunning than in the photo I saw of them. The carriages take a ride along the historic buildings that surround the traffic circle and then the horses pick up a trot as they head down Duke of Gloucester Street toward the dock where they will meet the reception boat.

"Is it my imagination, or does the whole wedding party seem to be made up of happy couples?" I comment, watching how they all seem joined at the hip.

Logan laughs, watching the horse pick up pace. "Not your imagination at all. Maeve and Jack are a couple, of course. Then there's Lacey and Mick, and Lacey's sister Vi and Joe—or Captain Shey to me."

"Captain?"

"Yep. A SEAL commander. I may be out of the military, but the guy will always be Captain Shey to me. The other two couples in the party I don't know. Must be from the groom's side." He gives a nod at the crowd of people headed toward Main Street. "Do you want to walk to the boat? Or we could catch a cab."

"Let's walk," I say, content to tuck my arm inside the crook of his and enjoy the evening. I'm wobbly on Cass's borrowed heels, but the sight of the stars sparkling above us as we saunter slowly down the brick-paved street is the perfect remedy for my aching toes.

Logan doesn't seem in a rush, and neither am I, as we pick up conversation with a few of the other guests headed toward the reception.

There are so many people here who recognize Logan from his time in the Navy. Again, I try to envision him as the Lieutenant Commander he once was, wiping my mind clear of images of him in his t-shirts streaked with dirt and paint and the khaki shorts that always are stuffed with things like drywall screws or a tape measure. My eyes gaze at him in the light offered by the streetlamps and I can imagine it somehow now—him in a crisp white uniform issuing commands and taking charge. Taking risks I can't even fathom, simply because he is proud to serve our country.

How strange it still must be for him to have separated from the Navy and the SEALs. The military is more than a job; it seems to be a way of life. And even to my untrained eyes, I can see how foreign a civilian lifestyle must seem in comparison.

By the time we reach the boat dock, Maeve swoops Logan into a hug. I would feel a hint of jealousy—she's simply that gorgeous and I'm only human—but before I can, she tosses him aside and pulls me in for an embrace, too. "So glad you could come, Allie," she says.

She knows my name?

"Logan has told me so much about you."

Logan told her about me?

"This is my husband Jack." She guides me to Jack before I can even answer her, and her husband gives me a warm hug. The guy is built from steel beneath his uniform, and I wonder if he's a SEAL, too. If I knew anything about all those shiny emblems they wear on their uniforms, I bet I'd be able to tell. But to me, they are simply eye candy.

"Thanks so much for coming, Allie," he says.

"I'm just so happy to be invited," I finally answer. "Bess is such a beautiful bride and they look perfect together. And her little girl is precious."

"She *is* precious, isn't she? She's my goddaughter, you know." Maeve tugs me away from Logan while sending him a playful wink, and he follows close behind as she introduces me around. My head spins from trying to remember all the names, but no one seems to mind if I forget a name or two in this crowd.

"They're so welcoming, Logan," I comment when we're finally able to sit down for dinner.

"It's a good crowd. Military tends to stick together around here, and on most bases that I've been on."

"It's like a big family," one of the other bridesmaids chimes in, leaning into our conversation as she approaches. Lacey, I think is her name, and she bobs her head lower toward us to talk. She and her husband were stationed in San Diego for a while, she tells me, and Logan and she talk fondly of the place he still calls home.

After the boat leaves the dock, I'm mesmerized by how beautiful Annapolis looks from the water in the nighttime. Logan points out the landmarks as we pass—the Capitol, the steeple of St. Mary's, and the yacht club, unmistakable by the swarm of expensive boats docked in front of it.

We later pass the Naval Academy skyline and he shows me Bancroft Hall, and the dome of the chapel illuminated against the dark sky.

I'm enchanted by this city, unable to pull my eyes from it until I smell the crab cakes that have just been placed in front of me by a white-gloved waiter, making my mouth water. As

I take my first bite, my eyes press shut as the taste of the lightly seasoned blue crab floods my taste buds.

That does it. Hell with Newton's Creek. I'm an Annapolitan now.

Later, Logan drags me—literally—onto the dance floor. I should be completely humiliated by the spectacle I'm making of myself. I'm a horrific dancer. But I'm having too much fun to even care as I stand next to Bess's little girl who is admirably trying to teach me the Electric Slide.

Logan pulls me close when a slow song starts, and I'm grateful to let the world slip away for a few minutes while I'm lost in his arms. For all the loud music, I can barely hear him speak. But when he holds me, I can feel his heart beat and I swear mine beats in perfect synchronicity.

After the bride tosses the bouquet, Logan whispers in my ear, "I'm dying to get you alone." The goodbyes and good wishes we share with the people I've met tonight are said in the haze of champagne, and we're on the water taxi again before I know it, snuggling close as the boat takes us toward our B&B in Eastport.

I must have staggered a little getting off the boat—I've always been a lightweight when it comes to champagne—because Logan lifts me into his arms and carries me the two blocks to our inn. I start to doze in his arms. But just as I do, I feel the soft bed beneath me as he sets me down.

I'm going to have a hangover tomorrow. And I don't even care.

CHAPTER 25

~ ALLIE ~

The upside of being a lightweight is that I get drunk off so little, I barely feel the pain the next day.

I'm lying naked in the soft queen size bed with Logan's arms wrapped around me and his chest at my back. He kisses my neck softly, murmuring words that have me moist with desire. I roll to my back to face him. His smile is like morning coffee to me; I need it for the day to officially begin.

"No headache?" he asks.

I shake my head no. What I'm feeling in my skull could barely be classified as a headache, and I don't want him holding back with me this morning.

There's something about waking up in a cozy hotel room with him, the bed a little too small to share with a man as tall and broad-shouldered as him. I love the way I feel more of his skin against me in this bed, and I'm ready to ask him to swap his king size mattress for something smaller.

"I can barely remember getting back here last night," I comment, images of the reception surfacing in my brain the same way champagne bubbles rise to the top. I've been to a few weddings, but honestly haven't ever been to one as much fun as Bess and Tyler's.

"You were a little tipsy."

"I don't remember. Did we…?" My voice trails as he grins at me.

"I'd like to think that if we did, you'd remember."

I laugh because he's right. "Well, I'm sober now, so I'm hoping you'll make it up to me."

An eyebrow raises. "Make it up to you? You're the one who drank too much. Not me."

"Oooh," I say quietly, nudging him onto his back. "You're absolutely right." I touch my lips to his chest and plant kisses down his abs leading to where he is already hard and ready for me. "So sorry about that, Logan."

"I'll forgive—" His eyelids slam shut and he silences himself as my tongue touches his cock. I taste his saltiness as I trace the head with the tip of my tongue and slide it downward along the outer edge of him to his root. A curse escapes him as I take him in my mouth. I can't take him in fully. He's too big for that. So I tap into my creativity and stroke the base of him with my hand as I move his cock in and out of my mouth.

My eyes look upward to see his reaction. His neck is arched as he reaches his hand to my hair. He's gentle with me, and not insistent that I even try to take him in deeper. But I'm desperate to bring him satisfaction and I ease him in a little more. I swallow as the tip of him reaches the back of my mouth and he fires off a curse, pulling me off him.

"Keep that up and I won't be able to stop." His voice is gravelly as he reaches for the box on the nightstand.

"You don't have to."

"I do. The best part of sex with you is feeling you shatter when I'm inside you. You won't deprive me of that."

He's sheathed himself and I'm still on top of him, straddling him as I take him in. I moan in satisfaction, feeling myself stretch to accommodate him. He feels so different when he's beneath me and I'm the one in control. I whimper at the feel of him throbbing inside me. Sliding upward, my body immediately craves his length again, and I drop myself down on him so hard I feel him ram against my depths.

"Careful, baby. I don't want to hurt you." His voice, his tenderness, nearly have me coming undone in that very moment.

My lips meet his as my body moves again upward and then down again. I'm so wet around him, it's stunning, making the motion so smooth and erotic. I wonder how fast he wants me to do this. Despite my vast knowledge of sex toys, there are so many things I really have yet to learn about pleasing a man with my own body. I want to learn all these things. From him.

Only from him.

"Tell me what to do," I say.

His eyes widen slightly as he looks at me.

"Do you like it fast or slow?" I ask, hoping he won't laugh at my question.

His smile is seductive. "Slow at first is nice, then fast just before I'm going to come. Fast and hard then."

"And what else? What else do you like?" I'm curious now.

"I love to suck on you when you're on top like this," he says, arching his neck and taking a nipple in his mouth. His saliva practically sizzles on my skin as I move my breasts closer to him.

I murmur, "I like that," and slide up and down on him slowly now, pressing him against my clit when he's deep inside me. My muscles start to tighten up around him at the sensation. I drive him in deep again and again till I feel my eyelids lower, caught up in the sensation of having him throbbing inside of me as I feel his teeth and tongue toying with my nipple.

He pulls his mouth away from my breast and I nearly cry in protest. My nipple is wet with his saliva and my breast is pink from the pressure. Against the chill of the AC, the bud gets even harder, just as he takes my other breast in his mouth and suckles.

I'm so caught up in the sensation, that I nearly have to remind myself to move again. He's spoiled me, I realize, always taking over in bed, letting me feel all the sensations without any of the effort. I crack a smile just at the thought of it.

What a wonderful way to be spoiled.

Lowering myself onto him again, I linger a little longer in the position, enjoying the pressure of where our bodies meet, and feeling my own need growing.

His mouth leaves my body again. "And I love to feel you come when I'm inside of you. It's the most incredible sensation, Allie."

I feel his cock throbbing just at the mention of it.

"Let me feel that now, baby," he says.

I rub against him more, with him so deep inside me. He grabs my ass and shifts me slightly, causing his cock to ram up against my G spot. "Logan," I cry out at the rush of need that suddenly consumes me. My channel seizes up around him.

"That's it, baby. That's it," he urges, as I ride each wave of sensation, thrusting my body against him. The moment my pulsating ceases, he pushes me onto my back and thrusts deep and hard inside of me.

"What you do to me, Allie," he says as he chases his own need now, driving himself into me so hard I can feel my own climax within reach again. Our bodies are slick as they move against each other, and every sensation seems magnified. Every nerve ending of my body is firing as my toes curl up and my pelvis arches.

My hands move to the span of muscles on his chest, then grazing along to his shoulders and over to his rippled back. So much power I feel beneath my fingertips as I caress him. So much power inside me, hard and desperate.

I can tell when he's going to come now—I know the feel of him that well. I can sense the moment when his cock gets so hard that there's no way he can hold back. And my own body instinctively rises to the same apex, ready to release the moment I feel him let go.

And let go he does, breathing out my name in unison with my cry as my body shudders beneath him, milking the orgasm for the pleasure it brings to every square inch of my flesh.

I've never actually had to run to catch an airplane. Most of the time, I tend to arrive way too early, playing games on my phone for at least an hour because I overestimated, again, how long it would take me to get through security.

Not so, today. Logan and I spent a little too long enjoying those last moments in our hotel room and found ourselves tearing across the airport corridor toward our gate. We literally made it within seconds before they shut the gate on us.

Well, maybe it was a minute or two. But when I tell the story to my friends, I'll definitely say it was seconds.

Now, safe in our seats, I can only laugh as my heart pounds in my chest.

"I really need to workout more if I'm going to be chasing airplanes like this," I say as I turn to him.

"I think our problem was that I gave you too much of a workout this morning as it is," he responds with a chuckle, giving my seatbelt a tug to make sure it's secure before he checks his own.

It's little things like that that I love most about him.

My heart pinches slightly at that thought.

My eyes catch a glimpse of the Chesapeake Bay after the plane takes off, and then it turns to soar toward the land-locked Midwest where I've spent my entire life.

Logan belongs near the water—in a place like Annapolis or his beloved San Diego. And it's only a matter of time before he outgrows this land-tolerant phase he's going through and realizes it's time for him to be where he is destined to be.

Far away from me.

I love my life in Ohio. Even though the lure of the Bay and the incredible scenery I enjoyed this weekend is tempting, Newton's Creek is where I've started planting my roots. I have my organization there, my two jobs, my wonderful friends. My memories of my dad.

I glance at him as he puts his seat in the reclining position, struggling to stretch his legs in the tight quarters. "Next time, you're not talking me out of first class," he says, darting me a meaningful look.

A smile eases up my face at the sound of his low, teasing laughter.

I'd leave the Midwest in a heartbeat to be with Logan, I realize. But would I regret it?

I give my head a slight shake. No matter. Logan's never even told me he loves me, much less asked if I'd be comfortable following him someplace other than Ohio.

The flight attendant passes me a soda and I thank her, grateful for the cool liquid to snap me back to reality.

It's hard to not think about the future after going to a

wedding, so I cut myself some slack, ripping into the small plastic bag of pretzels I've just been handed.

Logan passes me his bag. "I'm sorry we didn't leave in time to catch lunch."

"I'm fine. I'd much rather have been in bed with you than sitting in some airport food court." I can feel my heartbeat picking up its pace even at the recollection.

He intertwines his fingers with mine, and I look down at our hands, realizing how perfectly they fit together. His hands are so much bigger than mine, it should look like I'm being swallowed up in his grasp. Yet it doesn't. It just looks *right*.

"Thank you so much for taking me, Logan."

"You've said that enough already. Thank you for going. I never would have come if you hadn't joined me. Maeve told me specifically that she owes you for that. Anytime you want to visit wherever they happened to be living, you'll have a place to stay."

I grin. "Any chance I could convince Jack to take a job in Hawaii, then?"

He laughs. "Plenty of Navy presence there. Is that where you'd like to live one day?"

I shrug. "I've never even been there, so I can't really say. But I think it would at least be a nice place to visit."

"Beyond nice. It's paradise. Quite literally, paradise."

As our flight soars away from the coastline, Logan tells me all about the places he lived while he was in the Navy. I love to hear him talk about his past this way, with joy in his eyes rather than the fury and guilt I see when he talks about his final year with the SEALs.

His words have me on a journey to Monterey and Miami. To Germany and Australia. I settle into my seat, resting my head against his shoulder as he talks, his calm voice lulling me to sleep and my hormones getting me riled up at the same time.

I wonder how one would go about getting into the mile-high club while flying coach? A laugh bubbles up inside of me at the thought, but I tamp it back down, not anxious to interrupt the images of faraway places that Logan is painting in my head.

I am completely lost to him.

The landscape outside my window starts to look more familiar, vast stretches of crops sliced into perfect geometric shapes by rural roads. I'm excited to see home approaching, anxious to check my email and phone messages, find out how our dogs are doing, and tell my friends about the incredible weekend I had.

The best weekend of my life, actually.

I grip the armrests tightly as we begin our final approach. I don't mind flying. But the landing part kind of throws me. Seeing my white knuckles, Logan takes my hand in his, and immediately all the anxiety flows outward from my body. His presence has so much power over me.

Our plane touches down and the brakes slam, and I squeeze Logan's hand in response till we come to a near stop, taxiing slowly to the gate. He looks at me. "Welcome home, Allie."

"It's good to be home." With you, I want to add, but I don't. But it's undeniable. Home is so much better with Logan.

We're herded like cattle off the plane and toward baggage claim, and I pull my phone from my purse to check in.

I turn it back on and see a text message from my realtor pop up. *"Allie, I've got news. Call me."*

My heart lurches and I grab Logan to steady myself.

"Are you okay?"

"Yes, yes. I heard from my realtor."

"What did she say?"

"Just that she has news and to call her."

His eyes light up, and he seems as excited as I am right now. "Well, call her. Right now. I'll keep an eye out for the bags."

I punch in her number. As her phone rings, I overanalyze her text. If it is good news, wouldn't she just write it in the text? Or maybe she'd be more likely to want to tell me good news directly? I have no idea, and panic as she doesn't answer. It will kill me if I have to leave a message and wait for her reply.

"Jackie Swanson," she finally answers, and I sigh with relief.

"Jackie, it's Allie. I just got off the plane and got your message."

"Oh, Allie, I'm afraid it's not good. You were outbid. The property has gone to someone else."

I feel the tears welling up in my eyes and I search for Logan, needing to cling to something, someone. He's headed back my way, dragging our bags, with concern in his eyes when he sees my face.

As a tear drops onto my cheek, his face falls. He knows.

"I'm so sorry, Allie," I hear Jackie's voice in my ear, but I can barely respond. "I know how much you wanted that property."

I nod, even though I know she can't see it. "Thanks, Jackie." My eyes are locked on Logan and he wraps his arm over my shoulder and gives me a reassuring squeeze. *At least I have Logan.* The thought flits through my mind, as though a life preserver has been tossed to me as I drown.

But I wanted that kennel so badly I could taste it. It was my dream. And now that's all it will ever be.

"If it makes you feel any better, you never could have outbid the buyer," Jackie says in my ear. "It was JLS Heartland. You know, that big housing developer. They're tearing it down and building some houses."

My blood drains from my face. "Who? Who did you say?" I ask her, unwilling to believe it.

"JLS Heartland. They're huge around here. They're buying up a lot of land in Newton's Creek, I guess because it's caught the eye of commuters and land's cheap here. I'm so sorry, Allie. You can't win against a company like that."

I hear a whirring sound in my head as blood saturates my brain, making me light-headed. It's the same loud noise between my ears that I heard on the airplane from the engines. But my feet are flat on the ground. I reach out and touch the handle of my suitcase just to see if I can feel it, to convince myself I'm not having a bad dream. But I can feel the cool, hard plastic in my hand.

Logan's family's company outbid me. My mind races, trying to remember if I ever told his family about my plans for the bankrupt kennel. But I didn't.

I only told Logan.

"Again, I'm so sorry, Allie. You call me if you want to start looking at some other property for your rescue. I think it's a wonderful idea."

A wonderful idea that will never come to pass. I can't afford to buy land and build something new. I could barely afford the lowball bid I made on the foreclosure. "Thanks, Jackie."

I turn off the phone and am unable to look Logan in the eyes.

"I'm so sorry, Allie. I take it you didn't get it," he says.

"No." My voice is soft, breathless, with the wind knocked from my lungs.

"Someone else bid more?"

I can't answer him for a moment. I just stare at the dirty floor of the baggage claim and let the sounds of people coming and going flow over me. Finally opening my mouth, I whisper, "JLS Heartland."

In my peripheral vision, I can see his head tilt with awareness. "What?"

"JLS Heartland," I repeat, finally looking at his eyes, trying to see if he had any idea this could have happened. "JLS Heartland bought the land. They're tearing it down and building a housing development."

"Son of a bitch." The curse escapes him, and his eyes are daggers as he looks off into the distance somewhere. "Dammit, Allie. I had no idea they were eyeing that property."

I search his eyes, looking for deceit. But as always, there's none there. This is as much a shock to him as it is to me. "Did you tell your family what I was planning?"

He presses his lips together in thought, and shakes his head slowly. "No. No, I—" he pauses. "I know I told them you wanted to build a rescue kennel for your dogs." His brow furrows sharply. "I might have told them you bid on a foreclosure, though. Dammit, Allie, I'm not sure if I gave any details. But it would be natural for me to tell them."

He takes my chilled hand in his. "They never would have done this if they knew you were the other bidder, Allie. Even Ryan wouldn't. He's all business, but he doesn't skulk around behind people's backs. If he knew you were bidding on something they were interested in, he would have said something."

I look at him, my heart aching, knowing that he's trying to convince himself as much as me.

"I'll figure this out, Allie. I'll find a way to fix this."

I hear his words, but I know it's futile. I wrapped up everything I had in that dream, and now I have nothing to show for it but heartbreak.

CHAPTER 26

- LOGAN -

I step into the massive complex that is the heart of my family heritage and feel nothing but anger as I storm toward the directory. It says a lot about how often I come into this building that I have to look at the directory to even know what floor my brother's office is on. I haven't been in here in years. Nearly a decade, actually, and the place looks completely different now. It's a sleek modern fortress, intimidating and pretentious.

I spot the office of the CEO listed. *Top floor, of course,* I think, realizing I should have been able to guess that. My feet pound against marble floors that glimmer in the sun that shines through the floor-to-ceiling windows of the lobby.

Not a single fingerprint mars the mirrored elevator as I step in and press the button. My fingers are cold, wanting desperately to curl into a fist and punch my brother. Did he know? I want so much to believe that he didn't.

As the elevator doors open, I'm greeted by a slick granite reception desk and a young woman in the tight ponytail and trim suit who asks if she can help me.

"Yes, I'm Jacob Sheridan, Jr. and I'm here to see my brother."

Her eyes widen at that, and I'm partly surprised, having wondered if the people here even knew I existed. It wouldn't be their fault if they didn't. I've been the family recluse for so long, hiding out under the auspices of the U.S. Navy.

Nodding, she lifts her phone and tells someone I'm here.

She offers a seat to me, but I prefer to stand. I've got too much rage coursing inside my veins to sit in the soft chair she gestures toward, or sip on the coffee she offers to bring me.

An older woman approaches. "Mr. Sheridan?" she asks.

"Call me Logan, actually. I go by my middle name."

"Of course. I'm Deborah, your brother's assistant. Let me walk you back." She signals for me to enter the long hallway and I spot the imposing double doors at the end. So this is where my brother hangs out these days, I ponder.

"You look so much like your mother. You have her eyes," she says. She looks to be in her early sixties, the kind of woman who might have photos of her grandchildren framed and sitting on her desk. I decide to like her. "She's such a lovely woman—your mother," she continues.

We stop outside his door and she taps before she opens it for me. I spot him on the other side of a large mahogany desk, a desk I can imagine my father sat behind in the not-too-distant past.

"Let me know if you need anything, Mr. Sheridan," she says and shuts the door behind me.

"Logan." Standing, my brother looks concerned. "I don't think you've stepped foot in this complex since..."

"Since a long time ago, Ryan," I cut him off. "I'm well

aware. Let's just cut the bullshit for a minute. Does the name Newton's Creek Boarding Kennel ring a bell?"

He looks at me, apparently confused, as he sits back down. "No. Do you need a boarding kennel for Kosmo?"

I lean back on my heels, a hint of relief seeping into my gut. "It's a boarding kennel that went bankrupt a while back. Did I happen to mention it to you ever?"

I need to know. I need to know if I slipped about something that ended up causing Allie pain. It would kill me, but I need to know.

"I don't think so. Why would you be telling me about a bankrupt kennel?"

"You just bought one, Ryan."

Cocking his head, he frowns. "You mean the company did?"

"Yes, dammit, the company you're CEO of." My voice is thick with venom as I approach his desk.

His eyes narrow at my tone and he leans forward. "Do you have any idea how many acres we buy up every week, Logan? Oh, that's right. You wouldn't know, would you? Because you don't give a shit about our family business. So don't you dare come marching in here insinuating that I don't know what's going on in my company. It's all land to me, Logan. I don't give a damn if there's an old kennel on it or an abandoned motel or a tree house. We're after the land, not the buildings." He pauses, checking his temper as he leans back in his chair again. "So are you going to tell me what the hell is going on, or are you just going to interrogate me some more?"

I square my shoulders toward him, still on the offense. "Allie put a bid on a foreclosure. An abandoned dog kennel. She wanted to turn it into a brick-and-mortar presence for her rescue organization so that she could save more dogs."

Ryan's face sags noticeably as he nods. "I remember you

told me she was trying to buy something. But you never mentioned where." He emits a quiet curse. "So I take it we outbid her?"

I nod. "By a sizable amount, I'm sure."

"I didn't know, Logan." He moves his mouse, waking up his computer. "Where is it?"

"About three miles down Tyland Road. Two acres near the intersection with Birch."

He taps at his keyboard and frowns at what he sees on his monitor. "In between two farms," he says it under his breath, as if it's more to himself than to me. "Yeah, we bought it and the two adjoining farms. We've got plans for forty homes there. A clubhouse with a pool. It'll be a nice community, Logan."

I raise an eyebrow. "It'll be just as nice with a dog rescue on it."

Ryan heaves a sigh. "I'm sorry about Allie's plans. But there are other places where she can build a dog rescue."

"You're so detached from reality, aren't you, Ryan? She doesn't have the money for that. That's why she bid on that old kennel. She had enough money to fix it up, not to start fresh. Why the hell can't you just let her keep it?"

"*I'm* detached from reality? You're the one asking me to keep an old dog kennel smack dab in the center of our newest seventy-acre housing development. The barking alone will drive people away. It's not going to happen, Logan. I'm sorry. I feel horribly for Allie, but it's nothing personal. It's business."

"Maybe it should be personal, Ryan. Maybe we have gotten too damn big if we're buying up land without even thinking of the people it affects."

"We build *houses*, Logan. We're always thinking about people. We're providing affordable houses in safe, family-oriented communities."

"Affordable? That's such bullshit, Ryan. Half the guys I served with can't afford the homes you build, and they're protecting your freedom, for God's sake. You sit here in your slick new office with your Armani suit and build your houses for people in your world, not mine."

"Listen—"

"No, you listen. That little piece of land was Allie's dream."

He stares at me, his eyes seeming almost sympathetic. "Shit. You're in love with her."

"Yes, dammit." I know it's the first time I'm admitting this, and it annoys me that I'm telling it to my brother, not her. I should have said it a long time ago. But it's the last thing she wants to hear from me right now. "She's everything to me. And you've fucked it up, dammit." I give the chair I'm leaning on a shove, fighting back the urge to send it soaring across the room.

My breathing is tense and I need to get out of here.

"Where are you going?" I hear my brother over my shoulder as I head to his office door.

"To try to fix this."

CHAPTER 27

- LOGAN -

Allie is packing.

I watch in quiet disbelief as she neatly folds freshly washed clothes into the same suitcase that was on a flight home from Annapolis just two days ago, and it cuts my heart open.

How much things can change in the course of two days.

"This is crazy, Allie. You can't just leave."

"Logan, I need to get away."

"You were just away."

"Away from you." Her eyes widen, like she hadn't intended to say it.

"Okay, well, I've always asked for honesty," I say through my teeth. The fact is, she's been nothing but away from me the past couple days, always claiming to be busy, barely speaking to me. I know she's hurt and I don't blame her. But silence isn't going to fix anything.

I've been busy, too, trying to come up with a plan to make this right. I tell her that, and all I ever hear is that she doesn't want my help.

"Look, you didn't outbid me. So it doesn't have anything to do with you."

"Yeah, but it has everything to do with my family," I admit.

She rests her hand on a stack of shirts filling her suitcase. I hit the nail on the head.

"It was a business decision," she says, sounding reminiscent of my brother. "I don't blame your family."

"You just don't want to have to see them again." I say it matter-of-factly because it's what I'd feel. My family means a lot to me, and if she sticks with me, she knows she'll have to face the people who pulled the rug out from under her. There's no joy in that.

"You have a lovely family. I care a lot about them. But I'm not feeling too warmly about JLS Heartland right now, to be honest."

"Neither am I."

"Besides, I really have been needing to spend some time with my mom. I've let too much time pass. I was able to rehome Juniper and Sandy yesterday, and Cass took Rex off my hands because her spaniel should be placed next week."

"I could have taken the dog." It stings that she wouldn't even ask. I feel like she's cutting ties with me as quickly as she can. "You know I would have taken him."

"You've done enough for me." She looks up at me, tears in her eyes. "I really mean that, you know, Logan. You've done so much for me, and I—" She stops, pressing her lips together tightly into a thin line. "All of this would have happened anyway. I would have sold my condo and been sleeping on Cass's sofa all this time. You've only made my life better."

But I couldn't stop this from happening. "You're going to

get your shelter, Allie. I'll see to it."

Shaking her head, she presses her hand against my chest. It's the first touch I've had from her in a while, and it makes me want to pull her toward me, hold her close, and never let her go. But she steps back again before I can. "No. I'm not getting it that way. I've been skating along on your generosity enough. I mean it, Logan. Enough already."

I want to tell her I do it because I love her. But tossing the word at her right now would seem more like manipulation, a way of getting her to forgive my family and me, a way of making her want to stay.

"I won't be gone that long. Nancy doesn't care where I work from, so long as I have my laptop. And I'll figure out where I'm going to live while I'm away. I have the money from my condo now that it's not wrapped up in the bid."

"You don't have to move."

"Your renovation is almost done anyway. It's time for you to sell this place and move on."

Move on?

I have to remind myself that was ever my plan.

She extends her hand with her set of keys to the townhome. "I'll get my furniture out of here as soon as I can."

I close my fingers over her hand, trapping the keys back in her grasp. There's no way I'm letting her give those back without a fight. "Allie, I'm not worried about that. I'm worried about us. *Us*," I repeat, hoping she feels the weight of the word.

Staring at my hand still enclosed around hers, her shoulders shudder. "I just need some time, Logan. Time to let it all soak in. I'll still be around if you need me." Two tears trickle down her cheeks. "So if you can't sleep, you know who to call."

I pull her close, whether she likes it or not. "I won't sleep. Because I'll be finding a way to make this right."

CHAPTER 28

~ ALLIE ~

I'm taking the coward's way out, I figure as I flick on the turn signal at my mother's exit. It's childish; the bank didn't want to play nice with me, so I'm grabbing my dollies and running to my mommy.

How did I even think I was ready to take on a run-down kennel and turn my fledgling nonprofit into something bigger, more effective? I'm too young—just like Logan used to tell me.

And it stuns me that he was right. I *am* too young for him. He's a SEAL—faced down more tragedy in his 32 years than most people do in their lifetime. I'm just a silly woman with a useless degree and a dream that is bigger than my bank account. He knew the world would cut a person like me down to size, and he was right.

I just didn't think it would be his family taking the first slice of me.

I turn onto my mom's street and am greeted by rows of two-story colonials, each with the same stone and siding façade. It's a newer community. I'd almost wonder if it's a JLS Heartland development, but I think the houses are smaller here than is their norm.

My mom swings open the door only seconds after I pull into the driveway, not even giving me a chance to take a breath or prepare myself to see her again in this house that isn't my home. It still feels awkward to me.

She wraps her arms around me in an embrace that could only come from a mother. As I fight the tears, I'm reminded of Logan's mom—how welcoming she was to me, how truly excited she was about my mission with the dogs. Did Logan tell her what happened, I wonder?

I'll probably never know.

My mother pulls back from me only inches and touches a finger to the dark circles under my eyes. "Honey, you look exhausted. Have you been sick?"

"No. Just tired."

"Come on in. I'll make you some chicken soup, anyway," she says. Chicken soup can save the world, or at least my mother believes that. And truly, when she makes it up the way she does, I'm pretty convinced of it, too.

"New car?" she notes, glancing at the silver SUV as I pull out my bags.

"Yeah," I mutter. "A donation to my organization from someone."

"They donated a new car?"

She's checking out the leather seats and eyeing the dashboard that, to me, still looks more like it belongs in a sci-fi movie than in a car.

"You must be doing some things right for those dogs if you're getting donations like this, Allie."

Yeah, or spreading my legs for the right guy, I think, feeling a knot of disgust with myself.

"I'm so proud of you," she continues, oblivious that her words are rubbing salt in my wounds, and proving to me that I shouldn't have come here. I should have just crawled into a hole for a month. "You're saving lives, Allie. It's your dream and you're making it happen."

I burst into tears at the mention of my dream.

"Oh, honey, what's wrong?" she asks.

I tell her then. I tell her everything, first leaning against my car in the driveway till she leads me inside the house and sits me down at the kitchen counter. I'm so grateful that her husband isn't home now, and I can have a little time with my mom by myself.

I tell her about the wedding, Logan's family, and what happened with the foreclosure. I even tell her about the damn SUV, as she browns some chicken in olive oil to ready it for the soup. The loud sizzle and the smell of paprika and pepper soothe me as I pour my heart out to her in a way I haven't done since Devin dumped me back in college.

She slices an onion and the scent wafts my way, giving me a good excuse for the tears in my eyes.

"It sounds like you really love him, Allie."

The lump lodged in my throat almost blocks my admission. "Yes."

"Have you told him that?"

"No. Neither one of us has said it," I answer begrudgingly. "And why bother? We were doomed from the start."

"Why is that, do you think?"

"He's never going to stay in Newton's Creek. I think he regrets ever moving there—did it on impulse and now he's just figuring out his next move. He belongs on the coast somewhere."

"And you think you belong in Newton's Creek?"

I nod firmly.

"Why?"

I really don't want to tell her the truth. "I miss Dad," I say vaguely instead.

She nods, turning down the heat on the stove and sitting beside me. "And what else do you miss?"

"I miss our house. I miss being able to feel close to him around every corner."

She lowers her head. "I moved from that house for all the same reasons you wanted to stay."

"What do you mean?"

"We watched you grow up in that house, Allie. Together. All the milestones you reached were with your dad at my side. You remember racing down the staircase to see the tree on Christmas morning, but I remember sitting with your dad watching you race down those stairs. You remember the swing in the backyard, but I remember putting it together on the hottest day of the summer with your dad. You remember riding your bike in the neighborhood Fourth of July parade that ran in front of our house, but I remember sitting with your dad on the front porch as you rode by. He was always there for me. For us. And it was such a blessing. I couldn't face another moment in that house without him."

"You really loved him, didn't you?" I'm remembering what Logan said now, how he thought my mom might have married so soon again just because she couldn't stand the idea of being alone after being with someone she loved for so long.

"I loved your dad in a way I could never love another man. He gave me you. He gave me my best memories. He gave me the best chapter of my life." Tears are pooling in her eyes. "Don't get me wrong. I love my husband now. He's a good man, Allie, and he showed me that I really can laugh again and feel a warmth in my heart again. But it's a different kind of love for a different phase in our lives." She takes my hand as it rests on the counter. "What kind of love do you feel for Logan?"

I shake my head, trying to find words. "Something so powerful. I know it hasn't been that long that we've even been together, but when I'm with him, things feel so right I can't even put it into words."

"Do you picture your life with him?"

"It's hard not to."

"In Newton's Creek?"

I shrug. "Anywhere."

"Then it sounds to me you found your home. Your home is with Logan."

I sigh. "I don't know how I'd face his family again. It's even worse that they didn't know. Now I'll be poor, pathetic Allie. I don't want to be that to them."

"That's ridiculous. You're a capable young woman who is saving the lives of countless dogs. There is nothing pathetic about you."

"I don't want their sympathy."

"Then tell them that."

"And I don't want their charity either. I know it's crazy, but I feel like Logan throws his money my way too quickly, like it's nothing to him. I know him, Mom. His last words to me were that he was going to fix this."

"So, let him."

"That's not what I want though. I can't even stand driving that car because it reminds me of him. I don't want more things that I depend on to be somehow attached to him. I'd be just like you with the house, you know? Unable to get away from his memory after he leaves."

"You're assuming he'll leave then."

"Yes," I say without hesitation.

"Allie, you are a passionate person. You've always felt

things so deeply. You find a mission and you think you're the only one who can accomplish it the right way simply because you feel its weight so deeply in your heart. You're so much like your father in that way. I've seen all that you've accomplished and it amazes me. It makes me proud. But you're wrong to think you're the only one who feels things so deeply. That you can't share your load with someone else." She pats my hand as she stands. "Take some time. Cry it out. Lick your wounds. But promise me that you won't go through life thinking that you have to do things alone."

She kisses my forehead, and glances at her watch. "It's 5:00 in some part of the world right now," she says with a smile. "How about a glass of wine?"

CHAPTER 29

- LOGAN -

Sitting in my car, staring at the unassuming house with its terracotta tile roof and stucco exterior, my heart rate is doing double time.

I want to call Allie. I *need* to call Allie. I haven't heard from her since she texted me to tell me she arrived at her mom's, and I know that hearing from me right now is the last thing she needs.

What she needs is for me to fix what my family's company did to her dream. But everything my brother has been telling me the last three days is right. I can't expect him to build an entire development around a rescue kennel to satisfy a girl I've known for a matter of months. And as much as I'd like to swoop in and buy a couple acres and build her a new kennel, I know that throwing my money at this problem isn't what she wants.

Hell if I can figure out what would fix this, though.

A breeze gusts through the palms in front of the house, drawing my eyes to the blue sky above me, streaked with thin, wispy clouds. I stare into the sky, feeling that there's a perfect solution somewhere out there for me. For us. But it's out of my reach, blocked by the guilt I've used as a crutch these past years, making me weak and vulnerable.

Allie doesn't need me like that.

Which is why I'm staring at this house right now, reluctant to see what's awaiting me on the other side of the door. Or who, I should say.

I can talk a good game about fixing things with Allie. But what I really need to fix is myself.

I inhale deeply, and leave the protective confines of the rental car I picked up at San Diego International Airport. The warmth of the sun feels differently here than it does in the Midwest. The summer air is crisp, not as thick with humidity. The scent of a honeysuckle alongside the front porch reminds me somehow of Allie with its sweetness, and gives me the determination to rap lightly on the door.

A woman answers it, looking more radiant than she did when I last saw her as she buried the man she loved.

"Clare. I'm sorry to just show up like this," I begin.

"Logan." She pulls me into a hug. "You're always welcome. You know that. Come in, come in," she urges, letting me in through the doorway like a lost dog.

"I got Lucas's graduation announcement," I say.

"Amazing, isn't it? He's gone and grown up on me."

"He looks just like his dad," I comment, then wondering if I was right to even acknowledge Torres right now. I don't want to make her cry. But her eyes are bright as she looks at me.

"He does, doesn't he?"

I nod awkwardly. "Clare, there's something I wanted to

give him. I really hope you don't mind. But I wanted to do it in person rather than just send it."

"Logan, you really shouldn't have. You don't have to get him anything for graduating."

"I do. It's something I think his dad would have wanted him to have."

She cocks her head, curious, and her eyes drift slightly, probably remembering her husband. "Lucas," she calls over her shoulder. "There's someone here to see you."

I hear his footsteps on the stairs and gaze at Lucas as he enters the kitchen. He's grown since I saw him last. Not taller, but broader, stronger. Like his dad.

His eyes meet mine and I see the recollection.

"Do you remember Logan, honey? He served with your dad."

"Sure," he says, reaching out his hand, more cordial than his father ever would have been. Torres was more of a fist bump kind of guy, always joking, playing pranks. His son seems more serious, and it's no wonder with what he's already seen in his life.

"I'll leave you two alone," Clare says, retreating to her living room.

"Good to see you, Lucas," I tell him, feeling strangely intimidated by this kid who's so much younger than me. The guilt swells in my head, and the pain of memories pool behind the dam of my soul, ready to flood. I clench my teeth together, willing them to subside.

"You, too," he replies. "I remember you from the funeral. You were with my dad when he died."

"Right before he died," I say, feeling the need to be specific. "I was about thirty feet away when it happened." When he got shot, I want to say, but I think he knows without my saying.

"I wanted to give you something since you're headed to

college." I reach into my pocket and pull out a check. I know it's a guilt gift and I'm shamed by the knowledge. But I also know he'll need the money.

His chin drops when he sees the number written on the check—not much to a guy like me, but plenty to a young man starting off in life. He thrusts it back to me. "It's nice of you, Logan, really. But I don't need it. Special Operations Warrior Foundation is covering my tuition."

I smile at the knowledge. The group covers the tuition of the children of fallen Special Ops warriors—SEALs, Rangers, and the like. I make a mental note to send them a check, too.

I nudge his hand away from me again. "You'll still need it. There are plenty of expenses that they won't be able to cover. Invest it now, and buy yourself a house later or something. Please. I insist."

He nods stoically, and I know right away he's not the type of kid to blow it on something foolish. I'm glad for that. I don't need him buying a souped-up sports car with it and wrapping it around a tree. I've got enough guilt already.

He sets it down on the counter in front of him, still looking a little shell-shocked to have a windfall of cash.

"There's something else I wanted to give you." I pull out a small box from my cargo shorts. "After my last mission with the Teams, the one right after your dad died, I was awarded the Silver Star. I never felt right getting it without your dad standing there with us. Your dad should have been with us on that mission. I want you to have it." I open the box.

He's silent as he looks at it, his finger tracing its laurel wreath.

My chest broadens as I inhale sharply. "And I wanted to say how sorry I am, Lucas."

His eyes dart up sharply from the medal. "Why?"

"I could have saved him. I should have saved him. I—"

He cuts me off. “You couldn’t have made it back to him in time.”

I search his eyes and wonder how much he knows. “I carried Crosby back to safety first.”

“Because he was shot in the neck. He was worse off than my dad was.”

Looking at him, I realize he must have heard the story of those final moments from one of my SEAL brothers. “Crosby died anyway. If I had taken your dad back—”

“—you would have done everything that you’re trained not to do,” he interrupts. “You needed to take the most wounded man out of danger first. He couldn’t fend for himself. My dad knew that. You didn’t know he was going to get shot again.”

The wisdom this kid has stuns me. “But I still wish I could have saved him.”

“So do I,” he says, and I think he’s talking about me until he continues. “I could have had him quit, you know.”

I feel my eyes soften, seeing the pain in his eyes, pain I recognize too well.

“When I was about fourteen,” he tells me, “I was pissed he was leaving us again, you know? Going back into the field. I was playing baseball back then, and was having a really good season. I wanted him to see me through it. For once, I wanted him to be in the stands watching me win. I cried and shouted and slammed doors. Finally, he told me what I wanted to hear. If it was causing me so much pain, he’d give it up. Leave the SEALs, the Navy, get a normal job like other dads.”

I watch him as he talks, hearing a story Torres never shared with me.

“I was happy for a while. But I saw him put on his uniform the next day to head into base, and I couldn’t let him do it. I couldn’t let him put in his separation paperwork. I knew he loved being a SEAL too much. And for the first time, I knew he loved me even more than he did the SEALs. That was all I wanted to know."

He sits at the counter, his eyes falling to the Silver Star again. "If I had just had him get out then, he'd be alive right now."

I sit beside him, watching his eyes trace the outline of the medal. "It's not your fault. You gave him his freedom to do the work he loved. I can't even imagine how proud he must have been of you in that moment." I feel a lump in my throat at the thought. "Lucas, he was always so proud of you. The last thing he would have wanted was you thinking it was your fault."

A grin inches up his face as his sad eyes meet mine. "Right back atcha," he comments.

I lay my hand on his shoulder, a smile warming my face. The kid is smarter at his eighteen years than I am at my thirty-two.

Damn, he is going to make a hell of a mark on this world. I can tell.

The sun sparkles on the waves as I stare out at the Pacific Ocean from my perch on La Jolla Shores. The boulder I'm sitting on is hard and moist from the salty sea spray and even though I can't see any sea lions in my line of sight, I can smell them. I can definitely smell them.

The sand is speckled with footprints of humans and other sea-loving creatures, and the water washes a few more away each time it surges up from the ocean to the shore.

I've always loved it here, but it's not my favorite spot in San Diego. I can't choose a favorite. There are too many vistas that have tugged at my soul in the years that I was stationed here. But this is definitely one of my top five.

It's the ocean I love the most about this place, though. I love the idea of it—this vast body of water that somehow touches so many shores around the world, interconnecting with other bodies of water and luring beach goers from countless countries and cultures. The people I see right now, dipping their toes in the sand and diving in between waves, see the ocean as a place of recreation. Other people, more directly tied to the seas, see it as sustenance. Some see it as a threat. But we're all tied to it somehow, it seems.

My heart feels strangely lighter now, with yesterday's visit to Torres's son behind me. The guilt that ate away at me seems to have abated, at least for now. And I hope the feeling lasts, even though I know somehow it will still come to me in the night for many years to come.

I'll keep in better touch with Lucas Torres, I decide with a nod, making a commitment. And I feel free now to come back here to the place I've always believed was my future home, as though the shores here were constructed by some higher power just to welcome me.

Only it doesn't feel like home now. Not the way it used to. And I realize that I need a certain someone sitting beside me for it to be home.

I need Allie.

Now that I've made things right with my past, I need to make things right for my future.

I pull myself off the boulder and let my feet sink into the sand below, gazing out to the horizon again and vowing that I'll come back one day.

I head to my car and make the tedious drive to the airport in morning traffic. I was only in San Diego one night, but it was enough for me, which is an odd thought seeing as I used to say I'd never get enough of this town.

But the only thing right now that I can't seem to get enough of is Allie. She's still at her mom's, I'm sure. I'm almost happy to give her the time she needs to think, because the plan that is brewing in my head has needed a few days to percolate.

I'm grateful for the Wi-Fi they offer on flights these days, and I take full advantage of the six hours on the plane to do a little more research.

The sun is halfway to the horizon by the time I pull my truck into a space in front of my townhome. A surge of anticipation fuels me as I prepare to make my brother an offer that might change the direction of my life.

I open my front door to empty silence, without the light clicking of Kosmo's paws on his way to greet me. He stayed the night at my parents so that I could make my spontaneous trip. My mom said it's the least she could do considering what happened with Allie, and from the look in her eyes I could tell she would rather I chased after Allie than gone to San Diego.

But I had a mission, and I still do. For the first time since I left the SEALs, I feel that sense of a mission. It's not Allie's mission, which is why it feels so special to me. It's my own. It's unique and I'm hell-bent on making it happen.

I slap some water in my face and put on the suit that I might be wearing a lot of in the weeks to come. I hate suits, but I don't even mind, if I can get what I want by wearing it.

The sun is lower still in the sky as I pull up to JLS Heartland. In my suit now, I feel a little more a part of the place, a little less rough around the edges.

I approach the receptionist and her eyes widen appreciatively as she gazes at me. I guess suits must work almost as well on women as military uniforms.

I hope Allie likes the look of me in a suit.

"Hi. I'm here to see my brother," I tell her, waiting to see if she remembers who my brother is. She obviously does, because at the press of a couple buttons, Ryan's assistant is striding down the hallway toward me.

"Hello, Mr. Sheridan. Was your brother expecting you?"

"No, he's not," I say. I guess I should have called, but I'm hoping the element of surprise works as well on Ryan as it does in an enemy attack.

"He's just finishing up a conference call. Can I get you some coffee while you wait?"

"No, thank you," I reply, taking a seat in the chair she offers me. In my head, I'm spelling out the points I need to make, practicing as though I'm readying myself for a job interview. It's ridiculous, of course. It's just my brother, and the company name bears my own initials. I already know there's a place for me here, but I'll be asking a lot in return.

Ryan opens the door to his office, his eyes nearly popping from his head at the sight of me in a suit. "Logan. Come on in."

He shuts the door behind me. "So, a suit? Are you reporting in for work or something?" His tone tells me he's joking.

"I might be."

His eyebrows raise now, as he sits at his desk. "Are you serious?"

"It depends. Ryan, I've done a lot of thinking about what happened a few days ago. And you're right. I don't know anything about this business. I've always been more of a field guy. I don't even know why you're suddenly buying up land here in Newton's Creek, when the company's been hell-bent on being a nationwide presence."

"It's for Dad, Logan. You know how he needs to keep his toe in the business. It keeps him alive. But he can't travel to job sites like he used to. I thought we'd start a few projects locally so that he can still feel a part of things."

I nod, having figured that out for myself. "Dad can't travel right now, and you've got a daughter who is moving in with you this month. You're not in any position to be traveling to job sites and making sure our name isn't attached to bad developments." I inhale. "But I can. I don't even blink at travel. God knows I've done enough of it during my time in the Navy. And I may not know much about the paperwork and legal aspects of our business, but I can tell when things are going right and wrong on a job. And I'm a good leader. I've got plenty of people who will vouch for that. I can make sure we've got good teams working for us, keeping our brand strong."

Ryan looks stunned. "Logan, that would be—"

"Wait." I hold up my hand. "Before you get all warm and fuzzy, there's a lot I'm going to ask for in return."

He eases back in his leather chair and steeples his fingers. "I'm listening."

"First, I want JLS to be a leader in caring for the people in our communities. I want to set up a foundation."

"A foundation?"

"Yep. And in every development we have, I want to be able to offer a handicapped accessible house to a wounded servicemember living in the area. We've got developments in 32 states. We can really make a difference, Ryan."

I can't read his face as he looks at me, so I barrel on. "The government offers some assistance to veterans disabled in the line of duty. But it's not enough to set them and their families up in a house where they're not struggling to do the simplest things, like making a meal or brushing their teeth. We build houses, Ryan. We can do this without even blinking."

He waits a moment, maybe to see if I have anything else to say. I do, but I decide I need some feedback from him first.

"It would make us look good." His eyes are thoughtful.

"We do get some publicity problems, buying up tracts of land like we do. We've got our share of enemies."

I grin. "Then what better friends to make than the military?"

He nods slowly. "I like the idea."

"There's one other thing I need," I quickly add.

His gaze drops to his hands, as he reaches for a pen to toy with the same way he did back in high school, spinning it around the top of his fingers. "Why do I think this next part has to do with Allie?"

"Because you're my brother and you know I don't do wrong by people. I can't leave things the way they are. I'm not asking you to give her the old run-down kennel, though."

"Thank God for that."

"I did a little looking online and saw you bought up forty acres off the highway."

He nods. "Yes. We're putting in some more affordable housing." He narrows his eyes on me. "Because some people seem to think we only build houses for the rich."

I want to laugh, but I can't afford to miss a beat in my proposition. "I want five acres of that land adjacent to the highway."

"For what?" he asks, even though I know he knows.

"For a rescue kennel. I want it built by JLS Heartland Foundation, a donation to our community. Something big enough for not just dogs, but cats, birds, the whole gamut. The acreage next to the highway isn't best suited for homes anyway. It's too noisy. You stick a bunch of middle class homes there and you'll look like a tyrant—saving the good land—the quiet land—for the rich. But a bunch of animals aren't going to care about the noise, and the extra traffic will only help get them homes faster. You use that land to build a rescue organization, you'll look like a fucking hero."

"Five acres? Allie's plot that we bought in between the farms was only two."

"Five," I say adamantly. "Enough so that there's a noise buffer between her and the development."

"You drive a hard bargain. And I suppose you'll be negotiating your salary next?"

I smile, knowing he's going for it. "I promise I'll be gentle."

He laughs. "But enough to care for a wife and a few kids down the road, if things work out the way you've planned, I'm betting."

"Maybe so," I answer.

If I'm lucky.

CHAPTER 30

~ ALLIE ~

With my windows open, I hear the familiar crunching of gravel that greets me as I turn onto Logan's driveway. His truck and convertible are parked in front, along with two vans, one marked with the name of a plumbing company, and the other belonging to the painters.

It's hard work as usual here, I think with a sigh, and I can imagine Logan in there with them, finishing up #5 so that he can get these lovely homes on the market and move on.

He's been busy, I'm sure. Too busy to email or call or even manage a quick text. I know I said I needed time. But I didn't really mean I needed dead silence from him either.

I feel a little more like my old self after the week at my mom's, even though my sleep isn't quite up to speed. But the late nights I spent sitting on her back porch listening to the quiet of suburban Cleveland gave me time to re-envision my dreams without the foreclosure. There are still dogs I want to save.

My stepdad spent some time on that porch with me, too, telling me about some funding options I should consider that might put me within spitting distance of building a new kennel sometime in the future. He's not my dad, but I've discovered he's a really great guy and I can learn a lot from him.

I pull my luggage out of the back of my SUV and walk up to my door, knowing it won't be *my* door much longer. A vacancy came up in Cass's apartment building, and I'm planning on signing a lease tomorrow. I can't take on as many dogs while I live there, but it's the best I can do right now.

Swinging open the door, I see things the way I left them and I head to the kitchen to get a drink. The summer heat has me parched and I'm planning on spending the rest of the day catching my breath, sitting down by the water. It soothes me, the same way it does Logan, I guess. I just don't require as much of it.

Something catches my eye on the kitchen counter—a large sheet of paper rolled up and fastened with a red bow. Something for me? I glance over my shoulder hesitantly.

I just stare at it, confused, till I hear the door open behind me and a familiar voice over my shoulder.

"Open it," Logan says.

I turn and fill my eyes with the sight of him. He looks as tired as I feel, but there's something different about him. I can't quite put my finger on it.

"Logan," I say softly, hoping for some kind of affirmation from him so that I can run into his arms. His presence floods my senses, and I ache to be held by him—the feeling eclipsing any ache I felt when I lost the kennel.

My eyes search his, and I hold my breath, hoping he'll

open his arms or even step toward me. But he just stands in the doorway and repeats, "Open it, Allie."

It's only then that I remember the roll of paper in front of me. I look at it again curiously as I pull the bow.

It resembles a blueprint, but it's on a large sheet of thick white paper. An artist's rendering shows a building on the left side of the poster-sized sheet and an aerial view of the same building alongside a highway on the right.

I glance at him, bewildered. "What is this?"

"It's a rescue kennel alongside Rockbridge Highway."

I shake my head. "There's no kennel along Rockbridge Highway."

"There will be in about a year. JLS just settled on that land and we're deeding five acres of it to your organization. There will be a development adjacent to it, hopefully filled with people who want to adopt dogs."

The air rushes from my lungs and I raise my hand to my forehead. This isn't what I wanted him to do, I remind myself. It's everything that I want, yet I don't want it this way.

"No, Logan. I'm so grateful—really I am, but this isn't right. You can't make your brother do this."

"I'm not making him do this. I'm doing it myself. I've agreed to start working at JLS."

My jaw drops an inch. "Oh, Logan. Your family must be so happy."

He smiles. "My dad is over the moon about it. And my brother is… well, relieved to have some help. Hannah's moving in with him next week. Maybe if I can learn what I need to quickly enough, they can squeeze a good vacation in before the school year starts."

"But are *you* happy?" I never pictured Logan as being content behind a desk. Not to mention living with some semblance of permanence here in Newton's Creek.

"Not yet," he says, stepping toward me. His hand touches my waist and the other reaches to the side of my face. He traces the line of my cheekbone to my ear and tucks a lock of hair away as he pulls my face closer to his. My heart melts and my knees buckle as he supports me with his arm at the small of my back. Tears fill my eyes and I watch him through the haze of their moisture.

"Now I am," he says, lowering his mouth to mine and letting his soft lips touch me.

My soul fills to overflowing as I taste him, the kiss soft and sweet till I feel him part my lips with his tongue. I angle my head, letting more of his skin touch me, and feeling myself come alive again.

I feel the tears in my eyes threaten to fall, and he moves his lips from my mouth, lightly kissing my eyelids as I shut them.

"I've missed you in more ways than I thought possible," he tells me, edging out the insecurities that still lurked in my heart. "I've wanted to call you every minute of the day, but I knew you needed time. Besides," he smiles, "I've been busy while you've been away."

His gaze falls to the rendering stretched out on the counter, and mine follows.

"Logan, I can't accept this from you. I need to build my own dreams. I can't rely on you to do it for me."

"Why not, when you've built my dreams for me?"

My brow creases as I look at him.

"Allie, before I met you, I was a man without a mission. I was just living day to day. For some guys, that would be fine. But for me, it was suffocating. I've never lacked direction in my life, and since joining the SEALs I've never lived without meaning. But you showed me that risking my life as a SEAL isn't the only way I can make a mark on this world. I see what you've accomplished and I want that for myself."

I shake my head. "But this is my dream. Not yours."

"I know. And it's only a small piece of what I have planned at JLS Heartland. We're huge, Allie. Hell, even *I* didn't know how big we were till Ryan ran some numbers with me this week. We're solid enough that it's time for us to do more than just build homes. We've started a foundation."

"A foundation?"

"Yes, and this is one of our first donations to the towns where we build. The first of many, and I can't wait to tell you all my plans."

His eyes are filled with an excitement I've never seen in him. It's almost childlike, and it warms my heart.

"It's already a done deal, Allie. Nothing you can say will stop it, so I'm placing a huge gamble on the hope that you'll help us make this real." He taps on the paper. "And make it *right.*"

I stare at the rendering. It's a bigger kennel than the bankrupt one I had tried to buy. It's fresh and new and everything I could have possibly hoped for.

He strokes my cheek. "Will you make this place a reality with us?"

Tears stream down my cheeks and my lips quiver. A part of me—call it pride or stubbornness—tells me I should resist. But I remember what my mother told me about letting others share my dreams, to respect that they can feel the same passion I do, and to learn to share my load along with my joys.

Besides, when someone hands you your dream, you'd be a fool to not grab it.

So I grab.

"Yes, Logan. Yes, I will."

His smile is bright, framed in his kissable lips. He cocks his head. "You promise?"

He needs me to promise? Seriously? "I promise."

Relief settles into his shoulders as he takes both my hands. "Good, because there's something else I need to say, and I don't want it to influence you one way or the other."

I feel my stomach tighten up at the sudden nervousness I see etched around his eyes.

"I love you, Allie. I am completely, 100% in love with you. And I know this might be a little too soon for you to hear this—"

My breath catches. *No, not too soon at all.*

"—but I can't imagine my life without you. I have plans at JLS, but I have plans right here with you, too. I love you, Alexandra. You are my most important mission now. Building a future with you. Spending the next few months convincing you that I'm not the jaded former SEAL I once was. Making you see how perfectly we fit so that I can drop on my knee in front of you one day and beg you to be mine forever."

My body presses against him and I cradle his face in my hands. I can barely recognize the pure joy in his eyes as he speaks, and every piece of me wants to get to know this man —just as he is today, looking ahead to the future.

I lean in to kiss him, but he pulls away slightly, pressing his finger to my lips. "I know now that there are things I need to do in this world, but all I keep thinking is how much better it would be if I can do it all with you. Will you stick with me, Allie?" He taps the sheet of paper on the counter alongside of us. "Will you let this be the first of many great things we build together?"

"Yes," I cry through my tears, savoring the warmth I feel pressed against his body. "Because I love you too, Logan. I love you, too."

He lifts me into his arms, swinging me in a half circle, and carries me out of the kitchen.

I hope I know where we're headed, I think as my smile

presses against his soft lips and my body aches to feel him against me, with nothing between us.

No, I correct myself. I *know* where we're headed. And I couldn't be happier.

FROM THE AUTHOR

Thank you so much for reading *More, Please*! As an avid reader myself, I know there are many books available to you, so I'm deeply grateful—and very flattered—you took a chance on mine.

If you enjoyed the book, I hope you will consider reviewing it. I'm an independent author, so your reviews *literally* help me sell books and bring me that much closer to the day when I can quit my "day job" and do this full-time.

I hope you'll continue the **Homefront: The Sheridans** series with its next books, *Full Disclosure* and *Faking It*, as well as learn about another branch of the Sheridans with the **Homefront: Aloha, Sheridans** series.

In my mind, I often revisit the places and people in my books. So, from time to time, I love to share with my readers **free bonus scenes** I've written. Please check my website at www.KateAster.com/bonuses to see my latest.

I'd like to thank my husband and my entire family, who are my inspiration, for their unyielding support and patience ... to my dear friend Chuck for his Navy expertise ... to

Wanda for her much-needed local insight … and to Danielle for her sharp eyes. You are all fantastic!

Most of all, my thanks go to my readers. You are my cheering squad—and every time I think I can't write another book while still juggling the obligations of family and my other (exceedingly uninspiring) career, I get an email or a review from one of you that tugs at my heart and urges me on. I can't tell you how much it means to me! You also help point me in the direction of more stories you'd like to hear, as so many of you did when you wrote asking for "more, please" about the character of Logan, who was mentioned very briefly in *The SEAL's Best Man*. I am always thrilled to hear when one of my minor characters piques your curiosity!

I love to hear from readers. You can contact me at my website at www.KateAster.com and also sign up to find out when my next book is available.

Thanks again for your unwavering support!

BOOKS BY KATE ASTER

~ SPECIAL OPS: HOMEFRONT SERIES~

Romance awaits and life-long friendships blossom on the shores of the Chesapeake Bay.

SEAL the Deal

Special Ops: Homefront (Book One)

The SEAL's Best Man

Special Ops: Homefront (Book Two)

Contract with a SEAL

Special Ops: Homefront (Book Three)

Make Mine a Ranger

Special Ops: Homefront (Book Four)

BOOKS BY KATE ASTER

~ SPECIAL OPS: TRIBUTE SERIES~

Love gets a second chance when a very special ice cream shop opens near the United States Naval Academy.

No Reservations

Special Ops: Tribute (Book One)

Strong Enough

Special Ops: Tribute (Book Two)

Until Forever: A Wedding Novella

Special Ops: Tribute (Book Three)

Twice Tempted

Special Ops: Tribute (Book Four)

BOOKS BY KATE ASTER

~ HOMEFRONT: THE SHERIDANS SERIES ~

When one fledgling dog rescue comes along, three brothers find romance as they emerge from the shadow of their billionaire name.

More, Please

Homefront: The Sheridans (Book One)

Full Disclosure

Homefront: The Sheridans (Book Two)

Faking It

Homefront: The Sheridans (Book Three)

BOOKS BY KATE ASTER

~ HOMEFRONT: ALOHA, SHERIDANS SERIES ~

Even on a remote island paradise, a handful of bachelor brothers can't hide from love when they leave the Army.

A is for Alpha

Homefront: Aloha, Sheridans (Book One)

Hindsight

Homefront: Aloha, Sheridans (Book Two)

Island Fever

Homefront: Aloha, Sheridans (Book Three)

BOOKS BY KATE ASTER

~ BROTHERS IN ARMS SERIES ~

With two U.S. Naval Academy graduates and two from their arch rival at West Point, there's ample discord among the Adler brothers ... until love tames them.

BFF'ed

Brothers in Arms (Book One) - available now!

Books Two, Three, and Four

are coming soon.

Sign up at my website at ***www.KateAster.com***

to be the first to hear the release dates.

BOOKS BY KATE ASTER

~ FIRECRACKERS: NO COMMITMENT NOVELETTES ~

For when you don't have much free time… but want a quick, fun race to a happily ever after.

SEAL My Grout

Firecrackers: No Commitment Novelettes (Book One)

Available now!

Novelettes Two, Three, and Four

are coming soon.

Sign up at my website at ***www.KateAster.com***

to be the first to hear the release dates.

LET'S KEEP IN TOUCH!

Twitter: @KateAsterAuthor

Facebook: @KateAsterAuthor

Instagram: KateAsterAuthor

www.KateAster.com

Made in the USA
Columbia, SC
10 September 2021